The Book o

CW01642945

For Norman

Preface

Written by Cameron Crane

Does everybody skip the preface? I must have skimmed every preface I've ever came across. Why do I need to read this Regular Joe's opinion on a book I haven't yet read? Shouldn't I save the story of how to book came to be until after you learn what it became? Anyways, while I do have some things to say here, I'm sure you'll do okay if you skip this part of the book. Though, if I had to say something, while you're here and I have your attention, just know that you're probably not going to like this book. That's not a good selling point, I realize, but it's the truth- this is a very odd book. If you haven't heard of Norman before, or know what this is based from, then I suggest reading this next paragraph, because I'll try my best to explain to you exactly what you're signing up for.

Norman is a simple man. He's divorced, with a son who doesn't feel like giving him a call too often. Norman wears sweatpants to the grocery store. Norman lives by himself with his cat, who is also named Norman. Norman is not very creative. He likes to eat chicken on Fridays because it's a treat, and likes to eat beef on Mondays, since beef is his least favorite type of meat, and Monday is his least favorite day. In all regards, Norman is the physical embodiment of vanilla ice cream (in a bowl), and plain eggs. This book, in all its glory, tells the daily life of Norman, spanning one year. Each of the 365 stories within the book vary, as it is written by hundreds of writers and contributors from the website reddit.com, under the subreddit /r/lifeofnorman. There lies the home of Norman- an online community for the average bloke, where anyone who's uncreative enough can tell their own story about this fictional character. Because this is story being told incrementally by hundreds of different people, the book becomes less about a narrative, and more so an experience of getting an insight into sixth type of conflict in a story- man vs nothing in particular. That's the real reason I feel the need to stress the monotony of this book- it's meant to give you a daily insight into Norman, with stories ranging from slap-stick humor, to dealing with depression. With all of the large events of Norman's life stuck firmly in his past, the book is more about how he came to be the person he is today, and how easy it is to become like him too.

Anyways, there's the truth. There's tons of content within this book, from a remarkably talented group of writers, all willing to let their stories be published for free. I can talk about why it would be a good thing for you to buy the book: all the profits are going to cat shelters. That seems like a strange thing to decide to donate to, as I'm sure hundreds of people are eager to tell us about the other thousands of burning charities that could use the help, but we decided to fight this battle. The first one the book's profits will be donated to is VOKRA (Vancouver Orphan Kitten Rescue Association) in Vancouver, Canada. It's a non-profit volunteer shelter with a proven track record for being very considerate and kind people, and I thought they would be a wonderful choice. The plan is to donate ten thousand dollars per cat shelter, so long as the money for the book keeps coming in.

In Norman's life, there isn't many things that cause him happiness. He's content with most aspects in his life, but staying happy is something that he struggles to maintain on a daily basis. The source of much of Norman's love comes from having his cat (again, also named Norman). At the heart of it, that's what this book is about. That's why I wanted to put it together. If Norman can find happiness in a feline companion, giving the same opportunities to others seems like the best way that we can pay homage to the fictional character.

I should have had this book published a long time ago. I grossly underestimated how much work and time it would take to get this project seen through to the end. Over the past three years, Norman has become a big player in my life. It's hard for him not to. While there's 365 stories in the book now, I've also read countless others, perhaps even thousands. I think that the delay of the book being published has a lot to do with how much Norman has grown over time. After awhile, certain mannerisms of Norman are forgotten, and he develops a new way of thinking. For example, in the very, very beginning, Norman was a funny cut-out from an Australian newspaper ad. It was about a man, named Norman, who complained about a music venue for being too loud, even though *that* Norman had lived beside that venue for many years. It read, "Does that make Norman a dickhead?" with "Yes, it does." written underneath it.

So, at first, the stories were written in spite. His normal life, his wife leaving him, his cat being named after him- all this was to paint a miserable picture of the Australian. But somewhere along the line, things changed. No longer was it poking fun at him for living monotonously, but pointing out how we're all pretty much in his shoes. Because of that, collecting stories became more complicated. I couldn't just tell a really long joke anymore- it was about *him*, the newfound protagonist who dug himself out of his shallow character description, and giving these stories the treatment they deserve.

Every now and then, I'll get an email from someone who reads a lot of Norman stories. The person will tell me how grateful they are for the stories, and that because they understand Norman so well, these stories become a diary of sorts for people to let out their emotions. It helped them get through dark times, made them laugh and cry, and at the root of it all, that's what it's all about. Cats too, but really, it makes me unfathomably proud to be able to give something to people that can bring them a lot of joy, and sadness, through a mundane existential crisis.

Maybe this book isn't for you. Perhaps you're fortunate enough to live a life that's not nine to five, Monday through Friday, January to December, twenty-five to retirement. This book will either click, or it won't. And that's okay. But I hope you'll come along for this mild rollercoaster ride. A rollercoaster that's not exhilarating, without loops and drops; just some nice, subtle turns, with a pond in the centre, and ducks.

HAPPY NEW

January

Norman Attends a New Year's Party

January 1st, A Sunday

"3... 2... 1..."

The moderately sized crowd of office workers counted aloud and cheered, sharing the moment of midnight striking the clock, welcoming in the new year. The shouting was hushed momentarily, giving a chance for everyone to hug and kiss each other in celebration. In the corner of the room, standing near the cubicle he sits in every other weekday, was Norman.

Norman did not receive a kiss or hug during the celebrating. Instead, Norman was terribly preoccupied with two other tasks; one of those involved him brooding about how tired he was. He knew that they would be there until midnight, as that's how New Year's celebrations normally worked, but for someone who was used to being asleep by 10PM, this was a jarring experience.

The second thought that preoccupied Norman's mind was that he didn't know what to do with his hands. Earlier in the evening Norman had helped himself to a glass of punch. There was beer provided for the party, but Norman didn't like drinking all too often, unless it was a cooler, or a coke. The punchbowl was still filled to the brim, so Norman helped himself after much thought as to which cup he would like to use, or which orange slice to put in his cup. He wasn't normally this picky about cups and fruits, but he needed something to do. His co-workers were far younger than he was, himself being in his forties, and the ones that were in their forties were far too drunk for Norman to converse with. Instead, he opted to sipping on a glass of punch, grasping it with both hands, and spacing out the sips to once every few minutes. He didn't want to be seen going for a second glass- he didn't want to appear greedy- so he carefully drank what he had, as if he was on his last canteen, lost in the desert.

Before the countdown even began, Norman had run out of punch. He felt strange grasping an empty cup with both hands, so he made a trip to the trash can to empty it. While he was there, he noticed the garbage was overflowing. He took the full bag and threw it in the dumpster outside, when he discovered that someone had made a terrible mess of the parking lot as well! By the time he made it back to the party, after cleaning the parking lot and salting the sidewalk, the countdown had started. His hands were empty.

His armpits were far too sweaty to raise them above his head in celebration, so he opted out for a slow, methodical clap.

"3… 2… 1…"

The kissing and hugging ended. People dispersed. Norman stopped clapping. He headed for the door.

Norman drove home in his Daihatsu, perusing the radio-stations to keep busy at stoplights. Christmas music was still playing. Norman thought about stopping to buy a few pieces of jerky from a convenience store, but then remembered the leftover pork from the night before. He had forgotten to put it in plastic wrap, but Norman was okay with this. Now, it would more closely resemble jerky.

Norman unlocked the front door to his apartment. All quiet- just like he left it. As he switched on the lights, a pattering of furry feet made its way into Norman's arms.

"Hi buddy! Miss me?" Norman gleefully said to his cat, also named Norman. "What a day," Norman confided.

The cat purred curiously as Norman cut off chunks of the homemade jerky. Once the meat was lodged in his teeth, Norman gave the rest to Norman, flossed his teeth, and then he went to sleep.

Norman's Resolution

January 2nd, A Monday

It was January second, and Norman had just realized he hadn't chosen a New Year's resolution yet. He'd missed the first day of the year already, but he could just make that up by skipping and doing it next year. But then he would start a dangerous trend of always starting on the second... The thought made Norman stressed.

"From now on, I shall live every day to the fullest!" Norman declared.

Norman sat in his couch and turned on the television. He would later have breaded chicken for dinner.

Norman Gets a Cup of Water

January 3rd, A Tuesday

Norman sat on his couch. It was Tuesday night, and Norman never missed *CSI: Crime Scene Investigation*. About halfway through, a commercial came on.

Suddenly, Norman realized that his mouth was getting dry. *I'm thirsty*, he thought. Debating whether to sacrifice his comfortable position on the couch for a drink, Norman decided it was worth the effort.

Norman jumped off Norman's lap as he briskly walked to the kitchen. Norman wanted to make it back to the living room before the commercials ended. Reaching for the cabinet, Norman selected a medium-sized glass. *I am thirsty*, he thought, *but not that thirsty*.

Norman decided it was worth the risk to skip the ice, so he could save time. Norman placed his glass under the faucet. Norman didn't mind tap water. As the glass began to fill, five seconds turned to ten--and ten to fifteen.

Finally, the sense of urgency overcame him. Norman elected to cut the flow short, leaving the cup half empty. Or half full, as Norman called it. Being careful to maneuver his glass so it wouldn't spill, Norman quickly returned to his place on the couch. The commercials had not yet ended.

Norman took a sip of his lukewarm tap water, as Norman leaped onto Norman's lap. *That's better,* thought Norman.

Norman Becomes Confused by Geography

January 4th, A Wednesday

Norman was socially engaging with a co-worker that was talking about his cousin's travels to Dubai. Norman may or may not have implied during that conversation that Dubai was a country. He didn't remember exactly if he actually said something along the lines of "*Yes, it sure sounds like an amazing country*," or if he had just thought about saying it.

That night he couldn't sleep for hours, thinking about the conversation. Norman was very good at geography in high school, had always loved maps, knew a lot of different flags and absolutely knew Dubai was not a country.

Norman decided to never socially engage with that same co-worker again.

Norman Eats Out

January 5th, A Thursday

Norman was in the habit of having dinner at an Irish pub not too far from his home on Thursdays. The wait staff there were polite and knew him just well enough to make quiet, shallow inquiries as to how he was doing. Norman always said, 'Just fine, thank you' regardless of how the day had been or how he was feeling.

It was a ritual of sorts, just like the fish and chips he got every single time he ate there. He had started with the fish and chips a long time before, when he first came to the pub, and had stuck with them more for the sake of comfort and routine than anything else.

He knew how his meal would taste before it arrived, and could already see the process laminated upon the surface of his mind. On some deep, nearly subconscious level this bothered him, but never enough for him to order anything different. It was always the fish and chips, followed by apple pie á la mode and then the check.

The process of payment was just as mechanised as his meal.

Fish and chips and apple pie cost seventeen dollars and thirty cents, tax included. Norman knew this in the same way that he knew his address, knew that the hair growth treatments he was trying were not working, and knew that his son would not return the call Norman had made to him that morning.

Norman always paid in cash so he could leave without waiting around like he would if he paid via credit card. He always left a twenty and a five, and sometimes wondered if his servers looked forward to waiting his table because he tipped so well. He took one last sip from his water and promptly walked out, nodding at the inevitable request that he "have a nice day" from the woman behind the counter.

Later he would go to bed and sleep soundly, more or less, just like he did every Thursday night. Such was life for Norman.

Norman Goes into his Office Building

January 6th, A Friday

Norman was walking as usual to his building. Norman saw one of his coworkers walking towards the building as well. Norman noticed that their paces were the same and would reach the door at the same time.

Norman slowed down.

Norman Sees a Couple Flirting

January 7th, A Saturday

It's one of those restaurants where they place all the food in a long counter, you can serve yourself and then pay according to your meal's weight.

After filling his mouth with food, Norman aimlessly looked away from his plate. After some meandering, his eyes met a woman, sitting on a table by the wall across the room. *She's very pretty*, he thought. The young lady had a smile on her face, eyes shyly avoiding- and at the same time looking for- something ahead of her.

Norman placed another forkful in his mouth, and searched for the source of her smile.

At the table behind Norman, there was a man- also alone. His hands held a fork, but eating wasn't his focus right now, as indicated by the same smile and shy look-away-and-back combo the blonde performed.

The waiter came by and asked if he wanted something to drink. Norman was on a diet, so he ordered orange juice instead of soda. Norman distractingly proceeded to cut a piece of his steak, moving it around the plate playing with the rice and beans. When the chewing started, attention promptly returned to the people-watching routine.

The couple seemed to be getting shyer and shyer. But, with time, their locking eyes got longer, and the face-away got shorter. The woman now periodically grabbed a piece of her hair and did a random motion with it, her face now reddish.

Norman wondered what that interaction would look like when one of the two needed to eat. He pictured himself smiling with his mouth full of food, and that made him giggle a little. He tried not to though, as he worried people would think he was crazy for laughing at nothing.

The waiter came back soon after with the glass of juice and Norman thanked him politely. The waiter seemed to be a nice person; Norman planned to tip him well. He took a sip to see if it was good, and he liked it. Another mouthful of food and a piece of steak later, Norman's eyes once again floated around the space in front of him. The news was on TV, but he couldn't hear it. He tried to lip-read what the anchor said, but it was no use. Norman shrugged and ate one more forkful.

Shortly after, Norman paid for his meal and made his way to the restroom- after all, he needed to brush for the dentist appointment later that day. He took the brush and paste out of his briefcase and let autopilot do the deed. There were already two other men brushing their teeth in there, and it made Norman feel comfortable.

After wetting the toothpaste in the sink, Norman raised his head and saw himself in the mirror. He suddenly remembered the couple he had observed back in the restaurant. He wondered what the conclusion to that curious encounter was. Norman pictured the two of them happy together, and then he regretted not staying there to see.

That guy sure is lucky, Norman thought.

Norman's toothbrush touched his mouth, and he regretted having had that orange juice earlier.

Norman Takes Norman to a Cat Shelter

January 8th, A Sunday

Norman's cat, Norman, was sick. He didn't drink the water from his bowl and refused to eat any of his tempting treats. Norman knew what he had to do.

Norman took Norman to a cat shelter. Norman had done this in the past, as the cat would sometimes become blue and need attention from other cats. He let Norman drift away into the crowd of felines as he browsed the shelter, getting ideas for what sort of climbable furniture he could build for his cat once they went home.

As Norman carried Norman out of the shelter, he was confronted by the lady at the front counter, saying that he couldn't take cats without filling out paperwork or paying the fee for adoption. Norman explained that this was his cat, but she didn't listen. After she checked the number of cats in the shelter and that all were accounted for except the one in Norman's arms, the cat caretaker still didn't believe him.

Norman filled out the paperwork, paid the $200 fee, and readopted his cat Norman.

Norman Dials the Wrong Number

January 9th, A Monday

Few things in life were as convenient or satisfying as takeout delivery. The process of stating one's order, hanging up the phone, then watching the clock came very easily to Norman, who could think of no better way to obtain food on a Monday evening.

Norman liked takeout delivery.

With a practiced motion, he reached for the phone and dialled the toll-free number of the restaurant he hoped to reach. There was a brief pause, an electronic ringing tone, and finally, an unfamiliar voice. Norman was surprised when the telephone waitress - as he decided to think of her- asked for his credit card number before taking his order, but he provided it nonetheless.

Norman listened for a moment.

He hung up the phone. Norman did not like takeout delivery anymore.

Norman Takes a Nap

January 10th, A Tuesday

Norman exhaustedly flops into his La-Z-Boy, simultaneously pulling the lever to recline as he settles. The chair is too big for him, and the headrest pushes his head too far forward when upright, but it's comfortable when he reclines.

His breathing slows as the fan hums quietly above him and the stirring of the air begins to slowly wick up the perspiration from his forehead. His eyes follow one of the blades for a while as it makes its revolutions. He begins to lose focus; the blades merge into one. He blinks. Slowly. More slowly. His eyes fall closed.

Sleep's euphoria smooths away all the day's concerns, and massages Norman's limbs comfortingly deeper into the stuffing of his chair. It's been several years since he's thought of the chair as a gift from his ex-wife on their seventh, and last, wedding anniversary. It's simply his chair. And it's comfortable when he reclines.

Norman is Feeling Dangerous

January 11th, A Wednesday

Norman rolls down the window of his rusty car and sticks his arm out. He flattens his hand and makes it go up and down with the wind. He pretends his hand is a dolphin. Norman pulls his arm back in before it gets cut off by a stop sign. He has heard that this has happened to other people.

Norman Goes Shopping

January 12th, A Thursday

It was Thursday, so naturally Norman took his weekly trip to the supermarket. This week was beef week, and Norman picked out his regular items, in a moment of spontaneity stopped at the frozen vegetable section. He spent a long time thinking about the frozen carrots, pondering why carrots grow in the ground and why they are orange. Norman never came up with answers for these questions, and he left the aisle with a bag of frozen peas. Norman always hated carrots.

Norman Checks His Email

January 13th, A Friday

As soon as Norman opened his work email at 8AM Friday morning, he could see that he was in for a world of hurt. ***38 new emails.*** The bright red words beamed from the screen and pierced into Norman's tired eyes. He knew that he needed to get through all of them, but how?

He began. ***See the All New Summer E-cards from FunnyECards.com!*** There were 15 new ones. This was only going to hurt his workflow, but he couldn't let it sit there. 12 minutes passed, and Norman, sweating shotgun shells, finally finished playing through the final E-card. He'd have sent them to someone but he couldn't think of anyone in his life who hadn't responded negatively to an influx of E-cards. He flagged the email for when he could make a new friend.

Norman quickly clicked the next email. ***Norman, please print the attached for our 9*** - Norman quickly clicked the next email. ***Amazon.com. Please review your recent purchase.*** Norman shook and released his mouse. He had recently bought a new bag of cat food, but the cat wouldn't eat it. Norman had a lot of opinions to share, and hardly enough time. "I don't have enough *time!*" he whispered angrily at Amazon.com.

Just as he began to gain composure, Norman's supervisor Steven walked by. Norman hurriedly shuffled yesterday's project of coupon clipping out of Steven's line of sight, but he knew Steven saw it all.

"Hey bud, have you had a chance to print off that attachment I sent you?"

Norman shook his head no. "So many emails. Could you just print it?"

Steven lowered his shoulders and his eyelids, said sure, and walked back to his cubicle. Norman went back to his Amazon.com review. He wanted to get a refund on that cat food.

Norman Makes it Safely Across the Street

January 14th, A Saturday

Norman hated when large puddles formed at the edge of a sidewalk, especially when he needed to cross the street. Sure, Norman's legs had the reach needed to hop over the puddle, but it made Norman uncomfortable, as that leap could lead to his death. What if a truck happened to drive quickly across, and Norman, the fool, took one large leap directly in front of it? He would look so silly when the obituary listed his apparent suicide.

Norman decided to take three small calculated steps instead. If he moved fast enough, the water wouldn't pour in the sides of his shoes, and he would retain his ability to jump out of the way of a speeding vehicle.

Norman made it safely across the street.

Better to be sorry than dead, Norman thought to himself as he sat at a nearby bench, letting his soaked socks dry in the sun.

Norman and the Spider

January 15th, A Sunday

It was a quaint evening. Norman sat on the couch, staring beyond the wall in front of him. Distracting him from his daze was a small spider, crawling along the living room floor.

Norman called to Norman, who was sitting atop the coffee table, to chase after the spider. However, the cat had no interest in the spider. Instead, he jumped off the table and ran into the kitchen. Rather than squashing the spider himself, Norman went to bed and hoped he would just forget about it.

Norman Observes a Holiday

January 16th, A Monday

Norman sat in his favorite coffee shop enjoying a good book. About twenty minutes in, an attractive younger woman walked in and ordered a latte. She sat down at the next table over, facing Norman, and began to enjoy a novel of her own. Norman looked her over, and found her to be absolutely stunning. She was maybe late twenties, early thirties, mid-length hair falling in a slight curl on her ebony shoulders, with piercing hazel eyes. Norman was so captivated by her unique beauty that he did not realize he was staring until the young lady looked up and smiled at him.

"Happy Martin Luther King Day!" Norman exclaimed before he could stop himself.

The young lady's smile suddenly became artificial. With her eyebrows raised, she politely declared, "thanks," before desperately burying her face back into her novel, turning slightly sideways to avoid any future eye contact with Norman.

Norman went home shortly after, feeling both somewhat embarrassed, but also somewhat bolder.

Norman Yawns at Work

January 17th, A Tuesday

Halfway through his day at work, Norman yawned.

"Oh no, don't start doing that!" a co-worker joked.

Norman chuckled. "Yeah, I know."

"Rough night?"

"You could say that," Norman lied.

Norman didn't have a rough night. Norman had gotten eight hours of restful sleep. Norman was just always a little tired.

Norman Tells a Lie

January 18th, A Wednesday

As Norman entered his office, he was greeted by Lisa from HR.

"Hi Norman, how was your morning?"

Norman thought about his morning. Today he had already poured cereal into his bowl before he realised there was no more milk left in the fridge.

"It was fine, thank you," Norman said politely. He did not know Lisa that well and did not feel like talking about his morning.

Norman Tries a New Nickname

January 19th, A Thursday

Norman was getting ready to go to a co-worker's retirement party when he had an idea.

As he was ironing his shirt, he realized that there would be several people at the party whom he had not met before. This co-worker, Bill, had worked in three different departments during his tenure with the company, and employees from all three groups would be there.

Norman had an opportunity to make a new impression. He could come across as cool and aloof, with a mysterious air. He began ironing faster as his excitement grew, imagining strangers asking, "Who is this guy? How have I never met him?" The key component of this plan would be a new name– 'Norm'. "Like Norm McDonald?" they would ask. "Yes, except I'm funnier," he would reply with a chuckle and a smirk.

With this strategy in mind, Norman strutted into the party. He saw Frank, his cubicle mate of two years, talking to an attractive woman Norman had never seen before. He strolled over to them, his heart pounding. "Hi, Frank."

"Hey." Frank looked a little confused, perhaps thrown off by Norman's newfound confidence. "Uh, Betty, this is my cubicle mate, um..."

"Norm– Norman."

Norman Gets in Trouble at Work

January 20th, A Friday

Early in the morning, earlier than what Norman would consider early, Norman received an email from his floor boss. It read:

"To Norma,
I'd like to speak with you in my office when you come to work this morning. Thanks.
Sincerely, Rich Tucker"

Norman didn't know what to make of the email. Richard had never written an email to Norman before; all contact he had with his superiors was through his supervisor, Steven. "I would like to speak with *you?*" Norman said aloud. He immediately dressed himself so that he could think about this conundrum with pants on.

Rich, Rich, Richard... he wouldn't use a casual name like that if he meant something horrible. Then again, it wasn't Richie either. Maybe he's just so-so about yelling at Norman. Maybe he would fire him.

Norman thought about all the mistakes he had made at work over the previous months. Nothing came up. He shows up 15 minutes early every day, he does his reports on time, he cleans up after himself in the lunchroom, and he doesn't mingle, unless someone else was to approach him. In other words, he doesn't mingle at all. Then he thought, *Of course! My God.*

Last week, Norman checked his personal emails. As usual it had been empty, so he checked his spam folder. As he did that, Steven passed by and said, "Hey bud, have you had a chance to print off that attachment I sent you?"

That must be it. That's all it could be. Norman remembers responding in a rude fashion. He was busy!

Before heading to the office, Norman quickly transferred work files into his spam folder, just in case Rich Tucker said, "Well let me see these so called work files in the spam folder!" or something like that. He moved three files, all from one week ago, comfortably in the mess of spammed emails.

Norman entered Rich's office the moment he reached work, as to rip it off like a Band-Aid.

"You wanted to see me, Rich?" asked Norman.

"Who are you?" asked Rich.

"... I'm Norman."

"Oh yes! I emailed you this morning... Right. I was going to ask if you can work an extra few hours tonight. Debra in services is taking her daughter to a birthday party, and she needs someone to cover her desk for a few hours. She suggested you, and that you probably wouldn't be doing anything with your afternoon."

Norman hastily agreed in a sigh of relief. At the end of his regular shift, Norman moved over to Debra's desk, where very little of anything occurred. Norman checked his emails. It was empty, but his spam folder had four unopened messages. Those would have to wait.

Norman Goes to Work

January 21st, A Saturday

Like any other day, Norman awoke without the help of his alarm (although it's always set to 6:00 AM, just to be safe), turned around to stick his feet on the brown hardwood floor, and looked out the window of his apartment. *Ahh, nice and tepid weather today,* he thought to himself. At least, that's what he presumed it was like on the other side of the adjacent building that has always blocked his line of sight. Like any other day, Norman took a seven -minute shower, put on a sharp yet tasteful wool ensemble, careful not to forget the cardigan, and grabbed a soft-boiled egg from the fridge for his breakfast. After giving Norman some affection, he left for his job.

That's odd, he thought, *the traffic sure is light today.* Upon arriving at 7:50AM instead of 7:54AM as usual, he played with his thumbs for a while in the largely empty parking lot to help pass the extra time. After walking to his cubicle past an uncharacteristically quiet office, Norman saw that the last day marked off his calendar was indeed a Friday. Using the process of elimination, Norman realized that that would make today a Saturday, a weekend.

It was a quiet and somewhat slow day, and Norman received curiously few invoices to approve. He did not feel comfortable processing the few he did receive without the oversight of Steven, who was not in the office. While leaving the office park at 5:00, Norman noticed that the day was not tepid at all, but rather bright and blustery. Upon returning home, his eyes hurt from squinting into the sun on the drive back. Norman poured himself a glass of soda and waited for *Wheel of Fortune* to come on.

Norman Almost Buys Fish for Dinner

January 22nd, A Sunday

Norman was eating chicken for the third day in a row. As the credits for CSI came on he took his one plate and one fork to the sink. He thought about going to the store. He would try something different. Maybe buy a fish, cook it, and even mix some into Norman's kibble. Norman Jr. used to love fish; his favorite was salmon.

While washing the dishes he thought about the fish dinner. He remembered how his ex-wife would crinkle her nose at the smell of fish. Then he thought about what he would say to the broad-shouldered butcher when he would grunt and say, "Chicken again?"

He walked over and opened the fridge to stare at its few contents. He settled on leftovers that he was not sure would make it to tomorrow, and a can of ginger ale. He opened the freezer and saw a frozen chicken dinner that came with a brownie for dessert. It had been on sale for $3.60 the last time he had gone to the store. He sighed in relief and decided not to go to the store. He did not want to disappoint the butcher.

Norman Ruins His Future

January 23rd, A Monday

As Norman purchased a single packaged pork chop from the grocery store, he bumped into a young, black haired woman. "Eating for one?" she asked playfully, nodding towards the pork chop.

"Yes!" Norman exclaimed eagerly. It was the end of the conversation.

Later that night Norman considered the life they could have had together. He could have said something along the lines of '*It's for two, if you'd wish*', or something similarly romantic. He thought about beating up a thief that would steal her purse as they left the grocery store. He would teach the robber right from wrong and raise him like a lost son, and she would love Norman even more for his nobility. The robber would become an unofficial uncle to Norman and the woman's child. The child couldn't be called Norman Jr, so he would have to settle on something like...

Norman began to regret his decisions. He could have said more than 'Yes!' He could have paid for her groceries; she did only have half a cart. Norman also regretted having his shirt buttoned up so high. Norman felt lonely when he went to sleep.

Norman Gets a Snack

January 24th, A Tuesday

Norman stood in the break room of his office staring at the vending machine. He often took more time than he would like to decide what to get for a mid-afternoon snack. The choice was always between a blueberry granola bar and an almond granola bar, but today he noticed a new flavour had been added: coconut. Norman had never liked coconut before, but he had never had it in granola form. *This could be different,* he thought to himself.

A woman entered the break room, jolting him from his thoughts. She walked toward Norman and stood behind him, waiting patiently to use the vending machine. Forced to make a decision quickly so as to not disrupt her break, he decided to try the coconut-flavoured granola and hurriedly punched in F9. The spiraled cage whirred into life, bringing the granola bar forward to the edge of the shelf before it stopped, and the salty snack slid a short way before becoming caught on the end of the cage. Norman was not sure what to do. Normally the granola was deposited into the bottom of the machine where he could grab it, and if it caught like this he would softly tap the machine and it would drop. *I'm sure I would need to give it a solid smack to get the granola,* Norman thought. He raised his hand in a fist, ready to hit the machine.

The woman waiting behind him coughed, and Norman was reminded that he was not alone. Not wanting to be a nuisance to the woman, he lowered his arm and walked back to his desk without the granola bar.

As he opened the door to leave the break room, he heard several thuds. The woman followed him out while eating a coconut granola.

Norman Takes Control

January 25th, A Wednesday

Norman (the cat) was being particularly bothersome one Wednesday afternoon. While the cat had long forgotten what it did to make his owner so irritated, Norman had not. Annoyed, Norman grabbed the bowl of porridge that Norman had been lapping up, and emptied it down the garbage disposal. With vindication, Norman looked down at the cat and declared;

"Neither cat nor man shall eat this porridge!"

His pride was quickly overtaken with shame and hunger.

Norman Dates Online

January 26th, A Thursday

Norman sat quietly while his computer loaded the free dating website. His co-worker, Frank, had suggested he give it a try, citing a gentleman his sister had met as an optimistic anecdote of potential success. He eventually found a picture of himself that did not completely show the top of his head, left his profile blank, and began to browse.

Norman found a brunette around his age posing on a horse. He wondered if she would want to take him horseback riding, too. He'd never been, and he doubted he'd be any good. Norman sighed and closed the website. Online dating was exhausting.

Norman Mops the Floor

January 27th, A Friday

Norman wouldn't describe himself as a fan of ramen noodles, however due to the large amounts he could buy all at once, they were a staple of his weekly dinners. Tonight was chicken.

While opening the flavour packet Norman was overcome by a tickle in his nose. He desperately tried to fight it, but ultimately sneezed the entire contents of the powder packet onto the linoleum floor.

Norman frowned and filled a bucket with hot soapy water. He dipped his old mop in the water and set about cleaning the floor. Soon a warm chicken aroma filled the room. It was rich and delicious smelling. Norman even jokingly considered tasting the mop water.

After the mop was put away Norman reclaimed his now cold and flavourless noodles. As he ate them, he continued to enjoy the fading chicken smell.

Norman Flips His Pillow Over

January 28th, A Saturday

Norman woke up in the middle of the night feeling hot and uncomfortable. For some odd reason, he remembered the mail clerk in his office saying that his new girlfriend was "cooler than the other side of the pillow." Norman flipped his pillow over. *It is a bit cooler,* Norman thought before drifting back to sleep.

Norman Feels Disgruntled

January 29th, A Sunday

Norman was on the couch on a Sunday with Norman curled up on his lap. He was watching a rerun of *Wheel of Fortune* when he was struck by a realization: he had done nothing for the entire weekend! Norman was not, in fact, satisfied with his excessive usage of his electronic devices. As he looked back, he realized that the closest thing to physical activity that he had participated in was the walk from his car to the grocery store to pick up some snacks.

Norman felt like a slob. He was now determined to make up for his weekend of being a recluse by going to the gym for the first time in five years. But, as he started to get up, he remembered that Norman was on his lap and didn't want to disturb him. He also realized that his back ached, it was almost 7:00PM, and it was, after all, very chilly outside. Norman decided that he would rather see what vowels Jones would buy on the good old *Wheel of Fortune* rerun.

Norman Waves Back

January 30th, A Monday

Norman was walking down the street on his way home from work. He was behind a nice young man talking on his cell phone, which Norman didn't mind. After a short distance a figure, travelling in the opposite direction down the street, came into view. This person waved in Norman's direction.

Oh my, I think he's waving at me, Norman thought, *but what if he isn't? He may be waving at the man in front of me. But if he actually is waving at me- it would be rude not to wave back. However, if he's not it would be rather embarrassing.* After calculating his options, Norman decided to wave back at the man.

Lucky for Norman, the man was actually waving at him. It was an intern from his work.

Norman smiled the rest of the way home.

Norman Averts a Crisis

January 31st, A Tuesday

Norman buttoned up, straightened, and flushed. After the familiar splash came eerie silence. The lever hung limp.

Norman was frozen for a few moments and then, on a hunch, he slapped the tank. Something clicked and humming began.

He watched intently as the lever rose and locked in the ready position. He tried it gently for pressure, even letting out a trickle of water.

Norman sighed a sigh of relief. Crisis averted - for now.

February

February

A New Look

February 1st, A Wednesday

It was midday, and Norman decided he wanted to buy something new. He pondered the possibilities and decided to go to the nearby shopping center to look at today's outfits. He grabbed his umbrella and headed out. It was a sunny day as Norman stepped outside, perhaps he wouldn't even need his umbrella. Norman thought about leaving it, but decided against it. *After all, we can't control the weather*, he thought.

He strolled down the street, shaking his head in disapproval at the state of it. Norman wondered how it ever got so dirty. However, he was soon distracted as he arrived at the outlet and chose the first small shop he came across. Stepping inside, he was shocked to see a woman with short, pink hair and a pierced lip. Norman wondered if the lip piercing made it difficult for her to speak, but she didn't seem interested in talking to him, so he stepped over to a nearby rack, and proceeded to shuffle through the clothes. Norman tutted at the lack of fabric and bright colors included in the outfits. Norman thought to himself, *this simply won't do*, and promptly left the store without so much as a nod. Outside, he considered going to the next store, but decided he didn't need a change after all. Norman went home instead.

Norman Finds a Photograph

February 2nd, A Thursday

Norman's car had broken down a few streets from his house. He'd managed to coast onto the side of the road, and now he was walking home. The afternoon sun made him squint as he ambled across his side of suburbia.

The photograph's glossy surface caught his eye. It was next to a wheelie bin, lying on the curb. Norman picked it up, and realised it was incomplete; the left half of the photograph was torn down the middle. A cheery girl looked back at him. She had brilliant red hair and adorable freckles and looked to be in her late twenties. There was an arm around her shoulder, intruding from the missing right side of the image. The background was green and lush.

When Norman arrived home, he greeted and fed Norman, and made himself some macaroni and cheese for dinner. He placed the photograph gently upon his bedside table before he turned off the light. Norman dreamt he was eating macaroni and cheese with the girl in the photograph.

Norman Loves Pizza

February 3rd, A Friday

Norman pulled Thursday's pizza box from the fridge and walked it back to the couch. Norman loves pizza. As a kid, every birthday felt as magnificent and warm as the pizza that came with it. As Norman picked up a slice, he wondered if that was a real memory of his life or just something they were saying in one of the ads playing on TV.

Norman looked down at his knees and thought it was kind of funny that they looked like an old person's knees. Funny. The exaggerated voiceover of a car dealership ad faded out and the show was about to come back on. Norman smiled at the people on TV and tried to taste his mouthful of cold pizza.

Norman has his Window Cleaned

February 4th, A Saturday

A knock at the door introduced Norman to a man with a thick moustache offering a window cleaning service. For twenty-five dollars, he would rappel down the building and clean all of Norman's windows. Norman only had one window, but he agreed, as he didn't have a way of cleaning the window himself. The man said he would be back to collect payment when he finished.

Norman sat watching the window, waiting for the man to climb down. Eventually the man appeared, but began washing his neighbour's windows, positioned below his own. When the man arrived to collect payment Norman was too self-conscious to explain the mistake. Instead, he paid, and said the window looked the best it had in years.

Norman Drives Home in the Rain

February 5th, A Sunday

Norman was driving home in the rain from the grocery store. He never enjoyed driving in the rain because he was nervous that he would lose control of his car, but he was out of peas and needed some for his dinner.

As he pulled up to a light, he noticed the windshield wipers were moving in time with the music playing softly on the radio. He watched, mesmerized, until the wipers fell out of sync again. *Oh well,* thought Norman.

He continued home.

Norman Eats an Apple

February 6th, A Monday

It was a quarter past eleven and Norman was beginning to feel hungry. Luckily, Norman was prepared. He had eaten his breakfast earlier than usual and had brought an apple to snack on as insurance. Norman gingerly removed the apple from his lunch bag. He noticed a small sticker on the apple and peeled it off. He tried to put it in the waste basket next to his desk but it stuck to his finger. He tried to flick it off with another finger but it stuck each nail it touched. Norman considered wiping it on something but he didn't want to be a litter bug. Norman considered wiping it on himself but he didn't want to look like a fool. He stuck the sticker back on the apple and replaced it in his lunch bag. Maybe he would try again at lunch.

Norman Finds a Penny

February 7th, A Tuesday

Grocery shopping was one of those things that just had to be done. Norman made his way out to the car with this week's supply of oatmeal, bologna and cheese sandwiches, microwaveable dinners, and a special treat: a nice frozen pizza.

Norman carefully arranged his bags in the trunk of the car. When everything was just right, he pushed his cart back to the return. As he reached out to open the door of his car, Norman looked down. A dull, brown penny lay on the ground at his feet. Norman crouched to get a better look.

Tails.

Norman flipped over the penny and left it on the ground.

Norman Gets in Trouble with the Law

February 8th, A Wednesday

Norman hurried home from work. This was because he knew there would be a CSI marathon shortly after he got home. The shows would all be reruns, but Norman did not mind this because he was able to predict the culprit before the detectives could. He was usually right.

Unfortunately, he was so excited for the reruns that he didn't notice the speedometer creeping past the limit. He did notice the red and blue lights flashing in the mirror, though.

After Norman was pulled over, the officer asked Norman why he was going so fast. Norman started to explain about the CSI episodes, but the officer cut him off and told him a story about a friend of his who was killed by a drunk driver.

Norman thought this wasn't an applicable lecture as he wasn't drunk, but did not say anything. The officer then told Norman that he would not give him a ticket this time, but would be looking for him and would give him a ticket the next time. Norman thought it would be easier to look for his car and not him, but did not say anything, as doing so would help the officer find him and give him the ticket.

Norman returned home and found that, much to his disappointment, he had missed most of the first episode. Norman was upset, but then remembered the marathon started with a new episode, leaving the reruns untouched. He was not as bothered.

Norman Nearly Rear Ends a Parked Vehicle

February 9th, A Thursday

The sound of *The Deedles* coming through the speakers of his little car sounded fantastic. *"Here comes the fun,"* Norman mumbled along with whatever words he could remember. It was a long day at work and he simply could not be bothered to sing like he had been practicing all those mornings in the shower.

It was around 6:15PM, it was dark, cold and foggy. All Norman could think about was getting home, having a nice warm dinner and turning in for the night. He looked down at his cell phone to check the time. *If only we didn't have that last-minute meeting, I would have been home by now.*

Norman shook his head in frustration, barely noticing the large pick-up truck stopped at the red light in front of him. Norman slammed the brakes, his little car screeching to a halt. *Norman,* he thought to himself, *you really need to stop working yourself too hard.* The light turned green and Norman continued his commute home.

Norman is Pranked

<u>February 10th, A Friday</u>

Norman was sitting in his recliner when the phone rang, late in the evening.

"Hello?" asked Norman harshly.

He hadn't meant for his hello to sound so aggressive, but thought the thrilling action scene playing on the television might've affected it. He was already worried this call, with whoever it may be, would turn sour based on his rude beginning.

"Hello?" the voice said back.

Her voice sound much less offensive than his, and he was glad for that. *But who was she?* She sounded young, *like a little girl*, Norman thought.

"Hello?" Norman responded.

This time he was careful not to make it sound so harsh, but at the same time, tossed the ball back onto her court, as she was the one that called.

"Is your refrigerator running?" she asked.

Norman pondered the question, unsure of its answer. He stood from the chair, carefully tossed the blanket resting on top of him to the armrest, and went to his refrigerator. He opened it, and looked around. *Did the light mean it was working properly?*

"Does the light mean it's working properly?"

"Is it running?"

"Maybe. Does the light mean it's working properly?"

She hung up quickly, the phone clanging on plastic before cutting out. Norman was confused. He looked online to see if the light meant that the refrigerator was okay. It gave him various answers. Norman would have to call maintenance in the morning.

Norman Waits for Norman

February 11th, A Saturday

Norman waited, impatiently pacing back and forth by the window. It had been three or four days since Norman had left. Norman was worried. He missed Norman dearly. Every minute felt like an hour, every hour felt like a day, and every day felt like an eternity. Norman was becoming quite tired, but he would not sleep until Norman was home. Norman looked on, occasionally nodding off. Then a loud noise woke him up.

It was a familiar noise. Norman looked out just in time to see the familiar rusty car barely make it into the parking lot. Norman had come home! Norman ran to the door and eagerly awaited Norman to enter. Once Norman entered the apartment, Norman let out a great "Hello!" Norman smiled, gave Norman a scratch behind the ears, and went to sit in his favorite chair. Norman curled up on Norman's lap, and the man and cat fell asleep.

Norman Feeds Ducks

February 12th, A Sunday

Norman's rusty car spluttered and moaned as he pulled up to the shore of the lake that rested a few miles from his town. He walked around to the back of his car to grab his loaf of bread so that he might feed the ducks while staring out across the water.

Norman sat and ate the white bread himself. It was too cold for the ducks.

Norman Does a Good Deed

February 13th, A Monday

Norman drove home from work. On the way home, he saw a woman pulled over with her warning blinkers on. He thought back to an old video from high school auto class and figured that she must have a bad battery. Norman then turned around on the median and went to the auto shop.

Inside, Norman picked out the cheapest pair of jumper cables. While in line to the register, he thought about getting one of the air fresheners on display but decided against it.

He drove back, but the woman was gone. Norman figured it was for the best. He might have shocked himself jumping the car.

Norman went home and set the jumper cables and receipt next to his old ones. He convinced himself he would work up the courage to return them on the way home the next day, and parked in front of the store before deciding that he could use a spare set anyway. However, he felt self-conscious driving up to a business and then leaving, so he went inside and bought the air freshener.

Norman Cooks Some Chicken Wings

February 14th, A Tuesday

It was Tuesday night and Norman felt like cooking some chicken wings. He turned on the oven, arranged the wings on a pan, sprinkled on some cayenne pepper (he felt a little daring tonight) and placed the pan in the oven.

After forty-five minutes, he went to check on the wings and, after letting them cool on the counter for a few minutes, he tried one. He had made them far too spicy.

On his way back from Subway, Norman almost hit a fox with his car. The cayenne pepper from the wing he ate gave him heartburn later when he tried to sleep.

Norman Joins a Protest

February 15th, A Wednesday

When Norman bought socks, he bought black socks. He bought black socks because all of his other socks were black. He did not enjoy pairing things up - life was much easier when all of his socks were aesthetically apathetic.

But it wasn't just the colour. They had to be of the same brand: 'Filmores Black Socks'. And they had to be cotton-rich. He imagined the Kings of England wearing them in bed, swivelling their heels and soles together in shear delight.

Norman estimated that his socks' useful life stretched across about two years. Their relatively short life-span was the price to be paid for luxury. He had calculated that his socks of 2009 would soon be reaching their expiry date and so he had made an appointment with the menswear department.

A lot had happened in two years. Now, the elasticated landscape spanned shelves ranging from hiking socks to a grotesque hybrid of sock and slipper. Norman carefully negotiated his way to the 'no-nonsense' section.

He examined the rank and file of black socks and finger-walked his way to 'Filmores'.

Except they weren't 'Filmores'. They were a sock species called 'Flagmores'. Norman closed his eyes and squeezed the bunch. No, they were not the same. They were not Filmores. There were no Filmores.

Without thinking, he took one of the impostors in hand and made his way to the checkout. He rationalised: he wasn't complaining; he was merely asking. He was going to place the Flagmores on the counter and say, "Sorry to be a nuisance but I was hoping you could tell me where I can find a pair of Filmores." Perfectly reasonable. Perhaps putting them on the counter might seem a little combative, like throwing down the sock gauntlet. No, he was only asking: the Flagmores were for reference; they weren't a weapon.

He arrived at a queue and clipped himself in at the back. He wondered whether he could buy Filmores from the internet but that didn't feel right.

The counter was only two arm lengths away now. Only one customer stood between him and his question, an older woman wearing a silk kerchief around her neck. He craned over her shoulder and saw that she was buying a pair of Flagmores. The cashier looked pained. Silkerchief picked up the Flagmores and waggled them in the air like an eagle its prey.

"I've been coming to this store for over twenty years and you try and pass these off as the real thing?"

The cashier grimaced, "I'm sorry madam."

Silkerchief leaned in. "I don't think you understand. I came into town specially to buy Filmores. These," - she let the socks dribble off her hands onto the counter - "are of an inferior quality. I daren't use the term knock-off in an establishment such as this but these" - and this she whispered - "are second-rate."

The cashier stood unblinking as his hands found the phone, "I will speak to the manager."

Silkerchief crossed her arms: "O.K." She turned around and, seeing Norman's Flagmores, raised her eyes to the heavens.

The cashier delivered a strangled mutter into the handset as Norman tucked the socks under his armpit. "The manager will be with us shortly." he flat-smiled. The cashier motioned to Norman.

The complainant took a staccato step to the side and Norman fell into place. He looked to the cashier then back at Silkerchief. He felt the Flagmores swell in his armpit.

"Can I help you sir?" asked the cashier.

"Uh," Norman enunciated carefully.

"Do you need a bag for them?" the cashier pointed at the swelling.

“Uh.” Norman whisper-shouted. "I’ve forgotten something.” Norman swivelled on his heel and retreated back into the store. He found himself a column to watch from but was soon shooed away from his post by an idle security guard.

He wished people were more like his socks.

Norman has an Appointment

February 16th, A Thursday

Norman had awoken early, far before the sun had risen. He'd eaten some leftovers for breakfast, licking his bowl clean. He meandered aimlessly around the dim house until weak morning light began to sift through the curtains.

Not long after the alarm clock went off, which Norman had set the night before, Norman hesitantly entered the car. It smelt strange and off-putting. Once it began lurching about, Norman felt decidedly queasy. He arrived at a foreboding building, brimming with disturbing odours and frightening noise, where men in white coats manhandled him and fed him foul-tasting pills.

When he finally entered his house again, Norman felt disgruntled and vaguely violated. His sombre mood was softened somewhat after Norman scooped some tuna into his bowl as a treat. Norman loved tuna. He purred loudly in appreciation.

Norman Makes it to Work on Time

February 17th, A Friday

Norman woke up to the sound of his alarm. He'd dreamt that he was wearing new red shoes. One of his dream-coworkers had said they were stolen. Dream-Norman was sure they weren't. Still in bed, he thought about his dream for a few moments.

He got out of bed and went to the bathroom to brush his teeth before showering. While doing so he noticed his receding hairline. He stared at his hairline from various angles for a whole fifteen minutes, before he noticed the time and feared he'd be late to work.

He went to work without showering and made it there six minutes early.

Norman Goes Bowling

February 18th, A Saturday

Norman arrived at the bowling alley. Norman was very excited because he hadn't been bowling for a very long time, even though he loves bowling. He noticed that there was a very pretty redhead woman working the cash register, and he started to feel shy. He then noticed that there was a crane game in the corner where you could win a stuffed animal.

He decided he might as well kill some time and give it a shot. He set his eye on a pink elephant. He kept getting very close, but just couldn't manage to get it. After about seven tries, he realized he didn't have enough money on him to go bowling anymore. He started walking back to his car, wondering if that redhead woman would have decided to go for the pink elephant too.

Norman gets a Haircut

February 19th, A Sunday

Norman went into the town's second most popular barber shop. True, there were only two, but Norman thought that he should think positively.

"Go ahead and take a seat," the barber said as Norman walked in and took a seat. Norman waited half an hour, avoiding small talk with the other patrons.

"What do you need done?" The barber asked, staring at Norman's receding hairline. "O-oh, just, you know, shorter," he stammered out, gesturing at his hair. After the haircut, he tipped nicely and left without another word.

Norman Tries to Buy Some Cookies

February 20th, A Monday

Norman loves chocolate chip cookies. They had always been his favorite since he was a small boy. Growing up, his mom used to make them and he fondly remembers coming home to the smell of fresh cookies, hot out of the oven. There is a bakery shop near Norman's house and he enjoys occasionally stopping by, on the way home from work, to pick up some chocolate chip cookies that are almost as good as he remembers his mother's cookies being. Norman has never been able to make a batch of cookies without burning them.

This particular evening, as Norman stepped out of his decaying Daihatsu, he overheard some younger gentlemen talking about chocolate chip cookies. They entered the store ahead of Norman, and he gasped in exasperation. Norman approached the corner of the aisle with the cookies and, with a sigh of relief, found that there were two containers left. Before Norman could claim his own, the young boys promptly snatched both boxes between boisterous laughs, completely unaware of Norman walking down the aisle. Norman sighed again, deeper this time, and continued to walk past the posse, his eyes fixed straight ahead. He picked up a stick of cookie dough and returned to his car to drive home, to attempt once again to make the cookies himself.

Norman has a Friend

February 21st, A Tuesday

When Norman arrived home from work, he went through his regular Tuesday routine. Taking off his shirt, tie, and khaki pants, he began to change directly into his sleeping attire. He liked to take this time to reflect on some of the day's events. *Today was a good day*, he thought.

Norman had woken up at 6:15, happy with his decision for an early bedtime the night before. Traffic was mild, and Norman remembered seeing a bald eagle while on his way to work. Arriving a few minutes early, he found his favorite parking spot was open. It was the cozy spot, wedged into a shady corner of the building. He always felt a bit guilty not leaving it for someone else, but figured that today he had earned it by being early. "G'mornin', Normie," he heard as he entered the building. Norman didn't like the nickname that Randy had given him, but didn't bother to correct him, especially now that he had used it three times now. "Good morning, Randy," he replied to the good-natured custodian. Norman wondered if perhaps Randy disliked his nickname as well. He decided to call him by Randall from now on, just in case.

Norman was now heating up his chicken and mashed potatoes, leftover from last night. He had a lot of leftover nights ever since his divorce; he liked the large meals he had always made. Norman wondered if he could consider Randall a friend. *Perhaps I should have Randall over for dinner sometime,* he thought, *that way I might not have so many leftover nights.* But Norman knew he would not invite Randall over for dinner. He was used to his leftover nights.

Norman Needs a Change

February 22nd, A Wednesday

Norman was especially excited today. It was Wednesday and it was Norman's final interview for a prospective new career choice. After so many years of continued meritocracy, Norman came to the realization, after much careful and calculated thought, that it would be best for Norman and himself to seek a more fulfilling and financially profitable lifestyle.

Instead of his normal off-white button up and faded slacks, Norman felt it was appropriate to bring out some of his more formal attire in hopes of impressing the interviewers. Norman chose an off-white button up with blue vertical stripes and his matching, but faded, favorite blue tie. His son had gifted him that tie, it being the only gift Norman had from his son since he was a child, so he saved it for especially savory occasions such as this.

Feeling dressed up and overly-nervous, Norman left his home, feeding Norman as he left. He got in his Daihatsu, struggling to open the door, as the handle had broken the week prior. As Norman attempted to start his car, he had a startling realization. His interview had been the day prior and he had completely missed it.

Norman returned to his home, slipped his favorite faded blue tie back into it's proper place in his dresser drawer, sat down on his slightly squeaky twin bed, picked up the cord phone on his nightstand, and proceed to call his current employer letting him know that he would be back to work on Thursday.

Norman Fails to Find Love

February 23rd, A Thursday

One day, as Norman was walking into the library to return some books, he noticed an attractive woman walking out.

"Hello," he greeted her warmly. She kept walking.

Norman returned his books and looked for new ones, but didn't find any.

Norman Gets Stuck in Traffic

February 24th, A Friday

Norman had been trying to overtake a slow truck for about twenty minutes now. The pouring rain was beating down hard making visibility low, and the road was winding left and right without end. No cars were coming from up ahead, but Norman was never certain that it was safe. Behind him there was a long queue of angry fellow motorists, furious at his inability to overtake, and making their frustration known to him through honking the horns and flashing the headlights of their automobiles.

The road straightened, the sky cleared, and Norman finally started the slow creep past the truck with his rusty, little car. Once on the other side, the motorists behind him made the most of the opportunity to speed past him, get a good look at him, flail their arms wildly in a final attempt to release all their pent-up frustration, and disappear into the distance up ahead.

In the wake of the entire ordeal Norman felt like taking a break, and pulled over at the next rest stop. He emptied his bladder and filled his tank, and again he was on his way. Soon Norman was stuck behind the same truck again.

Norman's Little Friend

February 25th, A Saturday

Norman sat in his aged armchair. He painfully bent over and removed his shoes which were followed by his socks. It had been a long day and his feet ached. He lifted his left foot towards his right knee as best he could, joints aching even more intensely. He bent his head forward and watched as light from his lamp spilled onto his big toe.

There it was. That bloody verruca. It was hard to believe it had lived with him for over five years now. He had acquired it after a misguided attempt at getting fit by joining the local public swimming pool. He only went once and a week later had noticed his little toe travelling companion.

Norman had tried various treatments over the years. Freezing. Burning. Even cutting. Often it appeared to have gone. Weeks at a time. Without fail it always returned. *Persistent little bastard.* Norman had almost grown accustomed to it.

He came close to naming it a few times. It looked bigger today. It had blackened again. He touched it with his fingertip and it stung. He creaked to his feet and walked to the sink. Always careful to arch his big toe away from the floor, making for a strange walk. As he washed his finger vigorously he decided it was time to freeze his little friend again. It was time for it to hibernate for a few weeks. He'd see him again soon.

Norman Has an Epiphany

February 26th, A Sunday

Norman finished relieving himself and carefully zipped up his khakis. He was about to put the seat down when he had a thought: *I live alone. My wife has left. Norman Jr has left. Norman certainly isn't going to meow at me and tell me to leave the seat down. There is no one to tell me to put the seat down. I am a free man. I can do what I want, and a man wants to leave the seat up, because it's less work when he only has to pee.*

Norman put the seat down anyway, just to be safe.

Norman Goes to the DMV

February 27th, A Monday

Norman has been carrying around his driver's license for nearly 20 years. It is expired, faded, discolored and bent from being the "little spoon" to his many rewards membership cards. The other day he was embarrassingly turned away from the pub he occasionally goes to with his co-workers for having an expired license. So, Norman decided to go to the DMV to renew it after work. As Norman waited in line, he pondered whether "bald" would be listed as an option under hair color. He gazed at the picture on his old driver's license and reminisced his younger self and his flowing brownish blonde shoulder length hair and bushy mustache.

Norman looked up and realized he was next in line. He felt uncertain and worried. The middle-aged woman behind the counter glared at him over the top of her glasses as she monotonously muttered, "Next, please". Norman stepped forward and noticed on the woman's badge that her name is Norma. He calmly stated his intentions to renew his license to which she acknowledged and charged him $40 dollars. She asked him to step around to the other side of the waiting room if he would like to update his photo. Norman mustered a half-hearted smile headed to the exit door. He didn't have time to wait in another line for a photo. Norman needed to get home to feed Norman and watch *Wheel of Fortune*.

Norman Loves His Crossword Puzzles

February 28th, A Tuesday

Norman's fingers tingled, as excitement was brewing inside him. He parked his rusty, little car in the first spot he could find, ran toward his front door, opened and slammed it behind him, hurrying towards the breakfast table where he had always put the newspaper after reading it in the morning.

Today was a tough day at work, and he needed to relax in his favourite chair, forget all about his worries and do his daily crossword puzzle from the newspaper. It was almost a spiritual activity for Norman, his "high" - flying through dense white clouds of tricky questions and vague clues about celebrities and geography.

Norman stood in his lonely and empty kitchen holding the newspaper, a lump forming in his throat. The crossword has already been completed. *I must have done it sometime this morning,* Norman thought. Norman could be so forgetful sometimes. His eyes welled up with tears as a deep dark hole of despair formed somewhere inside him.

His kitchen seemed so empty now, so lonely. The desolation screamed at him.

Suddenly, though, the feeling of sorrow was transformed. Like a butterfly emerging from its cocoon, it transcended into a feeling of intense exhilaration as his eye fell on the date at the top of the newspaper. *How silly! This is yesterday's paper!* He whipped it across the kitchen in the direction of the trash can, and shuffled through mess on his kitchen table until he finally found his holy grail: today's newspaper.

Norman turns the page to the crossword puzzle to find that it had already been completed. He can be so forgetful sometimes.

MARCH.
RUSTY1

March

Norman Remembers

March 1st, A Wednesday

Norman laid in bed. He wasn’t comfortable. It was his pillow, and adjusting it only seemed to make things worse. His heart burn was acting up again.

Tomato sauce will do that, he thought. Norman made a mental note to take it easy on the tomato sauce.

His mind wandered, and he thought of a girl from school. Jane. She had had a thing for Norman. He remembered her trying to start conversations with him, laughing too hard when he made a joke, trying to catch his eye.... he had been oblivious, and why he remembered and realised it now, he didn't know. She had been plain but cute. Norman felt guilty. He decided he should look her up in the phone book.

"... Jane.... what was her last name? Jane Wes... Wal..."

Norman fell asleep.

The next morning Norman awoke. He remembered to take it easy on the tomato sauce. He did not remember Jane.

Norman Dip his Biscuit Too Far into his Tea

March 2nd, A Thursday

Norman's kettle reached the boil with a satisfying 'click'. Norman quickly placed a teabag into his favorite mug. He poured the hot water from the kettle into the mug, and while the tea stewed, he fetched some chocolate Digestives from a freshly opened pack. He removed the tea bag and added just a splash of milk. The liquid turned a caramel-brown. A perfect cup of tea.

Feeling quite pleased with his effort, Norman brought the cup and a plate holding his biscuits into the living room. Re-runs of a car show had been playing all day, and though he wasn't sure if Jeremy Clarkson was the best influence, he settled down to watch.

While his tea cooled, Norman thought it would be alright to eat a biscuit. He decided to dip it into his tea, something he wouldn't ordinarily risk. Gingerly, he lowered the Digestive into the brew. While he was doing this, the presenters of Top Gear were loading a caravan into a catapult. Distracted, Norman let his biscuit go too far into the tea and let it sit submersed in the tea for far too long.

The feeling of liquid against his fingertips snapped him back to his senses and he wrenched the biscuit from the mug. But he was too late. The biscuit broke and a large soggy section of it was left floating in his tea.

Norman was distraught.

Norman Gets Noticed

March 3rd, A Friday

A week ago, Norman had received a very nice email from the head of human resources. His steadfast attention to detail and meticulous attendance record had been rewarded with the honor of Employee of the Month. There was a cake in the lunchroom and his employee photo was hung on the wall by the water cooler.

At first, Norman had been thrilled with the title, but a few days later, he noticed a change in the people around him. People he didn't know were saying hi to him in the elevator. He was given the first cup of coffee at break time. Even Frank had been acting friendly towards him. He just wanted things to be quiet like they were before.

On the fridge that afternoon, he found a printout of his employee photo with block white letters printed over it in two lines. "WHAT WOULD NORMAN DO?"

Norman decided he didn't like being employee of the month.

Norman Goes to the Movies

March 4th, A Saturday

It was Saturday night and Norman wanted to treat himself. He remembered his co-workers sharing their excitement with each other about a new movie that was opening tonight. Norman really liked movie theaters, especially on busy nights, so he thought this would be a marvelous way to spend his evening.

The show started at 8:30PM, and as usual Norman liked to show up early. He sat down right in the middle of the theater and waited as all the other seats around him filled up with people eager to share the experience. He could hear their conversations as they waited; one man was talking about a new job he will be starting, and another group was chatting about the game that they all enjoyed. Norman overheard a young lady had just gotten engaged. She sat behind him so he couldn't see her but Norman imagined she was beautiful.

The movie started as the lights dimmed. Everyone went silent and watched the giant screen together, laughing at the same jokes and jumping when startled.

After the movie was over Norman went home happy. The movie was quite good but all he could think about is the beautiful new wife-to-be.

Norman Buys a Car

March 5th, A Sunday

It was 12:30PM on Sunday when Norman pulled into the dealership's parking lot. He exited his old rusty car and patted it on the hood much like someone would do to a horse at the end of a long journey.

He walked up to the dealership and held the door open for a young attractive lady in a business suit. She didn't say "Thank you." After her, a group of chatting business people passed through the door from the opposite direction. They also did not say "Thank you."

A couple more groups of people passed through the door he was holding; most of them ignored Norman but there were a few that expressed their gratitude.

Eventually Norman passed through the door but he noticed the reflection of somebody walking in behind him and got caught holding a second door open.

Once Norman was finally inside he was approached by a kind man in a business suit.

"Hi there, I'm John. John Wertz!" the man said.

"I'm Norman."

"What can I do for you Norman?"

"I'd like to buy a car."

"Do you know how much you're looking to spend?"

"Oh, not very much." Norman said.

John Wertz chuckled and slapped his hand on Norman's shoulder. "So, are you thinking somewhere around the $10,000 area?"

Norman calmly pulled away without saying a word and walked back to his old rusty car. John Wertz watched as Norman patted it on the hood before he got in and drove away.

Norman Finds Twenty Dollars

March 6th, A Monday

Norman's Daihatsu did not start this morning.

It's okay, Norman thought, as the weather was nice enough to walk in and he was always sure to wake up extra early for work so as not to be late.

After a long day at the office Norman began his trek home. Norman always looked at his feet as he walked. His mother used to nag him about his posture, but there next to the sidewalk laying in the gutter was a twenty-dollar bill. He wouldn't have seen this if he were looking straight ahead!

Norman remembered that he had to buy cat food for Norman.

As he entered the pet store on his way back he decided to buy a nicer brand of cat food this time. Normally he always bought the cheaper brand, but today was different. Upon arriving home, he had a diet ginger ale, fed Norman his fancier cat food, and watched CSI until nine o'clock.

As Norman was falling asleep he smiled, knowing that he had used his good fortune to better the life of his furry companion.

Somewhere in his apartment he heard Norman throwing up.

Norman Runs an Errand

March 7th, A Tuesday

Norman needed real cat food, so Norman went to the store.

As Norman entered the store, he passed a couple. The girl locked eyes with Norman for just a second. She had red hair, was wearing a red jacket and hat, and had very blue eyes. Norman broke eye contact and continued on his errand to get Norman cat food.

That night, as Norman was falling asleep, the girl popped back into his head. His stomach fluttered a little.

Norman Has Deja-vu

March 8th, A Wednesday

Norman woke up and cooked himself oatmeal with a side of tea. As he went to work, he turned the radio to his favourite station, and hummed along to the songs.

At work, Norman sorted paperwork, responded to emails, and wrote several T4's.

As he drove home, Norman picked up a pork-chop and rice from the grocery store. He also purchased a packet of cat treats for Norman.

Once home, Norman turned on CSI and began his meal.

As he prepared for bed, Norman had a thought. *Have I done this day before?*

Norman tried to do something to make this day different from the others. Norman imagined himself in prehistoric times, fighting off a velociraptor.

Norman never had that mental fantasy before. Norman fell asleep, feeling accomplished.

Norman is Chased by the Cops

March 9th, a Thursday

Norman was driving home from work. He was a bit late already. He was tired and thought of just beeping up a microwave meal. Or maybe he would take out Chinese, but then again, he had already done that last week.

Suddenly he saw a cop car in his rear-view mirror. Were the cops following him? Or were they just on their way elsewhere? Oh God, had he remembered his seat belt? Yes, yes he had. The seatbelt light would have lit up otherwise, anyway. *Phew.* He took a right turn, making sure to use his indicator and looking everywhere extra carefully. The cop car went straight ahead.

After about half a mile, Norman could breathe again. He felt kind of guilty. As he passed the next crossing, he realized he should have taken a left for Chinese takeout. Oh well, he supposed a microwave meal would do just fine.

Norman Eats M&M's

March 10th, A Friday

Today at work, Norman's boss congratulated everyone on their hard work. Norman thought about this while driving home and, deciding he deserved a reward, stopped at the convenience store to buy a pack of peanut M&Ms. Norman liked peanut M&Ms.

Norman ate them later that night, until eventually he turned the small bag over and nothing came out. Norman looked in the bag and saw only the bottom. He was disappointed for a moment. But then he realized that the bottom has folded up a bit.

Norman straightened out the bottom of the bag and found three peanut M&Ms.

Norman was happy.

Norman Does Not Like His New Phone

March 11th, A Saturday

At 11:13 PM, Norman's new phone beeped.

Norman's bought this phone about two years ago. He still calls it his "new" phone, though, because he's never gotten used to it. He missed his old phone. His old phone had buttons, and no finicky touch screen. Also, the old one didn't beep when he forgot to charge it, thereby waking him up. But the salesman insisted this new one was better, so he never bothered going back to the old one.

Norman got out of bed and plugged it in. When he returned to bed, he found that he was no longer as comfortable as he was before getting up.

Norman does not like his new phone.

Norman Has Trouble Falling Asleep

March 12th, A Sunday

Norman went to bed somewhere between 9 PM and 10 PM, as he did every night. Usually, after a few minutes, he fell asleep. Tonight, however, he could not.

Remembering his childhood, and how his mother always prescribed a glass of milk when he had had trouble falling asleep, he rolled out of bed to pour himself a glass.

The expiration date on the milk was two days ago. Norman poured himself a glass anyway, telling himself that the expiration date was never accurate.

Norman had awful gas and couldn't sleep.

Norman Goes to Work

March 13th, A Monday

Norman was driving to work when he spotted a female co-worker walking in the hot sun. *I should give her a lift,* he thought. He quickly looked around his car; it hadn't been cleaned in months. Norman looked straight ahead and sped past his co-worker, hoping she wouldn't notice. He got stuck at a red light and looked out the window, making eye contact with his colleague before speeding off again.

Norman Gets a Papercut

March 14th, A Tuesday

As Norman browsed at a bookstore, he received a papercut. It was a nasty one on his index finger, bled a drop of blood onto his shoes and brought forth three tears. He thought of asking the girl at the counter for ... something. He wasn't sure, but perhaps he would have liked her to know what became of him browsing her books, though he decided that would come off as pitiful.

Later at work, the cut was done bleeding, but left a thin white line of spread skin on his finger. For the rest of the day he favoured his wounded hand, and used it in front of his co-workers any time he could; taking a drink from the water-cooler, photocopying, or simply scratching his ear as he spoke to his co-worker Lisa. No one seemed to notice his wound, but Lisa did notice his new tie. It wasn't a new tie, but he took the compliment anyway.

Norman Tries KFC

March 15th, A Wednesday

Norman was browsing Wikipedia using the random feature when he stumbled upon the Kentucky Derby's history page. After spending a few minutes reading, Norman decided he would try KFC for the first time in his life that night. Half an hour before he left work he ordered online for pickup, and at that moment he caught a whiff of perfume as the new intern, Sharon, walked by.

Norman couldn't help but think of her face as he took the bus home and arrived at his doorstep. Upon entering his apartment, Norman fed Norman only to realise that he'd forgot to pick up his order from KFC. Norman ordered pizza for delivery before sitting down to watch an old episode of CSI.

Norman Saves the Day

March 16th, A Thursday

Norman's long hair blew in the wind as his red '76 Mustang with black racing stripes screeched, turning to the right. Gunshots rang out as Norman drove into the alley. He looked behind him, as '*Eye of the Tiger*' blared on the radio. The dark sunglasses that he was wearing along with the bandana around his head made it hard to read his expression, but it was clear that he was ready to kick some butt. The car jolted to a stop; it had reached the end of the alleyway. The gunshots grew louder.

"Get behind the car," said Norman to the two supermodels in the back seat of his Mustang.

His manly voice was deep and gravelly, filled with an amount of testosterone only found in movies. The two supermodels hid behind the car as Norman stepped out.

It was a cold day, but Norman wasn't wearing a shirt. His muscles glistened in the wind; his pecs flexed as he pulled out his machine gun, and his six-pack tensed as he readied for action. His cigar glowed as the cars that were pursuing them got closer and closer. Norman pulled the trigger.

"Sayonara, suckers," said Norman as his gun spit out a storm of bullets.

All fifty of the cars that had been chasing him exploded, struck by Norman's massive twenty-five-millimeter bullets. The gunmen in the cars were thrown into the air, as ablaze as their vehicles. Norman turned away from the explosion, never looking back. Norman didn't look back at explosions. That wasn't his style.

"Oh Norman! You've saved us!" said the drop-dead gorgeous supermodels that he had just rescued.

"I think we should all make out now!" exclaimed the blonde. Norman flexed his muscles in preparation.

Norman woke up with a bad case of gas. He ran to the bathroom, thinking that he shouldn't have eaten a bowl of salsa nachos right before going to bed. Spicy food always gave him gas and really funky dreams.

Norman Looks at Chairs

March 17th, A Friday

Norman had spent the morning looking for a chair on the internet. He hadn't bought a chair before. All previous chairs had already been there, waiting for him.

He didn't need a new chair. He already had one chair in front of the television but sometimes Norman would be using it. So, he was really buying a chair for Norman, or himself, depending on Norman's mood.

He had asked for Norman's opinion, but he wasn't feeling very cooperative as he lolled on the armchair, and besides, it was clear which chair the cat had wanted.

So, Norman looked for a chair similar to the chair he already owned. There were lots of chairs that looked like his chair but each of them were slightly too different.

Norman leaped off the armchair and trotted up to see what Norman was doing on the computer. "Mewl," said Norman.

Norman saw his opportunity and ran back to his armchair, pursued by Norman who jumped onto his lap.

Everyone had the chair they wanted, for now.

Norman Takes a Walk

March 18th, A Saturday

Saturday, 6:30AM. Norman always allowed himself an extra thirty minutes of sleep on the weekends. Normally, after waking up, Norman would make breakfast and read the newspaper. But not today.

Earlier this week Norman overheard a co-worker talking about an article in 'Men's Health' that said, "Just half an hour of walking is good for heart health!". Not wanting to be unhealthy, and acknowledging his family's history of heart attacks, Norman decided he should try something new.

Wearing his grey sweatpants, he found a CD mix he had made five years ago in an old CD case. He put it in his CD player and stepped outside into the crisp sunrise morning. This first song was a good one. The neighborhood was quiet and Norman quite enjoyed his ability to walk in time with the song without feeling self-conscious.

Finally, he made it to the end of the block. His heart rate was up and Norman was feeling the blood flow and even humming along with the song.

As he made a right turn in a perfect power-walk stance, the song changed.

"True" by Spandau Ballet.

The shadow of painful memories suddenly gripped Norman's conscience. This was *their* song.

Maybe that's enough walking for today, thought Norman. He shuffled home with no music.

Norman Goes to the Farmers Market

March 19th, A Sunday

Every third Sunday, Norman's town hosted a Farmer's market, with vendors in the streets selling fruits, vegetables, and various sundries.

On a whim, Norman, despite his dislike for crowds, decided to investigate the market.

Norman was intrigued by a vendor selling loose tea. Norman purchased a bag.

Norman regretted his purchase later, feeling that tea bags are much more time efficient.

Norman put the tea in the back of his cupboard and shut the door.

Norman Was

March 20th, A Monday

For the third time Norman explained to the fellow at the copy counter why he wanted his money back.

The gentleman seemed to get angrier with each iteration of the story.

Yes, "Carl", as his name tag proudly seemed to proclaim, had laid out and runran the job. No, it was not his problem that Norman had purportedly misspelled his cat's name on the lost and found poster, and had 160 copies of a lost and found poster for a cat named Morman.

Norman had the receipt and job order, showing that the spelling was correct on it, but Carl would not listen to reason, or proof.

Norman left, rather than face the confrontation. His cat had come home the night before, anyhow.

Norman Gets Harassed

March 21st, A Tuesday

Norman was on his way home after finishing his second unremarkable day of work this week. It was raining lightly. Norman had failed to take the precaution of bringing his umbrella, so rather than risking further dampness he thought it would be wise to take the bus. Fortunately for Norman his route home did account for these eventualities, allowing him to take refuge at a bus shelter.

"Got any change, Mister?" inquired the leader of a group of youths whom Norman suspected were probably in collusion with the children who congregated outside of Tescos. Norman looked at his marginally wet shoes. He had change- of course he had- he was planning on getting the bus. Were he given the option, he would rather not give them his change.

"I've got a dollar," Norman lied; he had one dollar and eighty five cents, and a chocolate bar he didn't actually want - but he might later.

"Gives it then mate," the second in charge demanded. Norman handed over the money and continued waiting for the bus he was no longer sure he could afford.

"Ha-ha, wanker." the third snickered. The group walked off as the rain began to fall.

Norman missed his son.

Wistful Norman

March 22nd, A Wednesday

He felt comfortable with her - safe. Sure, she wasn't the girl Norman envisioned himself ending up with, but he understood that as a man in his twenties with thinning hair he wasn't in a position to pick and choose. She accepted him and his shortcomings, shared his sense of humour, and made him happy. They enjoyed summer nights together driving around aimlessly, with no direction; the same route Norman's life followed. He loved the way she would place her hand on his where it rested on the gearstick of his ten-year-old automobile. Her thumb gently brushing the back of his hand made his heart beat faster.

Norman gave a sigh as a siren outside his cramped bedroom snapped him back to the present. *Maybe someone will make me feel that way again*, he thought optimistically. It had been fourteen years since anyone had.

Norman Walks Home in the Rain

March 23rd, A Thursday

It was five o'clock - finishing time for Norman's work. He had left his car at home today in an effort to start living a healthier lifestyle. Norman saw his co-worker Lisa on the way out. Lisa tried to say goodbye but Norman didn't particularly like Lisa so he continued on past her. As Norman walked out the exit he noticed it was raining. Norman didn't want to ask Lisa for a lift so he walked home. Norman didn't make it home in time for CSI. It was okay to have bad days sometimes.

Norman Messages Ted on Facebook

March 24th, A Friday

Norman decided one day that he'd try to message his old friend Ted on Facebook. He typed the message 'Hi', and sat for a while waiting for a response. After ten minutes of waiting, it showed that Ted has seen the message. Two minutes later, Ted blocked Norman. Norman sulked himself to sleep because he didn't understand why his friend had done that.

When he woke up Norman checked his laptop again to see if Ted blocking him was a mistake. Unfortunately for Norman, it wasn't. Yet again, like in his high school years, he was lonely. Norman poured himself a cup of coffee and stroked his cat Norman.

"You're my best friend Norman," he said, and then proceeded to create a Facebook account for his cat.

Norman Wins the Lottery

March 25th, A Saturday

Norman had won the lottery.

The winning ticket was prominently displayed on his refrigerator, held in place by a magnet in the shape of an ice cream cone. Norman did not care for that particular magnet, which was why he had selected it for the task of holding his ticket in place. Better to give the other, preferred magnets the task of holding more permanent items.

Saturday morning came, and Norman rose an hour earlier than usual. He disliked deviating from his routine... but these were special circumstances. After taking care to sign his name on the back of the ticket, seal it in an envelope for safe keeping, and then hide it away in his coat's inside pocket, Norman made his way to the lottery office. He had been thinking all weekend about how to spend his winnings, and now that they were so close at hand, he could scarcely contain his excitement.

The woman behind the counter gave Norman a strange look, but she counted out his ten dollars all the same.

That afternoon, Norman ordered a cookie and a pickle with his lunch.

Norman Makes Hot Chocolate

March 26th, A Sunday

It was a Sunday night and Norman felt as though he deserved a treat. He searched through his cupboard for a moment before finding a sachet of microwave hot chocolate. He poured it into a cup and added milk. He only realised that water was supposed to be added after he mixed the powder into the milk; though he proceeded nevertheless.

Norman placed it in the microwave and set the time for ninety seconds.

While he waited he thought of his childhood. Snapshots of rice pudding and the innocent slap of bare feet on wet concrete made him smile; but only briefly.

His attention returned to his hot chocolate, which he found to be slightly less warm than anticipated. He probably needed a new microwave.

Norman Wakes Up Early

March 27th, A Monday

Norman woke up at 5:51 AM, feeling refreshed. He silently congratulated himself for waking up six minutes earlier than usual. He vowed to try for seven minutes tomorrow. He prepared for work, and found himself leaving the house eight minutes earlier than usual.

On his way to work, he marvelled at the difference that a few minutes made in traffic, and walked up to work fifteen minutes early. When he got to his desk, his boss reminded him that it was daylight savings time, and that he was forty-five minutes late. Norman agreed to stay for an extra forty-five minutes, in order to make up for the time he lost.

Norman sighed. When he got home, CSI was over.

Norman Uses a Public Restroom

March 28th, A Tuesday

Norman was driving home from work when he felt the urge to relieve himself. This was strange, because he never had to use the restroom on his way home from work. It seemed that he'd been using the restroom a lot more frequently. Norman felt that he should lower his water intake.

Eventually the need accosted Norman and he decided to stop at a gas station and use the public restroom. Normally he wouldn't make the stop, especially when it fussed with his schedule so heavily. However, he'd tried to risk it before and had to pay the price for it.

As Norman started to relieve himself, his eyes wandered across the stall walls. He noticed a phone number scratched on the wall saying, 'Call for some fun XOXO'.

Norman's heart fluttered for a moment; this was a welcoming invitation. However, Norman had learned that these numbers are never fruitful.

Still, he couldn't help but wonder ‘What if?’

Norman’s nose tickled, so he scratched it. He breathed in. It tickled again so he scratched it a bit harder. He breathed in again. Norman breathed even harder again, past the point of no return. His body contorted, propelling freshly made Norman mucus and saliva through the air. As his body convulsed and recovered, he felt the warm drops of urine soak into his pants.

Norman is Proud!

March 29th, A Wednesday

Norman had been staring off blankly into space while sitting in his kitchen. Realizing that the spot of sun he was sitting in and enjoying had moved, it was probably time to go and do something. As he was about to disembark from his chair, he heard a noise in the pantry. It sounded like something was climbing around in the bag of chips. Norman had opened the chips a few weeks ago while watching a whole afternoon's worth of James Bond movies, so they were stale anyway. That didn't matter to Norman though... there was a mouse in the pantry!

Slowly, he made his way over to the pantry door as the rodent continued rustling happily in the bag of chips. Norman pulled the door open as stealthily as he could manage. The mouse was alerted by a small sunbeam (which had managed to meander its way through the leaves on the tree in the backyard) and decided to make a run for it right by Norman's feet! This was a mistake for the mouse, though, as it soon found itself in a cat's mouth, about to meet its end. Across the room, Norman had been sitting watching the events unfold (as they have in countless kitchens through the ages). He smiled a little, prideful that Norman had completed another successful hunt.

Norman Walks in on a Meeting

March 30th, A Thursday

The conference room was double-booked this day, so Ted held his weekly budget meeting in the break room. As he reviewed the upcoming expenses, a couple of employees came in briefly to refill their coffee mugs.

One man, someone Ted recognized but had never spoken to, opened the door and began to walk in. Seeing that there was a room full of people, the man lowered his gaze and quickly turned around, letting the door close softly behind him.

Ted went on with the meeting.

Norman has a Joke for his Coworkers

March 31st, A Friday

Norman had a joke he liked. He had discovered it during one of his favorite rituals: briefly scanning books at the local bookstore without purchasing anything. The not-too-often felt feeling of excitement rushed over him when he realized he could tell this to his coworkers at the office.

Norman rushed home and began to practice his delivery. Every ebb and flow of the tale's diction was rehearsed. Norman's cat served as his victim. Hour after hour Norman crafted the perfect delivery to his masterpiece. He had everything down from the tone of his voice to his hand gestures.

Today would be the day Norman would tell the infamous joke. It was lunchtime at the office, and all the guys were just hanging around having small talk. Meanwhile, Norman was shaking in nervousness. For once in his benign life he had the opportunity to put a smile on someone's face. A joint moment of happiness....and he would be the origin. This was more than a joke for him, it was a milestone in his life.

Validation that he can be just like "the guys". Proof that he hadn't died after his wife and son left.

Once conversation died down at the water cooler, Norman seized to opportunity to tell the most important story he would ever tell.

"So guys, I heard this funny joke a couple of days ago..." he started casually. Everyone's eyes were glued to him. Norman had done it! He was becoming the center of conversation. The joke flowed from Norman's lips like honey. He savored the moment.

Just as he was about to deliver the punch-line, one of the more eccentric extroverted guys came up. He began to exclaim praise for the Raven's victory over the Steelers. Everyone shifted their attention to him and began to cheer and scowl at the win/lose. The conversation began to swell and soon, no one was listening to Norman.

Sad and desolate, Norman turned to fill up his water cup. He sipped on it. It was luke-warm.

April

Norman's Birthday Dinner

April 1st, A Saturday

Norman decided to treat himself to a nice dinner. It was his birthday, after all. He pulled into the parking lot of his favourite local pub, The Pub. It was more crowded than he thought it would be, and a few groups of people were waiting outside. Norman didn't feel like waiting for a table. He sat parked in his car for a moment and thought about heading home.

I'll just sit at the bar, Norman thought, as he headed inside.

Norman confidently strode into the restaurant, smiling at the hostess as he walked by. As he approached the bar, Norman saw that there were no empty seats. Not wanting to turn around in the middle of the restaurant and risk drawing attention to himself, Norman headed to the back and used the restroom before heading home.

He made himself a ham sandwich for dinner and then sat down to watch some TV. CSI was on. It was an older episode, but Norman still enjoyed it. He relaxed and absentmindedly stroked Norman's fur, quietly humming the happy birthday song to himself.

Gee, what a great birthday, Norman thought happily.

Norman Feels Proud

April 2nd, A Sunday

Norman sat by himself in a Chinese restaurant late one afternoon, after he had come home to find his fridge empty of anything sweet, or anything sour. The place was empty from head to toe and Norman took a seat by the window. In the room were two waitresses; an elderly Chinese woman and an elderly Russian woman.

"I don't know Lynn," said the Russian woman, with a deep tone of sorrow over her words, "yesterday I had more tables than today. Today, nothing."

"Why?"

"I don't know. Yesterday I had seven deliveries. Today I have three. Yesterday I had more tables. No customers anymore."

Norman felt invisible to the two women. Sure, it was only him in the restaurant, but he figured it a half glass full situation. She should appreciate his service, for what it was. The Russian woman came over to the table.

"How is your food?"

"Very good, so far." Norman didn't mean to come off skeptical. "I think it will be good the whole way through too!"

She ignored both remarks. She quickly made her way back to the other side of the room and sat with her friend. Norman considered that she didn't care for his service, since his plate was only seven dollars- a great rate for chicken balls and rice- but not great for business. He thought about the tip. Seven dollars was a small price to pay for a full meal, and left him ample room to leave a tip. Sure, it wasn't great white rice, and the chicken balls dusted in his mouth, and the waitress left him a bit unappreciated too. But she was just having a bad day, and maybe a five dollar- *seven dollar!* - tip could leave her feeling better.

As a fortune cookie and bill reached Norman's table, a family of four came in the door. The Russian woman rushed to their aid, laying out napkins and menus for the family. Norman cracked open his fortune cookie.

Someone will make you very proud.

Norman didn't know what to make of that, since he wasn't sure who could accomplish such a feat. His cat Norman made him proud everyday... could that be it? As Norman pondered over his small list of acquaintances, the little girl from the family climbed into her chair.

"I'll get you a seat booster, my dear!" cried the Russian woman, eager to help.

"No, I'm old enough- I can do it!" she shouted back. Her father smiled and patted her on the back.

Was that the person that would make me proud? Norman thought. Her small accomplishment meant the world to her, and the thought of that made Norman proud.

Norman made his way to the front of the restaurant with his bill.

"How was your food?" she asked monotonously.

"Excellent!" Norman answered. A faint twitch on her face could have counted as a smile. She handed him the debit machine.

Would you like to tip? the machine asked.

Norman typed in seven dollars for his tip, taking his total price to a square fourteen dollars. He handed back the machine to her.

She never noticed the tip, or at least if she did, she left no regards. Norman really hoped that she just didn't see it; in the hopes that late at night, as she did her bookings, she would notice the generosity.

"Have a nice day," Norman said.

The Meaning of Norman

April 3rd, A Monday

When Norman returned from his lunch break, he found his coworkers gathered around Robert's desk. Robert was showing them something on his computer. Robert turned and noticed Norman standing in the doorway. "Hey Norman, come and see this!" he said. Norman walked over to Robert's desk.

"What is it?"

"I got bored after lunch, so I looked up the meaning of my name on this website I found. It means 'bright fame.' That's pretty cool, right? You want to know yours?"

"I suppose so," said Norman. It did seem like an interesting bit of trivia.

Robert typed "Norman" into the search bar and read the description that followed. "'From an old Germanic byname meaning "Northman", referring to a Viking.'" Then he clicked the back button. "It says here that the Normans were the ones who introduced the name 'Robert' to the British. So, the people who made your name made my name famous. Isn't that interesting?"

"That does sound interesting," Norman said quietly. The other coworkers tittered at the strange coincidence. Norman stood awkwardly for a moment until someone else asked what their own name meant. Then he walked over to his own desk and went back to work.

Later, Norman was at home filling Norman's dish with cat food. "Did you know you were named after Vikings, Norman?" he asked. Norman took a bite from his cat food and seemed unconcerned by this news.

"I guess it isn't that interesting after all," said Norman. He prepared his own dinner and sat down to watch the newest episode of CSI. "This will be much more interesting," he mused.

Norman Gets Self-Conscious

April 4th, A Tuesday

Norman's drive home from work was a little out of the ordinary: not only did he not get startled by the radio ad with the car horn in it today, but his journey home was sprinkled with rain. It wasn't enough rain to warrant the wipers going full speed, but was too much rain for the slowest speed: the windshield would get covered in raindrops by the next go-round of the wipers, and he couldn't have that. So, Norman tried the second click. While it cleared the rain more to his satisfaction, the few drops that accumulated before being wiped again made him uncomfortable, so he clicked up to the third speed.

"My wipers are going pretty fast for this light amount of rain," Norman said to himself. "This looks silly." But this speed cleared the windshield to his liking. He sat back into the seat, secure in his decision. Then another car drove past, and their windshield wipers appeared to be going slower than his. Not wanting to look like a worried old fool, Norman set his wiper speed back down a click.

Norman's Car Breaks Down

April 5th, A Wednesday

Waking up earlier than normal to make it for a fast food breakfast before work, Norman first had to deal with a failing car. The engine, or whatever is in the front and under the hood, was making squealing sounds every time he twisted the key in the ignition. Before long, smoke began to billow out from the cracks of the hood, and Norman said, "Oh."

Norman stood in the parking lot by himself until another person passed by. Norman worked up the courage to shout out to a balder than himself man unlocking his truck, asking for help with his car.

"Sure, I can check it out," said the balder man.

Norman and the man clicked open the hood, both of them blankly staring into the smoking interior.

"You know," the balder man said, "I don't know much about cars really."

He left Norman to his lonesome self. Norman returned to his apartment, called a tow truck, and waited for the tower to arrive before leaving for work. The tow truck driver took his time hooking up the car, but Norman didn't feel it was his place to tell him how to do his job. By the time Norman got in a cab, he still had some time to get the fast food sandwich before work, but he didn't want to inconvenience the taxi driver by making him go through a drive thru. He reached his desk five minutes early, and for the first time in a while, he did not have to wait for the janitor to unlock the front doors.

Norman Uses the Lift

April 6th, A Thursday

Norman considered the buttons carefully.

Up and down. But he was on the ground floor. How could he be sure where the lift was?

He took the stairs. He didn't want to risk it. Plus, he preferred the stairs, much less complicated.

Norman Gets a Ride

April 7th, A Friday

Norman was flying down the freeway at an unreasonable speed. His co-worker had volunteered her teenage son to give Norman a ride to the auto shop where his car was in need of repairs. Norman was impressed with the boy's full head of hair, but disapproved of his disregard for traffic laws and lack of turn signal etiquette.

Norman held his medium decaf coffee between his legs because the cup holder was occupied with used tissues that he dared not touch.

As they neared the shop the boy slammed on his brakes, narrowly avoiding a collision, but spilling Norman's coffee all over his lap.

The teenager yelled at Norman for spilling on his upholstery and demanded payment to have his seats cleaned.

It was hard getting his wallet out of his pocket with his badly scalded lap, but the boy was demanding a reasonable price.

Norman is Late for Work

April 8th, A Saturday

Norman woke up startled and looked around. Norman was basking in the sun that peeked through the curtains. The clock said 9:15AM and he panicked at how late he would be for work.

Norman ran to the restroom to do his business, quickly rinsed his eye boogers away, and ran his damp hands through his thin hair. He put on a wrinkled shirt and the pants from yesterday. He thought about how the bus would take too long and prayed his car would start. The time was now 9:30 AM.

As he searched for the car keys he saw Norman was sitting at the front door. He let out a loud "meow." Then Norman realized it was Saturday. He was glad his best friend had known just what to say to calm him down.

Norman and the Cocoon

April 9th, A Sunday

Norman was watching an episode of CSI when he heard pawing at the window. "Coming, Norman!" called Norman as he muted the TV and got up to let him inside.

"What's that in your mouth, Norman? Have you been hunting?" Norman had brought trophies home before. Norman groaned a bit as he crouched to see what it was. It was a bright green butterfly cocoon.

"Oh Norman!" he exclaimed with a tone of shock and disappointment that surprised even him. Startled, Norman dropped the cocoon on the floor as he fled.

Norman picked up the cocoon and inspected it for a moment. It was surely dead, and he was suddenly quite saddened. *Gone before the world even gets to see your true beauty*, he thought. He walked to the kitchen and wrapped it in a paper towel before laying it gently in the garbage bin.

Norman let out a deep sigh and walked to the living room. He sat down, wrapped himself tightly in his blanket and watched three more episodes of CSI.

Norman Takes the Subway

April 10th, A Monday

Norman entered the subway car and immediately noted his shoes were sticking slightly to the floor. He walked toward the one empty seat, wincing as his rubber soles announced each and every movement. As someone who didn't often take the train, he wondered if he'd stumbled onto the realization of why everyone else was wearing headphones.

As he wedged himself between a punk rocker who had a two-foot gap between his knees and a college-aged girl whose face was buried in her phone, he considered taking out his recently purchased smartphone. However, the train immediately stopped and the group of teenagers who entered the car caused him to change his mind. He had not opted for the theft insurance.

Instead, he busied himself with not making eye contact while struggling to appear casual. He decided that averting his eyes without looking strange was too much a challenge, and resigned himself to staring at his feet. Four more seconds passed, and once again he felt conspicuous. Suddenly, the crisis passed. The teenagers had reached their stop and exited the train, reducing the threat of theft significantly. Norman took out his phone. It was dead.

Norman Signs a Birthday Card

<u>April 11th, A Tuesday</u>

Someone at work brought a birthday card to Norman's desk and asked if he would sign it for Carol's birthday.

Norman didn't know who Carol was, but decided to sign the card anyway. Norman tried to think of something witty to say, but in the end just wrote '*Happy Birthday Carol. From Norman*'.

Later, Norman saw some people eating cake. He supposed one of them must be Carol.

Norman has a Good Day at the Office

April 12th, A Wednesday

One day, Norman's colleague Robert brought his pet dog, Trouble, to work. Trouble was a one-year-old golden retriever pup with floppy ears and a lolling tongue. He instantly became the entire office's centre of attention. Trouble went around the office playing with all the employees while Norman went about his day as usual. Half-way through the day, when Norman was working at his desk, he felt something brushing his feet. He looked down to the see the little pup rubbing his head up and down his calves, before promptly jumping into his lap and settling down. Norman froze in place for a few seconds, before carefully running his hand over the dog's head a few times, and went back to work. At the end of the day, Robert came to Norman's desk looking for Trouble.

"Hey look at that! He's been sleeping here the entire time. All that playing must have drained him."

"Yeah. He's a nice dog." Norman responded.

"Thanks. He must really trust you to sleep like that."

On his ride back home, Norman thought about Trouble and how nice it felt to have him around.

After he got home and put out a bowl of cat food for Norman, he narrated the entire day's events: about Trouble, about how he successfully complemented Robert, and how much work he did because he didn't move from his place for the half the day.

"Maybe we should get a dog."

Norman looked up for a second and promptly went back to eating.

Norman Rides the Bus

April 13th, A Thursday

Norman stood at the stop early in the morning. He glanced over at the man on his smartphone, watching a video. Norman chuckled at the video before getting on the bus. He shuffled to his seat, stepping on the foot of a young woman. He apologized and pulled out his phone. He forgot to charge it last night while watching CSI. He started tapping away and swiping at the blank screen to trick the passengers into believing that he is a successful businessman who is texting several people. Norman stumbled getting off the bus and ignored the laughter behind him. Norman realised he got off at the wrong stop. It started to rain.

Office Potluck

April 14th, A Friday

Eleanor from accounting had imposed a birthday potluck upon Norman's office. Everyone was required to bring their favorite dish in celebration of the relatively unknown accountant. She had only ever ignored Norman, even refusing him the decency of simple eye contact. A personal office-wide email chain, explicitly against company policy, was clearly well received by his coworkers as they all had bragged about how good their dish would be. Norman was quite perturbed by the notion of event, especially since no potlucks or jamborees heralded his birthday just two weeks prior. Only Steven, the Canadian floor supervisor, had acknowledged him that day after catching him cram in a gallon of Slow Churned Eddy's midday in the supply closet.

Norman was determined to be as frugal as possible in preparing his dish. On Potluck Eve, a stop in at a Korean grocer produced seven cans of mixed kernel corn costing roughly three dollars. The cans' labels were in a foreign script beyond Norman's comprehension. De-canning the greasy, multicolored maize imitated a strange fragrance that was tamed with generous globs of thick Country Crock and kosher salt. The sun's glare on the commute into work was the extent of cooking the platter was afforded, slightly melting the margarine.

At the designated lunch hour, all of Norman's colleagues unveiled the pride of their offerings to the sacred communal meal. Beyond his understanding, everyone else had put significant time and money into the event. Despite reaping the smorgasbord bounties, Norman felt isolated and alone as no one seemed to notice his corn. Inserting and removing a serving spoon was the only attention the dish received. Ashamed, Norman took the neglected corn home early with himself.

There was no way to recoup the costs of the ignored food or the public humiliation. Later unburdened of pants and a dress shirt, Norman loafed across a lowbrow La-Z-Boy shoveling in great helpings of the vegetable into his mouth. The day's heat melted any remaining margarine chunks and graciously lubricated the repetitive grain as he consumed it in entirety. Lethargic from binging, Norman buried his remaining pain in police procedural television while imagining impossible scenarios of humiliating Eleanor.

Norman Makes a Salad

April 15th, A Saturday

Norman had read an article about the benefits of eating enough vegetables in Reader's Digest. After carefully weighing the article in his mind for a period of months, he decided to take the plunge. This was a deviation from his usual beef and chicken schedule, and he was scared, but also optimistic.

At the grocery store, Norman spent his afternoon examining each bag of lettuce for signs of mold or wilting. He had to make a difficult choice between iceberg and spinach leaves: he settled on iceberg. He found the tomato section and selected his tomato. He also stopped by the cucumbers and picked out a nice-looking cucumber. *No need to overdo it*, Norman thought, and proceeded to the register.

When he got home, Norman was excited to prepare the salad. It was then that he realized he had forgotten to pick out a dressing. *Oh well*, Norman thought, *I can go back to beef tomorrow*. The salad did not taste as good as Norman had hoped.

Norman Goes to Church

April 16th, A Sunday

After eating breakfast at the local diner - the one with poor food and the smiling waitress - Norman passed a church on his way home and decided to go in. He found a seat in the back and sat quietly with folded hands.

He half-listened to the sermon while checking out families that were scattered about.

It was when the congregation stood up that he felt his stomach rumble, a low syncopation inside his bowels. Norman concluded that the cause of his untimed gassiness was most definitely from the extra cheese that came with his omelette, and probably his double order of bacon. He tightened his butt cheeks and rose.

He joined the congregation and bellowed a simple church hymn. When the hymn was over he sat down, and with little or no control a small fart emerged from under him and ruffled his underwear. A smirk appeared over his face as he remembered a funny proverb: *He who farts in church sits in his own pew.* He snickered to himself, looked around, and slowly the grin on his face disappeared when he realized he was emphatically alone.

He left church early.

Norman's Special Evening

April 17th, A Monday

Norman was particularly excited for CSI tonight. The episode due to come in the usual rotation of reruns was one that he had never seen before. It was the only episode he had never managed to catch. Something had always come up. Last time, it was a vet appointment for Norman.

As he settled into his chair and the intro played, there was a knock on his door. He got up and answered it. Standing there were two very well dressed young men from the Church of Latter-Day Saints.

They started talking about religion. Norman was not particularly interested and was a little anxious to be missing his show. However, he didn't want to be rude to the very polite young men, so he smiled, nodded and made polite small talk for 45 minutes until the young men left of their own accord.

Norman went back to his chair, but the episode was almost over. He turned the TV off. *Maybe next time.*

Norman Buys New Shoelaces

<u>April 18th, A Tuesday</u>

After months of noticing the worsening fraying, Norman decided to take action and go to town to buy some new shoelaces. After purchasing the item, he was hungry and decided to walk back to his apartment. On his way back, he passed a pizza chain. Norman did a double-take and realised that pizza sounded pretty good. After a few intense seconds of internal conflict, he found that he was already too far away and didn't want people to think he was indecisive. He walked to his home as his stomach rumbled.

Norman Goes to the Talent Show

April 19th, A Wednesday

It was a rather nice day and Norman decided he would skip the reruns of CSI to go see the city talent show.

Norman arrived and saw many people performing magnificently, showing off their talents. Of course, due to his inability to be in a crowd, he watched from a park bench quite some ways away with a pair of binoculars.

Norman wondered if he could ever be in a talent show. He went home and thought about what his talent would be until 9:30PM. Norman forgot all about the talent show by morning.

Norman Pours a Good Glass of Water

April 20th, A Thursday

Norman stepped onto the kitchen floor. He made sure to drag his foot along the floor just a bit with each step he took.

Norman really liked the texture of the floor.

Norman opened his cabinet and retrieved his favorite glass. It read "Good Morning!"

"Good morning!" said Norman's humble smile to the cup.

Norman filled the cup with water from the tap. He drank about half of the water until he noticed the time. Norman was going to miss being five minutes early for the bus!

Norman set down his cup, grabbed his coat and took one last look at his home before leaving out the door.

Norman got on the bus and took his seat. He saw a nice young lady approaching from down the aisle.

Norman thought about greeting her, but the thought was interrupted.

Norman remembered the cup, sitting alone on the kitchen counter and abandoned with a portion of water to carry. He tried to recall just how much water he left in the cup.

Better make sure to drink the rest, Norman thought to himself.

Norman's Missing Meatball

April 21st, A Friday

Norman peeled back the plastic film from his Lean Cuisine spaghetti and meatballs, neatly folding the covering over on itself twice. He rested the film on the empty package that laid picture-side up on his counter; Norman knew spaghetti and meatballs meant five minutes in the microwave, and had long since foregone the "cook as directed" instructions.

Resting both index fingers opposite the outer rim of his meal, Norman made his way to the couch. Norman slid his noodles from right to left in the tray, coating the dry noodles in spaghetti sauce. He took a bite. It was on this first bite - all spaghetti - that Norman realized his dinner contained only four meatballs.

It had certainly not gone unnoticed to Norman in 2010 when Lean Cuisine reduced the number of meatballs from six to five. At first, Norman thought this was a once-off oversight. It had not been.

After dinner, as Norman washed his fork, he couldn't help his mind from wandering. He hoped this wasn't 2008 all over again.

Norman's Childhood Toy Set

April 22nd, A Saturday

Norman was going through some old boxes in the closet this morning trying to find some retro clothing for an upcoming party. At the bottom, in a small plastic box was a red toy plane. It had a spaceman pilot.

Norman's story for the plane was as follows: A spaceman has been sent on a mission to a space station but was too afraid of the rocket erupting into a fireball. So instead, he went and stole a plane from a nearby airport. He is currently running away from his past life.

For a fleeting moment Norman was once again a child. He was the spaceman. He was flying.

Norman's Rainy Day

April 23rd, A Sunday

Norman's Sunday morning was fairly normal. He woke up precisely at 7:00AM, fed Norman, cooked himself a green pepper omelette and drank his morning coffee.

The Sunday paper arrived at 7:27 and Norman saw that the forecast called for wind and rain, confirmed by the pitter-patter of raindrops hitting the sun-guard above his windows. After Norman was finished reading the funnies in the paper he pulled on some rubber gumboots, grabbed an umbrella and headed out the door to the grocery store.

On the way to the store he was hit by a violent streak of wind and his umbrella flipped inside out. *One more thing to buy at the store*, thought Norman ruefully.

After he finished loading up his cart he went back to the front of the store to inspect their umbrellas. One of the umbrella's tags boasted that it sported wind-resistant technology. Norman turned the tag over and looked at the price: $12.99.

"Excuse me ma'am. Does this umbrella really resist the wind?" he asked a passing clerk.

"Sure."

Norman placed the umbrella delicately upon the top of his shopping basket and checked out. The wind was still violently blowing outside. It was the perfect time to try out his new wind-resistant umbrella.

He pressed the button on the handle and the umbrella spread out above his head. He wrapped the grocery bags around his free hand and began the walk back home.

Once in awhile the umbrella would catch a current of air, but for the most part it did its job well. At the door of his apartment he wedged the handle of the umbrella in the underside of his elbow to reach for the keys inside his pocket. A current of wind caught the umbrella and lifted it out of his arm and into the air. Norman reached after it and dropped his groceries, but it was too late. The umbrella was already tumbling down the road.

Unpacking his groceries inside his house he found that his eggs had broken after he dropped the bag. Norman sat down at his table and reread the morning's funnies.

Norman has a Sick Day

April 24th, A Monday

Today Norman felt out of sorts. He had slept through his alarm, and had awoken a full eight minutes later than usual. His bones were achy and his nose was clogged with snot, so he lay awhile in bed deciding what to do.

At four past seven Norman eased himself out of bed, and shuffled to the telephone. He called in sick. His boss asked him for his surname, but otherwise seemed unfazed. Norman's excitement at the prospect of a free day was tempered by his ill feelings. He chose to treat himself to some yoghurt, but realised he had missed the use-by date by a day. He took two Aspirin with a glass of tap water instead, threw away the yoghurt, and nearly forgot to feed Norman before spending the rest of the day in bed.

Norman Almost Gets Hit On

April 25th, A Tuesday

"Go on Lisa, he looks all cute and alone."

Lisa was unsure. The gentleman stood at the bar was nursing a beer and not really talking to anyone. He was dressed in typical clothes from the fifties, as that was the theme of the party, and stood near others wearing similar but didn't really seem to be integrating with the group.

“Maybe he wasn't with them. Maybe he had been pressured into coming out. Who knows?”

Lisa looked at her friend Beth and said, "I don't know. Is he with those guys or not?"

Beth replied, "I think I saw him come in with them. Go and talk to him. He looks friendly."

Lisa still felt a little apprehensive. "But you're not sure? He could be a psycho. And he's almost totally bald!"

Beth blinked. "Alright, whatever. It's not a big deal."

Norman sipped his beer and wished he was at home.

Norman Finds a Coin

April 26th, A Wednesday

Norman was at the grocery store, buying cat treats for Norman. He did not want to go out today, but he felt he owed it to his cat. As he approached the cashier, the total came out to $4.79, which he thought was a bit high, but no matter. He paid with a $5 bill, and as he left with an anxious look on his face, he noticed that one of his coins he had received was no mere dime, but a rare 1797 dime that was worth approximately $10,000 to antique collectors. In a fit of excitement, he threw his hands up, and the dime flew out of his hand, hitting a nearby pedestrian. The angry person did not care for Norman's apologies, and threw the dime at Norman, bounced off his chest, and fell down a sewage drain.

Norman walked home and fed Norman some treats.

Norman Walks Home

April 27th, A Thursday

Norman was riding the bus home from work. Norman was not paying attention because he was thinking about the chicken dinner he will have when he gets home, so he accidentally pulled the cord a stop earlier than he meant to. He hoped that someone else will get off at that stop but when the bus stops no one does. Norman was too embarrassed to say anything, so he took the earlier stop. It was raining outside. Norman forgot his umbrella.

Norman Checks out at the Grocery Store

April 28th, A Friday

Before bagging Norman's eggs, milk, bread and vanilla ice cream, the cashier at his local grocery store asked, "Paper or plastic?" Norman, feeling quite confident yet indecisive, said "Surprise me". The cashier promptly bagged the groceries in plastic bags. Norman would have preferred paper, because he heard from last week's paper that it was better for the environment.

He exchanged pleasantries with the cashier, being careful not to say, "You too" when asked, "Would you like your receipt?" as he did last week.

Norman Gets a Package

April 29th, A Saturday

Norman was coming home from work. He slowly walked up to his front door and eyed a small brown package with black tape in front of his door. There was a bright pink Post-It that read, "Happy Birthday!" Norman's birthday had been a month ago. He worried it was a prank, but he decided to take the risk. No one had played a prank on Norman since high school, as far as he knew.

It was about dinner time, but Norman was too excited to eat. He took out a pair of sharp scissors and placed them on the table. He lightly shook the box but the gift didn't make a sound. Norman thought how nice a gift it must be if they had packaged it so well. He savored cutting the edges of the black tape. He slowly cut down through the middle of the box so as to not damage the contents. Then it was open.

The doorbell rang twice and someone knocked excitedly interrupting Norman's focus. Norman walked to the door and looked through the peep hole warily. It was a young boy from down the hall, Joey. He'd seen Joey before playing ball in the street with the other kids. Norman opened the door and Joey told him his aunt had accidentally put his birthday present in front of Norman's door. So, Norman handed him the box and started to apologize for opening it, but Joey had already run away.

Norman Takes a Walk

April 30th, A Sunday

Norman realized he was out of eggs. The grocery store wasn't far from his home and the sun was out, but not too hot for his liking, so he decided he'd walk. He pulled on his black sneakers (the ones reserved for his outdoor adventures, not the ones he wore to work), and ventured out the door.

After reaching the end of the first block, Norman thought perhaps he should have stretched.

After two blocks, he realised he'd forgotten his reusable grocery bags. He was starting to amass a rather large collection of plastic bags, and couldn't find any use for them.

At block three, he promised to himself that he'd bring them back to the store to recycle next time. Next time for sure.

Norman bought ice cream, some milk and a bottle of wine, in case he has friends over, and only realized he'd forgotten the eggs the next morning.

May

Norman Send a Typo

May 1st, A Monday

Norman, eager to get to his lunchbreak, made an error as he sent off an email to Eleanor in HR. Instead of ending his email with "Regards, Norman", instead he ended it with "Regards. Norman"

Norman didn't like coming off as brash. It was something he strives to fight everyday with his always tasteful and polite emails. They were professional, whilst being warm, like the first sip of coffee in the morning. No one has ever complimented Norman's bravado in his emails, but he had also hoped that his subtlety had a rippling effect through his coworkers' days.

However, Eleanor's ripple was more like a tear. Norman would have to wait until after lunch to see her response. Norman sighed and left for the breakroom to fix himself a cup of coffee.

Once Norman reached the pot and poured the mug, he saw that Eleanor was standing behind him, waiting for her chance at the Keurig coffeemaker.

This was his chance to make it all okay.

"Eleanor," Norman started, "Would you like my cup of coffee?"

Eleanor blushed right through her pounded cherry makeup. "Why, that's very kind of you Norman!"

Norman smiled and willingly sacrificed his cup of coffee. Eleanor helped herself to a few cubes of sugar and returned to her cubicle, while Norman stayed and fixed himself a second cup.

If the email brings her spirits down, Norman thought, *at least the coffee will help bring it back up.*

Norman Walks Home on a Rainy Day

May 2nd, A Tuesday

Having woken up just a little early, Norman decided to walk to work. It was very temperate this morning and he wanted to be sure to be extra tired when he got home so as not to wake up too early the next morning, too.

"Keeping the sleep cycle healthy," he said to himself as he laced up some tennis shoes and put his work shoes in a small bag, which fit conveniently in his briefcase.

The weather turned soggy mid-day, and Norman realized that neither pair of shoes would keep him dry on the walk home. Regardless, he was determined to sleep his full eight hours that evening and the exercise would certainly help him slumber.

Halfway to his apartment, he stopped at a convenience store and bought a fresh pair of Flagmores socks, changed them (as well has his shoes) and chuckled at how clever he was. He was dry and felt marginally better about his situation. Immediately upon exiting, he stepped in a rather deep puddle and was soaked to the bone.

He smiled just a bit to himself as he realized that taking these socks off at home for a fresh pair would feel doubly good as the first pair.

Perhaps he would jump in a puddle intentionally, just for fun. The thought made him smile.

Norman Takes the Bus

May 3rd, A Wednesday

Norman was on his way home from work. As he sat at the bus stop, Norman looked at the advertisement on the billboard across the street; it was for a women's clothing store. When the bus arrived, Norman noticed there was only one empty seat. Norman sat next to an elderly woman who smelled like talcum powder.

Norman exited at the next stop and waited for a different bus.

Norman Receives a Phone Call

May 4th, A Thursday

Norman struggled to climb out of his recliner as the phone rang.

brrrrrrrrrrrrrrrriinnngggg.

He muted his show and walked over to the phone.

brrrrrrrrrrrrrrrriinnn-brrrrrrrrrriinnnggg.

Norman was alarmed. The phone never rang like that before. Never had it skipped a beat to interrupt itself.

brrrrrrrrrrrrrrrriinnngggg.

There it was, back to normal, but how could he be sure? He waited for it to ring again.

brrrrrrrrrrrrrrrriinnngggg.

He still wasn't convinced. Maybe it was a hacker, someone who could steal all his banking information based on Norman's voice.

brrrrrrrrrrrrrrrriinnngggg.

Norman went to the kitchen and grabbed a knife.

brrrrrrrrrrrrrrrriinnngggg.

He felt a knife was a little too fatal; if someone did attack him, he would want to hurt them, but if he used a knife they would need stitches, and he didn't want to cause that kind of pain to anyone... He pulled the wooden lever off on the side of his recliner, gripping it like a club.

brrrrrrrrrrrrrrriinnnggg.

Norman prepared himself behind the doorway. His heart was racing so fast that he had to sit down and wait for the tech savvy intruder.

brrrrrrrrrrrrrrriinnnggg.

That was the last ring. Norman was confused. He sat back in the recliner, reattached the lever, and unmuted his show.

Norman is Concerned About the Amount of Blood in his Stool

May 5th, A Friday

It was a Friday morning. Norman looked down into the bowl; red everywhere. On the bus home the night before, Norman had seen an advertisement about middle-aged men and colon cancer.

Now his poop was bloody.

He wondered whether he should tell someone at work he was probably dying from colon cancer. Then he remembered the beet salad he had eaten for dinner last night. He put on the same socks he'd worn for the last three days and left home for work.

He had forgotten his bus pass in the bathroom.

Norman Feeds his Cat

May 6th, A Saturday

Norman absent-mindedly picked at his argyle sweater.

The whir-clunk-whir of his semi faulty radiator competed with the hushed dialogue emanating from the television. Even though he had never seen the people who lived next door, he was terrified of the awkwardness which would stem from a complaint about noise. He strained to hear the telly over his radiator.

Norman watched as a socialite on his favourite TV show fed her affable cat, which purred and rubbed up against her in a show of appreciation. Norman felt a twinge in his chest, he paused for a second and his lips curled upwards in a way that was imperceptible, even to himself.

Norman laid out some food next to Norman, but the cat merely stalked away.

Norman Thinks He Sees a Minor Celebrity

May 7th, A Sunday

Norman was walking down a small avenue one fair Sunday afternoon, as there was a produce and food market set up. While Norman didn't really enjoy most of the food being cooked there, and would probably never eat the produce before it went off, it was nice to simply walk around and absorb the atmosphere of the busy market.

As Norman went to buy a pretzel from one of the many stalls, he noticed out of the corner of his eye that a familiar face was buying some curry and rice. He instantly recognised the man as an actor from a ten-year-old sketch comedy show.

The man looked very flushed, was balding and his face was sagging significantly, but Norman was sure he was who he thought he was. Norman didn't particularly like the show, and this man was never in the funniest skits, but Norman still wanted to take a picture with him.

Norman scoured his brain trying to think of his name so he could claim to be a fan. It was Tim something-or-other. Or was it Alfred? Norman seemed to recall he had a short-lived stand-up career, and he had appeared in several commercials. He was usually cast as a person cooking on a barbecue or a dad playing with his child while a voice-over droned on about insurance.

As Norman continued to think to himself, the man bought his butter-chicken curry and white rice and walked off. The person selling pretzels raised her voice to get Norman's attention. Norman ordered a cheese-filled pretzel with light salt and no herbs. The man was not the small-time comedian that Norman thought he was.

Norman Calls his Mother

May 8th, A Monday

The phone rang four times before she picked up.

Norman's mother sounded as though she had been expecting the call, but still acted delighted when Norman wished her a happy Mother's Day. She moved straight into laying on a little guilt for not calling more often, and asking Norman how his life had been.

Truthfully, not much had changed in the weeks since Norman had last called his mother. Work was still boring, the dating scene was still dry, and his life goals were still elusive. Feeling a little disappointed in himself, Norman painted his life a rosier hue when describing it. This left him feeling more disappointed in himself, and he was glad that his mother filled in the silences for the rest of the call.

"...And get yourself a nice girl, Junior. I love you." Norman's mother finished.

"Don't call me Junior, Mum," Norman responded automatically. "Love you too."

There was a click, and the apartment suddenly seemed very empty and quiet. *Maybe I should get a cat or something.* Briefly, Norman envisioned just browsing the internet all day and not caring about what expectations people held for him. Then he remembered his father and shuddered. *It must run in the genes.*

He scrolled through his phone's contact list until he found a particular girl. She had bizarre ideas, strange clothes, and was generally very irregular. He usually didn't much like hanging out with her, because she flew in the face of everything that made his life comfortable. But right now, comfortable was the last thing he wanted to feel. Today, he wasn't going to settle for just being Norman Jr.

The phone rang four times before she picked up.

Norman Has a Funny Taste in his Mouth

May 9th, A Tuesday

Norman woke up one morning with a peculiar taste in his mouth. It was a parched feeling, as if he hadn't had water in days, yet it also had a metallic tang to it. It could have been something he had eaten the night before for dinner, but he had eaten nothing out of the usual: oven cooked chicken wings with a can of ginger ale.

As he brushed his teeth, he found the toothpaste didn't taste minty. It tasted almost sour, and dulled. His breakfast cereal, usually wheaty and crunchy, tasted bland, almost minty, in addition to the regular texture. He thought twice about it now. *What is wrong with my mouth today?* The taste persisted at lunch with a sub that tasted like heartburn pills, and a vanilla smoothie that tasted like watery milk.

Then came dinner. He didn't want to take chances. He finished cooking the other half of the box of chicken wings, with another can of soda. This time, his chicken wings tasted like chicken wings, and his ginger ale tasted like ginger ale. "Everything is back to normal!" Norman said aloud to himself, alone in his apartment.

Norman Eats a Bagel

May 10th, A Wednesday

Norman walked into the break room for his second daily cup of coffee to find that his boss had provided a variety of bagels for the office. Norman was rather pleased.

Norman grabbed a napkin, a small paper plate, and a plastic knife. Napkin in hand, he reaches for his usual, a plain bagel, but decided at the last moment to try an onion bagel instead. Norman debated trying the garlic cream cheese as well, but thought it might be a bit too much with the onion bagel. Norman placed the bagel and a small scoop of plain cream cheese on his plate. Norman then carried his bagel and coffee back to his workspace so he could be productive while he ate.

Back in his cubicle, Norman struggled to slice his bagel with a plastic knife and ended up with some crumbs on his desk. He gathered them carefully into a neat pile and swept them into the small trash can he kept nearby. Norman found he had only taken enough cream cheese to cover one half of his bagel, so he sandwiched the two halves together. Norman decided that onion bagels are quite good, if a bit strong.

After enjoying his bagel and coffee, Norman worried that his breath might smell from the onion bits on the bagel. He opened his desk drawer to look for the curiously strong mints he had bought the previous week, but could not find them.

Feeling rather self-conscious, Norman successfully avoided talking in the bi-weekly office meeting so as not to smell up the room with his onion breath.

Norman Joins Yoga Class

May 11th, A Thursday

Norman was walking out of the shops with a packet of salt and vinegar chips when he noticed a poster for yoga classes. A special deal was available for one free class. The number was the first thing he ever wrote down in his new notepad he purchased earlier in the day. Norman felt exuberant and excited at the thought of meeting new people, but his hands shook, the notepad dropped, and the wind carried it away. Norman thought about chasing after it, but instead he walked inside the shop and bought a new notepad. During dinner that night with Norman, Norman wondered what had happened to his packet of chips.

Norman is Hungry

May 12th, A Friday

Norman woke up at noon, as per usual, so Norman was not home from work yet. As he stretched, the dull ache of hunger filled his stomach. Norman remembered his bowl being empty when he had fallen asleep last night. *Why had Norman been so late?* Lazily, he made his way to the food bowl, anticipating the taste of whatever off-brand cat food Norman bought.

Norman was disappointed. He turned, making his way to the front door to wait for Norman to get home from work. Drifting to sleep, Norman dreamt of a full food bowl.

Norman Walks Norman

May 13th, A Saturday

Norman decided it would be nice to take Norman on a walk to the nearby park. Norman decided he would need a leash, so Norman couldn't run away during their walk. Norman went to Pet Warehouse and bought a plain blue leash for Norman. No collar was needed, as Norman had one already, along with tags displaying his name, address, and immunisations.

Norman returned home to find Norman asleep on the armchair.

Another day perhaps, Norman thought.

Norman is Relieved

May 14th, A Sunday

Norman was concerned that he hadn't seen Norman eating for the past few days, though his water bowl was certainly emptying steadily. Worried, Norman turned to the Internet for answers. He skimmed the first three hits he found on Google. The third informed him that cats who haven't eaten in three days risk organ failure. Alarmed, Norman decided to act immediately. Based on information gleaned from hits one and two, he determined that he should try preparing Norman's favorites: dry food with cat milk, wet food, tuna, cooked chicken, and baked carrots.

Norman set out his ingredients in a neat line, and arranged a delightful cat buffet. Norman sat on the windowsill, watching Norman's progress with keen eyes, but once the buffet was set out, he stayed curled up on the sill, and didn't move at all. He simply yowled once, and stayed put.

Thinking that Norman might want some privacy, Norman walked to the other room, and hid himself just beyond the doorway so he could peep into the kitchen.

There he saw Norman shoving his nose along the bottom edge of the fridge, then bracing against it. Suddenly, the door opened, and Norman disappeared behind it!

Astonished, Norman quietly crept back into the kitchen, and swung back the fridge door. He saw Norman, standing on his hind legs with his front paws on the lower shelf of the fridge, carefully examining a tub of low fat cottage cheese. Painstakingly nudging the tub against the side of the fridge, Norman popped the lid right off, and was soon noisily lapping at his cheesy prize.

Well, fancy that, thought Norman, as he stroked his smooth dome. As he approached his ear, his fingertips traced three tiny wisps of hair, still clinging on despite the odds.

Norman's Big Day

May 15th, A Monday

Norman sat at his desk gently bobbing his head. He couldn't find a comfortable place to rest his hands so he just played with his fingers absentmindedly. For an office full of ringing phones and papers being pushed, it seemed quiet to Norman. *It must just be the cubicle walls*, he thought to himself. The sun began to set and Norman's co-workers slowly filed out of the building and returned to their homes. Norman wondered what they would be doing tonight, and if it was similar to what he would be doing. Unenthusiastically, he packed up his bag and headed home where Norman would be waiting for dinner.

As the two ate together, the awkward silence made Norman uncomfortable. Earnestly he said, "I guess the 10-year anniversary of working somewhere isn't really that important." He took Norman's silence as agreement. Tonight, he went to sleep a little early.

Norman Gets Rebellious

May 16th, A Tuesday

Norman woke up and took his usual fifteen minutes on the toilet. He brought his phone with him so he wouldn't be bored. It seemed like a good time to see if he had received any likes on the picture he had posted of his cat.

He was excited to see that he had received three likes. As he sat there, Norman began to realise how ridiculous his enthusiasm was for the recognition he received on Facebook.

In that moment, Norman decided he needed a radical shift in his life. He needed to make a statement.

With a triumphant tap, Norman agreed to temporarily deactivate his account. He was really starting to do something with himself.

Norman Buys a Litter Box

May 17th, A Wednesday

That seems like a handy device, Norman thought to himself when he saw the ad in a newspaper insert, *and it's on sale, too.* He picked up the self-cleaning litter box at Pet Warehouse that afternoon and set it up, pleased with himself for making such a smart purchase.

By that evening, Norman felt frustrated. The cat had taken to the change quite well, but Norman had not. He missed the daily ritual of sifting and scooping. It calmed him. The original litter box was, for him, a sort of Zen garden.

He cleaned the new one and dropped it in a charity box later that night.

Norman Robs a Bank

May 18th, A Thursday

Norman awoke feeling anxious. He had never done what he was about to do, but something unnatural came over him. Norman was ready to finally live life on the edge.

He pulled up to First National Bank and began walking towards the front doors. "It's now or never," mumbled Norman as he grabbed the door handle with his sweaty palm.

Norman got in line and pulled out the folded note from his pocket as he waited for the next available teller. "Next."

Norman cautiously approached the teller's window and slid the note, complete with his clear written instructions, into her hands.

"I would like to withdrawal twenty dollars from Savings Account Number: 12816802, please."

Norman knew he should keep that money in savings, but thought it was time to live a little.

Maybe I could get another two cans of Coke, Norman thought.

The bank teller counted out the money and handed it to Norman. "Thank you for choosing First National, have a great day."

Norman folded the money into his pocket and walked towards his car. As Norman was sitting in the passenger seat he counted the money himself.

Norman counted twenty-one dollars. A sudden urge of guilt and worry swept over Norman. *Bank robbers end up in jail*, Norman thought.

Norman hurried back into the bank and returned to the teller to tell her of the awful mistake. "I'm so sorry, I didn't mean to take the extra dollar," Norman remarked as he handed her the money.

The teller counted the money aloud once more. "One, two, three.... twenty dollars. Sir, it's all here."

Norman became perplexed as he realized it was actually him who counted incorrectly.

"Uh, uh it's okay, no withdrawal for me today," Norman blurted out as he turned and walked hurriedly towards the exit.

Norman's Toilet Friend

May 19th, A Friday

Norman and Pete, someone who works on the second floor, only have one thing in common- they head to the toilet at roughly the same time every weekday. Before lunch, Norman would head to the bathroom, and as he left, he almost certainly held the door open for Pete to make his entrance. Pete would nod. Norman would nod. The duality between the two men and a toilet was perfectly balanced.

One day, Norman encountered Pete somewhere else aside from the men's washroom- the elevator.

Norman nodded. Pete nodded. What made this different was the lack of brevity in their encounter. It made Norman uncomfortable.

Norman nodded again.

Pete was now uncomfortable.

Norman asked Pete whether he thought *Crane* was written on all of the female toilets too.

Pete got out of the elevator.

Norman's Running Late

May 20th, A Saturday

Norman opened his sleep crusted eyes and squinted at his alarm clock, flashing 12:00. Confused, he looked at the wristwatch he slept with to see that it was already 9:15! Frustrated that his alarm clock didn't go off, he raced around his room trying to perform as many tasks at once as he could, but only succeeded to get toothpaste on his favorite shirt, forcing him to change into another.

He locked his door, double checked it, and then remembered that he had the day off. "I'm such a goof!" Norman exclaimed. He walked back inside and started to clean the mess he had made getting ready.

Norman Goes to Rent a Movie

May 21st, A Sunday

Norman looked around the movie rental shop, overwhelmed by the amount of choice he had.

As he walked passed the adult section as fast as possible, he peeked to the left, catching the cover of an erotic movie, feeling ashamed and looking away quickly.

Oh boy, I better choose something to watch as soon as possible, he mumbled to himself.

After carefully choosing a movie, Norman settled for a thrilling action movie. It's been a long time since he'd seen something new, and he started to feel excited for the movie night to come.

Norman is going to love this movie, maybe I'll buy some sweets for my special night, he thought with a smile on his face.

As he walked to the cash register, Norman grabbed one of the snickers that were displayed near it.

I deserve a little treat, don't I?

Norman felt happy, he had something to look forward to on this fine evening.

Ready to rent his movie, Norman gave it to the young cashier, along with his snicker bar.

"That'll be $10; and we will give back $5 once you return the movie. You have until next Sunday to do so." said the teenager in a groan.

Norman checked his back pocket, but felt nothing. A surge of heat went through his body, panicking and looking for his wallet in every one of his pockets, to no avail. Norman glanced at the movie box, then met the cashier's eyes to only nod and slowly leave the rental shop.

A cold breeze struck his face. *I guess I'll just watch some CSI after all,* Norman thought.

Norman Ponders Nighthawks

May 22nd, A Monday

It was the first time that Norman had seen the painting in person. He had seen it before, sometimes on the TV, others in print on postcards and t-shirts, and while they were still together, his ex-wife owned a printing of the painting. It hung in their bathroom, across from the toilet. Norman pondered whether the metal canisters held coffee, tea, or milk. He figured milk would be a strange thing to kept in a place made to trap heat, but milk goes with coffee, or tea, and it made more sense to him that at least one of them were dedicated to accessories for a beverage.

Norman then imagined how the bartender got out of the triangle at the end of the night. *Is he a bartender or a barista?* Norman thought to himself.

Norman then remembered his full bladder and quickly made it home to the safety of his own washroom. The next day, Norman thumb-tacked a Nighthawks postcard to the wall across from the toilet.

Norman is Conflicted Between Magnets

May 23rd, A Tuesday

Norman stood in front of the fridge magnet section of a Hallmarks. He had a dilemma.

One magnet packet had images of cats and puns written on them. "I'm feline fine," one read, beside the face of a remarkably content cat. "I'm not lion!"

Norman heaved a huff out of his nose in delight.

However, the second package of cat pun magnets had different sayings on them. "You've got to be kitten meh!" one read. Norman didn't find this one nearly as clever, and slightly insultingly simple for the audience. No breath was huffed. But this one claimed to have better magnet strength than the competitors. While Norman wanted the superior comedic magnets, he could not will himself to be so cheap. He couldn't help but feel attracted and repulsed by both magnet packets.

Norman decided to buy both. To his delight, he couldn't actually tell the difference in magnet strength between the brands. He put the lesser puns on the lower half of the fridge.

Norman Rebels

May 24th, A Wednesday

It was 9:16AM and Norman was sitting on a lightly padded chair in the office kitchen at work. His manager was giving a presentation. As the stream of words drifted through the room, Norman noticed that he felt rather tired. Odd, since he'd gotten his usual eight hours of sleep, and had drunk the same warm cup of coffee with cream that he always drank. A friendly bank teller had persuaded him yesterday to have a piece of hard candy, and he wondered sleepily if that could be the root of his lethargy. He'd read somewhere that too much sugar can affect sleep quality.

After a short time, Norman noticed that he was having trouble focusing on his manager's presentation, having missed the last few sentences. What's more, Norman felt a yawn coming on. Now, Norman is not usually one to draw attention to himself, especially in such a professional atmosphere. He started to become worried – what if his manager thought that Norman was not engaged with the presentation? Norman did not want to consider the ramifications of such a thought, and though he feared making a scene, the urge to yawn was creeping slowly but steadily through his body.

Then a strange and new thought occurred to Norman. He realized that he really *WASN'T* engaged in the presentation. He *WAS* rather bored by his manager today. *Perhaps,* Norman thought, *I AM willing to shake things up a little, and give a good yawn. Nothing big, nothing flashy, just a nice, satisfying yawn.*

As Norman considered it, he liked the idea more and more. He sat up and prepared himself for his act of rebellion. By this time, however, he found that he was much too excited, and the urge to yawn had left him entirely.

No more candy for me, Norman thought. *It makes me kind of wild.*

He listened attentively to the last three minutes of the presentation.

Norman’s Thursday Encounter

May 25th, A Thursday

Norman was walking home from work on Thursday, after five.

On the path home, he walked by some stores. In front of one of the stores, a lady, probably an employee of the store, offered him a sheet with coupon offers on it.

Norman looked at the sheet, and mumbled “Thank you”. The lady asked if he wanted to look at anything inside the store.

"We have some new products in today," she said.

He thought about it. He had wondered what it was like in the store. But he was already running late, since he usually only took ten minutes to walk home.

"Thank you," he said, "but I don't have the time. I usually get home at five-ten, and it is already five-oh-five. Thank you though again."

He continued to walk home. He got home at 5:12 PM, a few minutes later than usual. *It's okay*, he reassured himself. *It's okay to lose control sometimes.*

Norman Buys Some Candy

May 26th, A Friday

Norman glanced at the clock on his desk which now read 3:00PM. It was Friday afternoon and the work week would soon be over. Norman had put in a productive week at the office and was excited to relax with Norman while catching a CSI marathon on Saturday. In fact, all the excitement inspired Norman to do something nice for himself. He worked hard and the weekend was coming; Norman earned himself a treat from the break room!

Norman went to the break room during his usual break time and scanned the vending machine for a suitable snack. The bright yellow packaging in the top right corner was too vibrant and enticing to ignore. Peanut M&M's. They were perfect. Norman purchased his snack with glee and returned to his desk.

Norman munched on his candy while he worked through the afternoon when eventually Norman bit down on a brown M&M (his favorite) that was slightly smaller than the others. There was no peanut! Instead the M&M was simply filled in with extra chocolate, as if an oversized plain M&M had found its way into the bag of peanut M&M's. A smile widened across Norman's face as he savored the bonus chocolate. *It's like having two candies in one package!* Norman chuckled to himself.

Norman knew that he was going to have a great weekend.

Norman Gets Chinese

May 27th, A Saturday

With the last piece of General Tso's chicken staring at him, Norman pushed around tiny remnants of broccoli florets to form a circle around the now trapped, breaded meat. *There,* Norman thought, *it's not lonely now.*

This was the second time he had eaten from Chong's Garden this week, but tonight was different; they hadn't forgotten to give him a fortune cookie.

He fumbled with his thick fingers and cracked open the beige vessel, which he popped into his mouth, one half at a time. The stale taste reminded him of cold mornings as a teenager, waiting for the bus while his peers raced down the street to school in more fashionable ways.

He straightened out the paper and read, 'In order to discover who you are, first learn who everybody else is. You're what's left.'

He flipped it over to the back and learned how to say 'Rain.' A moment later, Norman sneezed and the last piece of chicken rolls off the plate and onto his new khakis.

Norman Loses a Sock

May 28th, A Sunday

It was Sunday night. Time to do laundry. Norman sorted his clothes carefully on the floor of his bedroom. One pile for whites, one pile for lights, and one pile for darks. He carefully gathered up the whites first, methodically pinning each sock to its mate. When he was finished, one sock remained, with its pair nowhere in sight. Norman added 'buy socks' to his to-do list.

Norman Makes a Mistake

May 29th, A Monday

The lady was yelling at Norman. Norman wasn't quite sure why. He thought back over recent events, as the lady went red in the face. She was quite a large lady.

Norman was on his lunch break. He had been walking to the bakery to pick up a pie, and had been pleasantly surprised to discover a shortcut on his route. Taking the narrow alleyway between the optometrist and the massage salon shaved a good five minutes off his travel time. He was on his way back when two people blocking the path held him up in the alleyway.

He'd asked them politely to move aside, but that seemed only to frighten them. The figure closest to Norman barreled past him, accidentally dropping his purse. Norman picked it up and called after the man, who darted back to snatch it from him before sprinting away.

Norman had felt rather good until he'd left the alleyway and the lady had accosted him. The lady was furious. Norman wasn't quite sure why.

Norman Finds Something New

May 30th, A Tuesday

Norman was looking for beef instant noodle cups when he spotted a new shrimp flavor, with real shrimp inside. He was feeling rather adventurous today, so he took the shrimp flavor instead. He put it in the microwave for three minutes, as the package instructed, and upon taking it out, discovered some of the water had spilled over.

Norman cleaned it up, and took his soup to his dinner table. He looked inside and saw the many small shrimp it had to offer. Norman feared the shrimp. He was afraid they would come alive in his mouth.

The cat had some extra food mixed with his cat kibble that night.

Norman Ponders Karl Marx

May 31st, A Wednesday

On Wednesday, one of Norman's colleagues from marketing, who he had not ever seen before, complained about his menial jobs and said something riveting about class war before dropping French words that Norman understood for a while, but eventually gave up trying.

Norman took the train home, and then sat with his legs akimbo on his comfy armchair and commenced watching an old episode of CSI. Suddenly, the name Karl Marx popped into his head. Norman had heard of him before but could not remember where and when. Was it the name of an ol' drinking pal of his dad's, or some wacko Hollywood actor, or a football commentator on PENS? Norman felt overwhelmed by his train of thought. After a few seconds of strenuous thinking, Norman finally remembered Karl was an old colleague of his. It was an all-around good day for Norman.

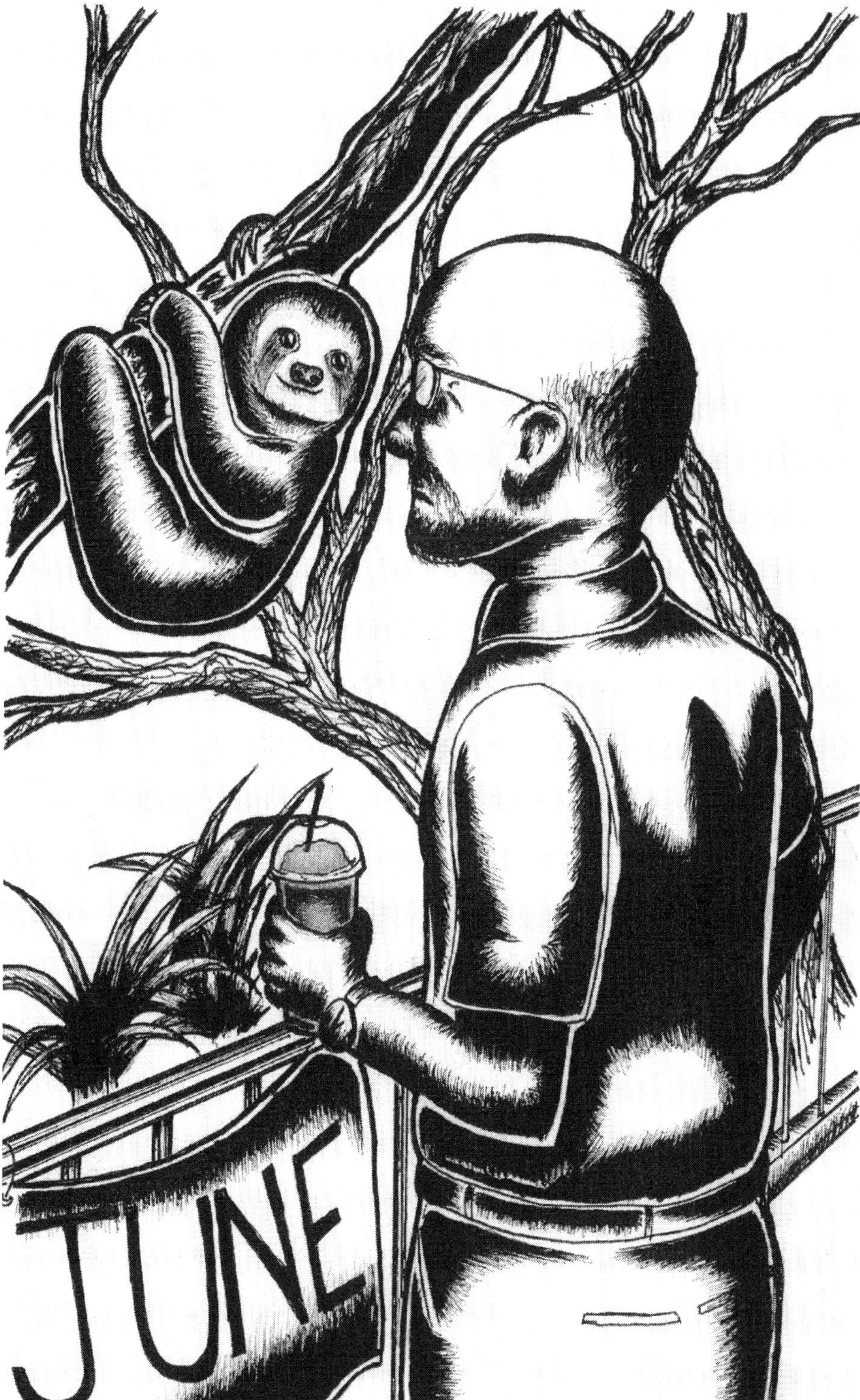
JUNE

June

Norman Surprises Himself

June 1st, A Thursday

Norman had just purchased a package of Werther's caramel hard candies, and he was enjoying them very much. As he left for the office in the morning, he stuck a single candy in his pocket. Then, he had an idea.

Norman put one candy in the inside pocket of all of his coats. Sweaters, blazers, even raincoats- Norman had enough for them all, things he hasn't worn in years, and perhaps wouldn't wear for years to come. *Sometimes it's nice to plan out surprises for yourself,* Norman thought.

Norman Makes a Big Change

June 2nd, A Friday

Today was the day things changed. Norman almost felt excited. He had no idea what prompted him to make this impulsive decision. He was nervous- what would people think of him? Too late- there was no stopping him now. Norman walked into the building. There was no going back now. He sat down at his desk, and nervously sighed.

Norman reached into his bag, and pulled out a picture of Norman. He gingerly placed the picture on his desk. *It feels good to be impulsive,* he thought. The adrenaline was still pumping through his veins. Then he realized something. The picture frame didn't go very well with his desk. He put the picture back into his bag. He would have to buy a new picture frame, when he went shopping next Thursday.

Norman's Watercooler Runs Out

June 3rd, A Saturday

Norman's finger turned pale as he squeezed the lever on his water-cooler that was sitting comfortably in the corner of his kitchen. *All dried up*, Norman thought.

Norman enjoyed owning a water cooler. With it, his water was always cold, and it didn't have that metallic tang that tap water had- it was almost as if his sink was laced with dirty pennies he's dropped in there over the years. It was most likely true. Norman sighed.

Only drips came from the cooler, and the drips only formed a tiny puddle in his mug. He made a note to look in to who this "Britta" person was and what she could do to fix his faucet, as well as writing down to purchase another jug when he went to the store. As much as he liked the jugged water, he felt terribly wasteful throwing away a giant plastic jug every week.

One time he attempted to make use of an old jug, and started to use it to collect coins. He saw on a television show that someone collected enough coins over the span of eight years that they bought a new Civic. Norman tried it, for a little while, but became desperate to find a tip for a pizza man one lazy Saturday. He couldn't reach for the pennies at the bottom, so he shook it over the sink to get access. Now he has pipes full of pennies. Norman sighed once again.

He savored the few drips of water in his cup, before refilling it anew from the sink.

The sink sputtered and moaned, shooting out the water. Norman let it run for a minute to get cold.

After a few minutes, Norman settled for lukewarm and prepared himself to drink the water.

Norman swished the cup, examining the water for blemishes.

It can't be that bad, Norman persuaded to himself. He put his mug to his lips.

Norman later made a note to pick up three jugs of water from the store, and inquired into finding Britta's phone number. The fact that the salesperson on the telephone was a man relieved Norman, but he was also slightly disappointed his couldn't pretend she was a young, pretty blonde.

Norman's TV Gets Interrupted

June 4th, A Sunday

Norman took another bite from his chicken wing, swallowing it along with a sip of ginger ale.

Tonight's CSI episode was one of the more exciting ones Norman had seen recently. He had seen this one three times so far, but still couldn't remember who the killer was. *Was it the mechanic?* he mused.

CSI cut away for the advertisements. Norman turned the volume down three bars. The ads were always very loud. Suddenly, the advertisement was interrupted by a lady with the words BREAKING NEWS plastered on the bottom of the screen.

The view of the lady cut away to a group of people. They were crying. Norman wanted to watch CSI, but it didn't seem as it was going to come back tonight. He turned off the TV.

That night, Norman couldn't sleep. Norman blamed the ginger ale. Next time he'd drink only half a bottle.

Norman Buys a Hat

June 5th, A Monday

Norman resented his baldness and figured it contributed to many of his woes. The 'right' hat could change people's first impression of him and reduce the amount of sunburn he received on his head during his short walks.

Norman was now gazing at the wide selection at the hat shop near his apartment. The friendly salesgirl had made several suggestions and he was appreciative of her attempts to help. Even so, he began to wonder if people would think it was weird that he was wearing a hat. Why had he not worn a hat before?

Norman decided to go home instead.

Norman Sees an Old High School Classmate

June 6th, A Tuesday

Norman stepped onto the public transit bus in the hope of having a fun ride. He rode often, sometimes just to stare out the windows and see the streets go by. Today, someone he knew rode on the bus too.

It was an old high school classmate- a pretty girl who was now a grown woman. She looked fine for her age- gray hairs hiding in a purple hat, and when she sat in the courtesy seating, Norman could only count the one roll of fat pressing against the bottom of her shirt. With her was a small boy, perhaps her son. Norman watched her, and as he still had his sunglasses on that day, he could do it incognito.

He decided against saying hello, or nodding, or even acknowledging her. Instead he sat and thought about the old days, while watching her own eyes to see if she would notice him. Several times Norman caught her gaze wandering to his end of the bus, quickly gazing at Norman. Norman felt flattered- perhaps she was admiring him! Though with a subtle frown on her face, he realised her expression was not unlike one's when staring at a pit stain on an unsuspecting passerby, or talking to a person who forgot to brush their teeth.

Norman took off his sunglasses and looked at himself in their reflection. The rolls of his chin were lit by the sunlight as easily as his balding head. His shirt had a chicken stain from earlier in the day. His tie was crooked. Norman put his sunglasses on again in embarrassment.

What Norman didn't notice, when the lady left the bus several stops later, is that she looked at him and smiled. When she noticed Norman's lack of a response, she hid her smile, ashamed. Norman stared out the window, watching a car's exhaust pipe leak onto the white lines near the stoplight.

Norman gets a Letter from his HOA

June 7th, A Wednesday

Norman,

We have received complaints from the community members that you have flooded the communal laundry room by loading too many of your items into one of the washers. We understand the desire to be efficient with your use of the facilities, but we ask that you divide your loads to ensure that this doesn't happen again. Please take care of the laundry room to give the next person a pleasant experience.

Thanks and all the best,

Kevin Garcon

HOA Community Leader

Norman only had enough quarters for one load of laundry, so he decided that Kevin was being unreasonable.

Norman Tries to Lucid Dream

June 8th, A Thursday

It was Thursday night and Norman was watching his old television. Staring mindlessly into the tiny picture-show box, Norman's eyes lit up as he flipped to the science channel. A program on lucid dreaming was playing. Norman had always been fond of controlling his dreams. Norman looked at the clock to see a prominent 7:30 PM.

It's too early to go to sleep, he thought.

Norman shrugged and followed the science channel's instructions for lucid dreaming, and went to sleep anticipating a night of wonders.

Norman woke up next morning to his alarm clock going off and no remembrance of dreams. Norman went through his usual morning routine before going to work.

Norman Feels Blue

June 9th, A Friday

Norman was having a bad day.

This morning, Norman, the cat, had vomited on the couch. Normally, this wouldn't bother him- he never found it a chore to look after his best friend. But today, he vomited on the daily newspaper as well- leaving his morning empty and without a crossword. *Just my luck*, Norman muttered to himself.

Later, at work, things got worse. Not only was it a Friday, but Frank, Norman's co-worker, beat him to the last creamer cup. Norman could have grabbed it first, but let Frank step in front of him, to be polite, and avoid taking something Frank might have had his eye on.

Like the creamer.

Norman was happy for Frank to have the cream, but that left Norman's coffee bitter. That left Norman bitter.

In the evening, huffed, puffed, and tuckered out, Norman went to his favorite pub- The Pub. He placed an order for chicken wings. They satisfied him- but not enough to sweeten his mood.

"Hey mister," said the red-haired waitress, "Just thought I'd ask you- we have an apple pie slice that someone didn't want with their order. Would you like to have it? It's on the house..."

Norman looked up to the waitress. She smiled warmly. The pie looked warm, too. Norman nodded.

"Here ya go, sweetie." she said.

From the window looking out of the kitchen, the red-haired waitress and one of her co-workers watched Norman inspect the pie.

He spun the plate around, carefully analyzing the slice. He grabbed the fork, cut off a piece, and took a bite. A warm smile came onto his face.

"He looks happy now!" said the co-worker.

"If he's happy, I'm happy."

Norman Goes Bicycle Shopping

June 10th, A Saturday

Upon arriving at the bicycle shop, Norman noticed a happy family eating dinner outside a nearby restaurant. The mother and son reminded Norman of his old family. Memories of his past surged through Norman's mind as he stared at the smiling couple and their son. Suddenly, Norman felt a sharp stinging pain. A bee sting snapped Norman out of his trance, and he remembered why he was here, just in time to see the cashier closing up the bike shop.

Norman Plays the Piano

June 11th, A Sunday

Norman walked through the busy mall, looking for batteries. He wouldn't normally go to the mall, it's too crowded for him, but he needed a new battery for the remote control to his television and the grocery store didn't have any.

As he was walking he passed by a piano sitting in the foyer with a sign that said, 'Play Me.' Norman walked closer to the piano, cautiously putting a hand on its gleaming surface. He wasn't quite sure that he should be doing this, but the sign did say 'Play Me' so he felt obligated to play something. He thought back to his high school band he was a part of: The Dusty Knucklers- he was the keyboard player.

Maybe I can still remember something from those days.

Norman felt a thrill of excitement course through him as he sat down on the cold stool. He put a finger out and pressed a key. Nothing happened. He pressed a little harder. Nothing happened. *The piano must be broken,* he thought, getting up from the stool.

Probably for the best, thought Norman as he walked away, *wouldn't want to make a fuss.*

Norman Smells the Past

June 12th, A Monday

As Norman walked down the street, his nose was met with an intoxicating aroma. It was the scent of deodorant. It was *Sure*, a brand that Norman once wore back in the 80's. He loved the smell- chemically sweet- and smelling it again brought him back to when he was a teenager himself. He remembered it reeking after a home basketball game, where he didn't score that night, or any nights, but tried his best. It reminded him of his date with Rebecca, and the awkward conversation with her father as he drove them to their first date.

Norman thought about the deodorant he wore now. There weren't many happy moments attached to it. *It has been a rather uneventful decade,* Norman thought to himself. Perhaps it was time for a change.

As Norman checked through the aisles for a stick of *Sure*, he was disappointed to discover that it was no longer sold. Norman left the store with something new- one called *Cool Sport*. It reminded him of his mother. *Perhaps this new smell will make the next decade more interesting,* Norman thought to himself.

Norman Exercises

June 13th, A Tuesday

Norman's doctor had told him to exercise yesterday, so he woke up early anticipating a nice jog. He put on his sweat-suit and laced up the running shoes he had purchased for $150 the night before, purely for his new workout routine. Leaving his apartment, he jogged awkwardly for a few minutes before doubling over, winded. Norman decided to walk instead.

He approached the intersection and stopped. The sign said he could walk, but a car had its blinker on, indicating it wanted to make a right turn. He waved at the driver to go ahead, but the driver waved back, urging him to go. Norman waved again, growing uncomfortable with the confrontation. The driver rolled down the passenger side window and yelled;

"Pedestrians have right of way, idiot! Now go!"

Norman turned back around and walked home. He logged his miles on a scrap piece of paper and wrote 'burned 10 calories' next to it. Norman planned to call his doctor the next morning and simply say; 'I did it'.

Norman Tries to Flirt

June 14th, A Wednesday

It was a hot day- an unusually hot day, in fact. Norman's air conditioning just happened to be broken, so he decided to walk through the park, hoping for a breeze or two. As he walked, he saw a beautiful woman. He found his mouth drying out and palms beginning to sweat. He watched her tie her shoes, and then he began to walk over to her. She stood up and saw him approaching. She asked how he was and he found himself stumbling over his words. She giggled and her cheeks blushed a deep red. He walked away, flustered. *Maybe next time,* he thought.

Norman's Ham and Cheese Sandwich

June 15th, A Thursday

It was a particularly sunny Thursday afternoon and Norman was in a good mood. He had slept well and his mind was at ease. He had no intention of spending any time outside but the stray rays of sunshine that made their way inside were still quite pleasing to him.

A *sandwich will be the frosting on the cake,* he thought. As he made his way into the kitchen, there was a knock on his door. This was all a bit too exciting for Norman.

After finding no one at the door Norman didn't wrack his mind for answers, instead he simply went to the kitchen for the sandwich that now had a new purpose: to restore the good spirits that the unclaimed knock somehow had managed to deprive him of.

The sandwich tasted good but Norman didn't quite enjoy the sunshine anymore that day.

Norman Buys a Grill

June 16th, A Friday

The grill came in a box, with nuts and screws and an instruction manual in every language. It took Norman a while to find the English section. He carefully built the grill and felt the same rush he experienced when he finished a jigsaw puzzle. Unfortunately, the grill was missing one leg, but eager not to be deterred, Norman propped it up with a stick and fired up the charcoal. As the charcoal lit, Norman grabbed a folding chair and sat down in front of his shiny new, peg-leg grill. No matter where he sat, the smoke blew in his eyes.

The coals seemed done, so he spread them and put on a whole chicken. Rubbing his hands together he sat back and listened to the sizzle. Within minutes it stopped sizzling. Norman lifted the lid; the coals seemed to not be as hot as he had thought. He finished the chicken in the oven and ate it standing up at the counter. It tasted dry.

Norman Tries a New Brand

June 17th, a Saturday

Norman was in the supermarket early in the morning. After placing a package of paper towels into his cart, he pulled his shopping list from his shirt pocket. As he ran a line through 'p towels', Norman noticed he had forgotten to find oatmeal. *Lucky I remembered,* he thought, *breakfast tomorrow would have been a nightmare.*

Norman pushed his cart over to where the oatmeal could usually be found. But, the shelf for the 'Unsweetened Original' flavor was empty. Norman looked at the shelves above and below: 'Fruit Medley' and 'Cinnamon Sugar'. Fruit was too tart for Norman in the morning so, on a whim, he picked up a box of 'Cinnamon Sugar' and proceeded through the checkout line.

The next morning, Norman was excited to try his new oatmeal. He woke ten minutes early and went straight to the kitchen. Norman emptied the packet into his bowl, added exactly one cup of milk, and heated the mixture in the microwave for three minutes. After letting it cool, he tried a spoonful. *That's much better than the kind I've been eating,* thought Norman. *I'll certainly get this from now on. Sometimes, trying new things is good.* Norman knew he was going to have a pleasant Saturday.

Norman Celebrates Father's Day

June 18th, A Sunday

For Norman, this Sunday was no more eventful than most others, though he had slept in a little longer than usual, snoozing twice instead of once. He had gotten up, showered, had breakfast, read the paper, then did some chores around the house while humming a rather annoying yet catchy song he had had stuck in his head for a few days now.

He was in the middle of doing the dishes when the doorbell rang. Curious, Norman dried off his hands and went to the door.

"Afternoon sir", the man in the UPS uniform said to him as he handed Norman a small but heavy package. As the delivery man was already on his way back to his van, Norman had just enough time to mutter "Thanks", all the while trying to remember what he'd ordered.

Still racking his brain, Norman put the package on the kitchen table and removed the brown paper around it.

"I don't know either, Norman", he told his cat that was looking at him quizzically.

In the package were three dark bottles of ale, centered around a big beer mug. There was plastic wrapping around it, with a little bow lint on top. Attached to it was a card. Norman opened it.

"Happy Father's Day, Dad! :) X Norm Jr. & Jess"

For what seemed like minutes, Norman couldn't move. He kept staring at the bottles, and felt a tear well up in his eye. He wanted to say something, anything, to Norman the cat or to himself or to no one in particular, but his throat was swollen.

That night, Norman drank two of the bottles from the beer mug. He didn't usually like ale, and these specific brews were sour and watery, but he drank them all the same and loved every swig of it.

When he lay in bed that night, he didn't know if his head was swarming from the beers or the happiness he felt.

Norman Holds the Door

June 19th, a Monday

Norman had just finished his Monday grocery shopping. He gathered his shopping bags and headed for the doors, looking forward to opening a fresh can of cat food for Norman. As he passed through the doorway, his coat pocket caught on the door handle and he paused for a moment to detach himself. A man who passed through the door after him thanked him for holding the door and continued on his way. Norman looked up to see that more people were approaching the doorway. He held the door open, allowing them to pass through unhindered.

Hours later, Norman opened his apartment door to find Norman meowing discontentedly. Norman opened a can of cat food and fed Norman. He wondered if cats need to make the same sacrifices that people do to be heroes.

Norman Enjoys the Rain

June 20th, A Tuesday

Norman opened the door to the dreary day outside. *A walk in the rain was just what the doctor ordered on this fine day*, Norman thought to himself. He carefully placed his feet in his rain boots, opened his umbrella, and ventured out. Norman stopped at the bottom of the steps in front of his house, looked the street up and down, and rubbed his chin thoughtfully. The open-air market was likely to be chaotic with people running to and fro trying to complete their shopping without getting too soaked. The downtown shops, as well, would all be crowded with strangers attempting to escape the rain. To Norman, the park was the only sensible option. After all, who in their right mind would be out at the park in this weather?

Chuckling softly at his own cleverness, Norman turned and walked up the street. As he neared the park, however, he was dismayed at the number of people who seemed to have the same thought as Norman. Umbrellas of all colors swirled, couples held hands, and children splashed in puddles.

As Norman looked about, a large frown forming on his face, he failed to hear the shouts of "Left!" coming from the biker behind him. Without quite enough room to get by, the biker's handle caught the edge of Norman's coat, sending him stumbling off the walkway and into a puddle. The cyclist wobbled and weaved, but regained his balance and kept going, looking back at Norman only long enough to give him the finger. "A fine day, indeed", grumbled Norman as he got back up.

Norman picked himself back up and turned to head home again, just as a small child ran screeching by. Another child's mud ball missed the intended target, splattering Norman in the face. Norman turned red with anger, but the children were off in a flash, and the internal tirade that was half formed in Norman's head smoldered. Norman retreated to his apartment, refining his speech to the children's parents about social responsibility, removed his rain boots, set his umbrella in the stand, and went to make a cup of tea, only to find that he was out.

Norman Loses his Wallet

June 21st, A Wednesday

It was Wednesday night, but Norman decided to get his shopping done a night early. He was feeling adventurous. He picked up half a dozen of his favorite frozen entrees (Salisbury steak with peas and carrots and a brownie) and proceeded through the self-checkout line.

As Norman was waiting for the bus, he felt his right back pocket and noticed his wallet was missing. He went back to the store and mustered up the courage to ask the clerk at the help desk if anyone had turned in a wallet. As she began to answer, Norman turned and walked away.

He keeps his wallet in his left back pocket on Wednesdays. Norman decided he won't go shopping on Wednesdays anymore.

Norman Learns of Local Singles in his Area

June 22nd, A Thursday

After learning about local singles in his area, Norman's old computer had finally gone kaput; spitting out a low wheeze as the viruses overwhelmed the machine.

Norman's old university roommate Danny now works in IT, something Norman pursued as well, before dropping out of college when Junior was born. He never knew what happened to all of his classmates, and he thought it would be nice to hear from Danny again, to catch up about the last two decades, and to see if he could fix his computer problems as well.

Norman's calf cramped horribly as he stood up from his swivel chair. Norman limped to his kitchen to see if he had any ice, only to see that he forgot about the chicken he set aside for dinner yesterday.

Norman fried the chicken with a side of fries and a ginger soda. Norman wasn't normally a fan of ginger soda, but it reminded him of staying home from middle school when he had the flu. Longing for the nostalgia of sick-days, Norman ended his night by calling in sick to work for the next morning.

Norman Takes a Walk

June 23rd, A Friday

Norman didn't like the smell of the apartment because Norman vomited on the recliner. He decided to clean it up later.

Norman took a walk to get away from the apartment, and saw that it was sunny. He checked the time and it said 6:03PM. As he walked, he tried to walk only on lines on the ground. A pretty woman passed him. Norman looked down and stopped walking on the lines.

Norman Gets Some Pie

June 24th, A Saturday

It was early evening when Norman looked up from the paper. He looked down to make sure he did not read the ad wrong. *No*. There it was. Plain as day.

"Today only- apple pie slices- 50 cents."

This was the bakery Norman passed nearly every day to and from work, but knew that the normal prices were much too high for his budget. He had overheard co-workers complain that the coffee there was no good either. But this special deal gave Norman a chance.

"It's not too late, I can make it before they close." Norman said aloud, feeling good that his Saturday would not be spent entirely in his flat.

"I'm sorry, but our apple pie sold out pretty early this afternoon," the clerk kindly told him. Norman steeled himself and ordered a slice of blueberry-rhubarb pie and a cup of coffee. He had come all this way, after all.

Nearly finished with his slice, Norman felt a tap on his shoulder. It was the clerk, holding another slice of blueberry-rhubarb pie in a to-go box. "We're closing, and have a leftover slice if you would like it."

Norman smiled and sipped the not-awful-not-great coffee. "Thank you." Today was a good day.

Norman Messages his Son on Facebook

June 25th, a Sunday

Norman hesitated before typing his son's name in the search-bar. After all, his friend request status had been pending for the past eight months. Perhaps he had just forgot.

In his profile picture, Norman Jr. had his arms wrapped around a smiling woman in a yellow sundress. Long, flowing hair that reached her waist in waves. Norman was proud that his son could find such a beautiful woman.

In the message field, Norman typed,
"Hello, son! It's been awhile since I've heard from you. Just wanted to see how you were doing! Don't be a stranger!"

Norman hit enter and waited. Inside, he already knew that his son wouldn't respond, but he waited anyway.

Unfortunately, Norman's intuition wasn't wrong. A box appeared beneath his message, indicating that his message had been "Seen." And the next day, it remained seen. The next day, and the next.

After the fourth day, Norman knew not to bother checking his Facebook inbox. Instead of typing his son's name in the search bar, he sighed and looked to his cat, wondering if he would miss him if he died.

Norman's Lunch Break

June 26th, A Monday

Norman checked the time on the bottom right side of his computer. It read 12:00, marking the start of his half-hour lunch break. He locked his computer to be sure nothing compromised his files, then walked over to the break room. After retrieving his lunch from the office refrigerator, he went over to his usual seat at the corner table. As he sat, he heard two coworkers make plans to sit outside for lunch and enjoy the unseasonably warm weather. Norman wondered if he should take his lunch outside, too. After a moment, he decided against it since his lunch was already unpacked.

Norman Visits the Zoo

June 27th, a Tuesday

Norman read an article in the newspaper about the brand-new tiger exhibit at the zoo today. He decided it would be fun to pay the zoo a visit after he finished working. Norman had only been to the zoo once, in elementary school with his class.

There was a crowd around the tiger exhibit. Norman decided he would look around the zoo and then come back when there were less people. He bought a slushy and sat down to watch the sloths. The sloths moved very slowly and always looked tired most of the time.

Norman went back to the tiger exhibit. There was still a large crowd watching the tigers. He decided that he would come back next week to try and see the tigers. Norman went back to the sloths to wave goodbye.

Norman Watches Frasier

June 28th, A Wednesday

Norman sat on his plaid couch watching an old rerun of *Frasier*. He chuckled half-heartedly at Niles becoming dopey after taking too much allergy medicine. Norman kept his voice low so as not to startle the cat. He then had the realisation that he needed to sneeze. He hastily walked over to his coat to retrieve his handkerchief. The loud noise woke his cat. Midway through fumbling in his coat pocket he realised that he no longer needed to sneeze. He sat back down on the couch and took another bite of his casserole.

He felt guilty about waking his cat.

Norman Considers Suicide

June 29th, A Thursday

'Death at one's own hand,' read the crossword clue.

Norman was on the bus and had the distinct suspicion that someone was reading over his shoulder. He could feel light, strawberry-scented breath at the nape of his neck. The bus was on the way home, and it was a Thursday. Norman worried that perhaps people were getting ready for the weekend.

Norman re-read the clue. It was clearly 'suicide'.

"Have you considered suicide?" suggested the strawberry voice.

Norman turned slowly and hid his shock under a prim smile.

"Yes," he whispered.

Norman Goes for an Interview

June 30th, a Friday

After three weeks with a silent phone, Norman had almost forgotten about the job that he'd applied for. Suffice it to say he was quite surprised when the phone rang and a voice on the other end asked him to meet for an interview.

Norman eagerly agreed and ended the call with a large smile. The interview was to be Friday at 2:00PM sharp. He went to bed early so that he would have ample time to prepare.

In the morning, he took the remaining money from his last paycheck to a nice clothing outlet and bought a simple button up shirt and a striped tie. He gave himself a once-over in the mirror and nodded in approval before buying the clothes. After the purchase, he was left with fifteen dollars, just enough for a cab.

He called a cab over and told the man where to go. They'd just pulled up to the address when Norman's phone began to ring. Norman handed the cab driver the ten dollars that he was owed and answered the phone.

"Hello, Norman?"

"Yes, this is Norman."

"We're sorry, but we wanted to let you know that we've just filled the position you are interviewing for. Please do not come."

Norman slowly lowered the phone and tapped the cab driver on the shoulder.

"Would it cost about ten dollars for us to go back the way we came?"

The cab driver shook his head. Norman exited the cab to begin the long walk home.

July

July

Norman Goes to a Yard Sale

July 1st, A Saturday

It was a particularly bright and sunny morning. Norman decided not to waste such a nice day inside, so he went for a walk.

A few blocks from his home was a yard sale. Norman hadn't been to one in years. He stopped to see what was available. Old pairs of shoes, a toaster, a box of magazines for ten cents each. There wasn't much that he found appealing.

Then an item on the table of knick-knacks caught his eye- a cute little ceramic skunk holding a flower. Norman smiled for a moment. It reminded him of a gift he had given his ex-wife back when they were dating. It almost looked the same, except Norman gave her a ceramic squirrel holding an acorn. He began to wonder if she still had that little squirrel, but he quickly put that thought out of his mind. Norman didn't like to dwell on the past.

He walked away from the yard sale back to home, lost in thought.

Norman Watches TV

July 2nd, A Sunday

"Capitals," said the handsome man. Norman imagined what it would be like to be on TV, but soon found himself uncomfortably anxious at the thought.

"This city was the birthplace of military leader Simón Bolívar," said Trebek.

"What is Caracas?" asked Norman.

The handsome gentleman repeated his question, and Norman chuckled softly to himself. He had watched a rerun of the episode earlier that day.

Norman Meets a New Co-worker

July 3rd, A Monday

Norman sat in his cubicle staring at his computer screen. He'd been entering figures for what seemed like hours. Days like this made his mind wander to other activities, like taking a walk in the park or settling in for takeout and a CSI marathon, or–

"Well, who's this good-looking fella?"

Norman abruptly came out of his daydream to see Kelli looking at a photo of Norman the cat. Kelli had been hired just a few days ago, and was quite friendly and attractive. Norman had never spoken to her before, but it was fair to say that he was smitten.

"Oh, um, well, that-that's my cat. His name is Norman too!"

Norman became immediately self-conscious and could feel himself begin to sweat. He could smell her perfume as she set a fresh stack of reports on Norman's desk.

"Well", Kelli said, "Norman looks like such a sweetie! He reminds me of my fiancé's cat. Well, see you!"

Kelli's words hung in the air as she walked back to her office. Norman let out a sigh and gazed at the photo. Kelli was right. Norman was a good-looking cat.

Norman Buys Groceries

July 4th, A Tuesday

Norman was pushing his cart through the seemingly endless aisles of a grocery store when he passed a lone brunette woman in the soup aisle. She glanced at his direction with the barest quirk of a smile. Norman jerked away his gaze towards his favorite soup, hoping the woman would not think that he was staring at her. A few minutes later they passed each other again in the snack aisle, this time both avoiding eye contact. *Crisis averted,* Norman thought to himself.

Norman Gets a Call

July 5th, A Wednesday

Today Norman sat at home after a long day of work. It was 6:23 in the afternoon on a Wednesday, and he was bored. He'd surfed the channels for any CSI reruns, but came up empty.

He settled instead for some show on the travel channel, which he always found interesting. Today it was about a young traveling couple in Paris showcasing sights, and then about a rugged mountain climber in Nepal.

Suddenly his landline rang. *Who could it be?* he thought, somewhat excitedly. He had to stop himself from answering it immediately. *Don't want them to think I wait by the phone all day*, he thought. He picked it up and counted in his head: "One ring, two rings, three..."

As he did so the anxiety of talking to the possibly unknown person flooded his mind. *What would I even say?* He hurriedly forced himself to hit the button and mumble “Hello.”

Silence. They must have hung up right before he picked up. Norman was relieved.

Norman Eats Cereal

July 6th, A Thursday

Ever since he was a child, Norman had been in the habit of eating his cereal dry. This was not because he didn't like his milk; instead, it was because he preferred the cereal to stay crunchy. He found the texture of soggy cereal to be exceedingly unpleasant, though he could never tell you exactly why.

Today, he decided to eat it with milk. This was after waking up in a much better mood than usual. Most mornings Norman woke up tired, and the only thing that got him out of bed was the knowledge that he needed to feed Norman before he started pawing and howling. Today however, Norman woke up with a smile. He didn't believe it at first, but when he saw himself in the mirror he knew it was true; there, running across the width of his face and looking a bit out of place, was the bare trace of a smile.

He tried to think of the cause of the smile, but nothing came to mind. He decided that he must have had a good dream or something. That seemed to make sense. He couldn't remember the dream, though, but that was nothing new. Norman stopped remembering his dreams a long time ago. Sometimes, like right now, he wished that he still did.

Nonetheless, Norman felt emboldened in his newly-found good mood. He felt adventurous, and hungered for some sort of change. Then, perhaps because he was actually hungry, his mind turned to cereal, and he decided that this would be his first step into a new life. He would become a man who ate his cereal with milk.

When he opened the fridge, he was happy to find that he indeed had some milk. He had bought skim milk by accident though, which was not his favorite. He looked to see if another carton was hiding somewhere, but could not find one. It looked as if skim milk was truly all he had.

Norman changed his mind about the cereal. He decided that it wasn't worth it, so long as he didn't have good milk. He poured himself a bowl and chewed slowly, staring at the cracks forming in the kitchen wall. He felt the dry bits of falsely-colored corn products cut the roof of his mouth. However unpleasant, it was a familiar sensation, so Norman didn't mind much.

Norman Misses his Stop

July 7th, A Friday

Norman arrived at his bus stop at exactly 7:35. Arriving five minutes later would mean that if the bus was early, he would miss it. Arriving five minutes earlier would mean that the previous bus would see him and expect him to get on. When his bus arrived at 7:45 he took his seat and put on his headphones. Norman had read the previous day that wearing headphones makes it seem like you don't want to be disturbed, and it seemed to be working so far.

Norman was enjoying his morning commute when unexpectedly, the bus pulled over at the stop before his and a beautiful woman stepped on board. Norman stared out the window and heard the woman sit down next to him and pull out a book.

Norman’s stop was next.

The closest 'stop' button to signal the driver was located just next to the woman's shoulder. Norman analysed all the ways he could press the button without seeming creepy and decided to simply ask her to press the button for him. Norman bit his lip, rolled his shoulders and turned to ask her, only to see headphones clamped over her ears. She didn’t want to be disturbed either.

The woman pressed the button seven stops later.

Norman Stumbles upon a Garage Sale

July 8th, A Saturday

As Norman was walking home, after getting some groceries, he stumbled upon a garage sale. He wanted to walk past it, as it was drizzling outside. As he walked by, he couldn't help but notice an old radio. Norman's mother used to listen to that same radio all the time when he was growing up. It made him think of the times when he'd be playing with his toys while his mother ironed clothing. He was filled with nostalgia as he reminisced his youth. He must've been standing there for a while, as the owner of the garage sale approached him.

"You interested in that ol' radio?" the owner asked. Norman only had a ten-dollar bill on him, so he figured he couldn't afford it right now. After a brief pause the owner started again; "Ehh, you can have 'r for... Let's say seven bucks." Norman imagined how the radio would fit perfectly on his empty night stand, how he could remember his youth every night before he went to sleep. Norman smiled.

He was already carrying his groceries in one hand and the radio would be quite the load. Surely his arms would be pretty tired by the time he makes it home. He politely refused the offer and walked off. He could've been home right now. He might even miss the first few minutes of the reruns he planned to watch.

Norman Answers the Phone

July 9th, A Sunday

The phone rang... once... twice... and on the third, Norman picked up. "Hello?" he spoke into the receiver, but it was too late, as the person on the other end had disconnected. Norman sighed and went back to brushing Norman.

It was only ten minutes before the phone rang again and Norman waited, again, until the third ring to pick up. "Hello?" Norman repeated blandly into the phone four times before he decided that the person must have hung up again.

This time after hanging up, he turned the TV off and pushed Norman off his lap. Norman moved to the window, with a cup of coffee in his hand and when the phone rang again, Norman never picked up.

Norman Makes a Prank Call

July 10th, A Monday

Norman was browsing the internet one morning when he came across something interesting. He squinted to read it. It appeared to be a conversation between two people.

"Is your fridge running, sir?"

"Yes."

"Can you catch it?"

Norman smiled. He read some more. This was an example of a prank call, where somebody calls someone else pretending to be somebody important but is calling for the sake of a joke. *I could do that,* Norman thought to himself, all the while forgetting how easily he had been pranked in the past. He picked up the phone and dialed a random number.

As the phone rang, Norman tried to think of a company name that he could use. The person on the other end picked up.

The conversation began.

"Hello?"

"Hello!"

"Yes?"

"..."

"Is anyone there?"

"Yes. This is Norman. Incorporated. Norman Incorporated. I'm... we're calling to ask about your refrigerator. Is it running?"

"No."

"Okay."

The man hung up. Norman put the phone back in its cradle and went to eat breakfast.

Norman Almost Buys New Socks

July 11th, A Tuesday

Norman went shopping. He didn't like shopping because there was the chance that he might see someone he knew and would have to think of something to say. But he needed socks.

Norman perused the sock collection, marveling at all the different types of socks there were. There were crew cut and ankle socks and black socks and blue socks and socks that let your feet breathe and wool socks and-

Norman shook his head. He decided to think it over at home and come back another day.

Norman's Slippers

July 12th, A Wednesday

Norman was tired. It was just about time to head to bed, and he'd had a long day. He was dressed in his typical summer nightwear: striped white pajamas, a navy robe, and burgundy slippers.

Soon after Norman's marriage had ended, he sought to clear any reminders of his ex-wife from his home. The slippers were the exception--she had bought them as a late wedding present on their honeymoon. Despite his usual rule of exile, he couldn't find anything comparable to replace them and was stuck with the reminder of her.

As Norman sat down on his bed, he looked at the slippers and sighed. He felt defeated. It was time for bed.

Norman Solves a Puzzle

July 13th, A Thursday

The puzzle was dusty, and had obviously been sitting on the bookstore shelf for quite some time. Norman picked it up, interested in its shiny cover. He had an urge to pick up a puzzle as entertainment for the weekend.

Norman used to solve these puzzles with his son, Norman Jr, and missed the opportunity for thought. He purchased the puzzle and continued on his way, performing his various errands until he got home. When he got home he opened the box, slowly pouring all the pieces out onto the table. It was rather expansive.

This puzzle would prove quite hard to solve. After several hours of working to put the pieces together, Norman only had a small portion of the puzzle done. Norman (the cat) had been laying on the table near him for the majority of this time, and had begun to occasionally step on and around the puzzle pieces. Norman rose from his chair, poured Norman's favorite cat food into his dish, and sat again, staring intently at the puzzle.

Slowly, the pieces fell into place. As the picture began to come together, Norman felt satisfaction in his solving of this puzzle, and once it was done, enjoyed having relived something he formerly had done with his son. After solving the puzzle, he walked to his home phone, and began to dial his son's number. A woman answered, saying her name was Laura.

Laura explained that Norman had the wrong number. It seemed Norman Jr. had changed his number. Norman said thank you to Laura, and then hung up. He checked his clock.

It was ten thirty.

Norman went to bed, reminiscing about his son.

Norman Thinks About Getting a Dog

July 14th, A Friday

Norman stepped off the bus after a visit to the grocery store. It was beef week, and he had one lone shopping bag slung over his arm. Norman usually looked at the ground when he walked, but today he happened to look up. There was a young man walking a dog ahead of him. It was an impressive dog, perhaps a shepherd. Norman imagined himself putting a picture of the dog on his desk at work. Perhaps the new intern would notice and think he was the type to have a powerful dog.

The dog approached and sniffed at Norman's shopping bag. The owner yanked on the leash, muttering an apology, and Norman nodded. He was suddenly embarrassed. Norman scurried up to his home and opened the front door. He imagined that the dog was very impressed by the meat for his evening meal, and that he would make a fine dog owner.

When Norman walked into the house, the cat was lazing about on the kitchen counter. Norman was usually on the counter when Norman came home, even though he'd been told cats didn't belong on counters. Norman sighed and shooed his cat down onto the floor. Of course, he couldn't get a dog, he realized. It would upset Norman's routine.

Norman Goes to the Pictures

July 15th, A Saturday

It was raining outside. Norman thought that he might go to the pictures.

He caught two buses to get to the theatre and walked through the doors smiling. Gazing up at the options, the choice was obvious. He walked to the counter and asked for an adult's ticket for a new action movie and a medium ginger ale. It wasn't starting for another fifteen minutes so he strolled into a nearby bookstore to pass the time.

He picked up a book about boats. Norman always had liked boats. He looked at the pictures of the giant water-crafts and smiled. He turned the page and began to read.

Norman kept reading on the spot, until the store owner informed him they were closing. He bought the book and strolled home. It had stopped raining, and Norman thought about the lady at the movie counter. He might see another movie next weekend.

Norman Reminisces

July 16th, A Sunday

Norman was cleaning out his closet when, behind piles of boot-cut jeans and corduroys he no longer wore, he came across a dusty old shoe box. He carefully took the box out and blew the dust off the top, smiling at his teenage handwriting spread out across the box cover, spelling out 'memories'. Norman hadn't looked through these in a long time.

He opened the box and sifted through the various keepsakes, a smirk planted firmly on his face the entire time. He took each object into his hand, running his fingers along their surfaces, transporting himself back to each archived moment.

He did this with every item in the box, until he came across an old blue polka dot hair clip. He racked his brain, but he couldn't remember for the life of him where it was from. *It must've gotten in there by accident*, he thought. Norman walked over and threw it into the garbage.

A few minutes later he came back, sleeves rolled up, and retrieved the clip from the trash, putting it back into the box.

It would come back to him eventually.

Norman Reads the Paper

July 17th, A Monday

Norman was pleased with the shade of his tea that morning. It was a slightly darker brown than last Monday when he had lost concentration and added too much milk. He liked to wait for approximately one more minute for his tea to reach an optimal drinking temperature before he would begin to sip.

Norman gingerly unfolded that day's copy of the Daily Informer; a reasonably priced newspaper that had a well-balanced crossword suited to his ability. On page four, Norman noticed a spelling mistake. He circled it with a red pen and wondered if anybody else had noticed it. He sipped his tea and grimaced; perhaps he should have waited another ten seconds.

Norman Writes a Bestselling Novel

July 18th, A Tuesday

Norman stumbled into the kitchen to look for a pencil. He finally found it in a drawer underneath a yellow screwdriver.

He couldn't find any lined paper and almost gave up before remembering that he had a supply of napkins in his cupboard. It was unconventional to use a napkin for a reason other than mopping bits of food or drink, but it was all right to make one exception today.

He licked the end of the pencil and put it to the napkin. It smeared and tore through the thin paper. Norman tried again, making a weak vertical line. After a bit of effort, Norman had the first word down. His mind raced with the possibilities.

It seemed like a good start, but Norman didn't want to ruin what he already had by going in the wrong direction. The famous man on the telly had said that before he had written his bestselling novel, he thought very carefully about what he was going to write. Norman knew as soon as he saw the interview that he could write a famous book, too.

Norman looked at what he had written and thought very hard. It was hard to tell whether it belonged best at the beginning or the end. It was good either way. He decided it was safest to ask for an outside opinion.

"Norman," Norman said, "would you like to hear a story I wrote?" Norman did not respond. He was sleeping on the arm of the couch in front of the telly.

Norman frowned at the napkin. Now it seemed like more of a middle. A lot of things seemed to be just middles.

Norman chastised himself for getting caught up in the moment. Norman had certainly met quite a lot of people that were very interesting. Perhaps one of them would become famous instead of him. The more he mulled it over, the more he liked the idea.

Perhaps not everyone needs to be remembered, Norman thought, before settling into the chair, draping his arm around Norman, and letting the napkin fall to the carpet.

The single word on the napkin fell facedown.

"The

Norman Steps Out

July 19th, A Wednesday

Norman sat down at a booth in the back of a small café a few blocks from his apartment. It was a fine day, though a bit sunny for Norman's tastes, and Norman had resolved to get out instead of staying inside. As Norman looked absentmindedly over the restaurant's decor, a waitress came over.

"Hi, welcome to Café Christiano! My name is Helen. Can I get you something to drink?" she asked as she handed Norman a menu.

"Um, I'll just have water, I suppose." Norman replied.

"Coming right up!" she smiled as she walked away. Helen looked to be in her early 30s with a fair complexion and was quite tall for someone with her slender build. Her hair was cut rather a lot shorter than Norman usually liked, but it framed her face well. *She seemed quite nice*, Norman thought to himself. Something in her demeanor and her friendly greeting made Norman picture being able to be great friends with her.

"Alrighty, here's your water sir. Can I get you something to start with?" Helen startled Norman, who had been lost in thought. He realized with some embarrassment that he had been too busy daydreaming to begin looking at the menu. He quickly opened to the appetizers and looked at his options.

"Do you need more time?" Helen the waitress asked.

"No, I, uh..." Norman stammered. He was beginning to get nervous now. He didn't want to embarrass himself in front of his new friend Helen.

"Well I... um, I mean, what do yo- what would you recommend?" Norman asked. Helen thought for a moment.

"I really like the hummus platter. It comes with pita chips and assorted vegetables and the hummus is made fresh in house each day. It's really tasty!" *Hummus?* Norman had never tried hummus. He didn't even know what was in hummus. Still, if Helen liked it, maybe it was worth a shot.

"Yeah, that sounds good. I'll have that."

"Okay, I'll put your order in." Helen replied. Norman watched her as she walked away. He felt butterflies in his stomach start to take flight. Here he was, eating at a new restaurant, making new friends and trying exotic international cuisine! This had all the makings of a great day. Norman sat in anticipation for about five minutes before Helen the waitress reappeared.

"Alright, here's your hummus platter. I'll be back in a bit to take your meal order. Enjoy!" Norman looked down at the food before him. He was greeted with a large plate of what looked like tortilla chips, but not quite, and what looked like onion dip, but not exactly. There were also carrot and celery sticks. Norman recognized those. Norman exhaled.

Here goes nothing, he said to himself. He picked up one of the chips, scooped a medium bit of hummus onto it, and took a bite. He started chewing. He stopped. Norman didn't like it. He kept chewing. Norman still didn't like it. He swallowed with some difficulty. He was now sure that he didn't like it. The texture and taste reminded him of paste which reminded him of junior high. Norman didn't like junior high. He looked down at the platter and started to panic. He knew he couldn't finish it, but he couldn't send it back. What would Helen think? She had said it was her favorite. Not eating it would be a slap in her face. Norman nervously wrung his hands trying to decide what to do. He didn't have much time- Helen had said that she would be back in a few minutes and then she would see.

Norman had an idea. He took out a small pack of tissues that he kept in his pocket and removed the tissues from the plastic wrapper. Norman looked around to make sure that nobody was looking at him. He picked up his spoon and began scooping the hummus into the wrapper. Norman's heart was pounding now. He had to be quick, Helen could be back at any moment and he couldn't bear for her to see this. Norman scooped the last of the hummus and quickly put the wrapper back in his pocket. He unfolded several napkins from the holder on the table and put the chips and vegetables into them before balling them up and shoving them too, in his pocket. Norman looked up, heart still racing. Helen was nowhere in sight. He breathed a sigh of relief.

Maybe Norman will like the hummus, he thought to himself as he took a sip of water to calm his nerves. Norman hated wasting food. A few moments later, Helen the waitress reappeared.

"Are we ready to order? Oh! You finished your hummus already. That was quick. How'd you like it?"

"It was good."

Norman ordered chicken fingers.

Norman Goes to the Movies

July 20th, A Thursday

Norman was going to the movies.

Once he had browsed the newspaper for show times, he hopped on the bus to the theatre. He wasn't sure he'd make it on time, but he did. He bought some popcorn and took a seat in the dark auditorium. The screen told him to turn off his phone, so he did.

Norman glanced at the other people in the theatre. He wondered who they were and why they also chose to see this movie. He really hoped they enjoyed the film.

Soon the movie began, and Norman quickly realised he was in the wrong theatre. But he didn't leave. *Lots of people worked hard on this movie,* he thought. He didn't want those people to feel bad. He also feared the other moviegoers would feel put down, because this movie wasn't good enough for Norman.

He watched the whole movie. It was about ghosts. It scared him. By the time it was over, he didn't feel like seeing any new movies, so he exited the theatre and turned on his phone again. No one had called.

Norman Misses Out

July 21st, A Friday

Norman was falling in love at work. The new intern, Donna, was everything Norman liked in a woman.

"Hi, how are you?" she would say in the mornings. Norman would smile and say, "I'm good!" he thought his response may be profound in its simplicity.

Norman tried his best to figure out what made her tick. *Does she like flowers?* Norman picked up a plant from the lobby and placed it by her desk, to see how she would react.

She liked ham sandwiches for lunch. Maybe she found little piglets cute. Norman would intentionally buy two ham sandwiches for lunch, but never worked up the courage to give her the second one. He had had two ham sandwiches for weeks.

One day, as Norman came to work, he went to greet Donna.

"Hi, how are you?" she asked. Norman was about to muster out an "I'm good", when he noticed a ring on her finger. It turned out Donna had her diamond ring in the repair shop for the last few weeks.

Norman went home early that day. He couldn't stop thinking about what he could have done differently. He could have met her years ago, before she had even met her husband. Norman certainly wasn't occupied then. He could have given her flowers, have been more attractive, and done more to get her attention. He could have been better than 'good'. Norman felt upset.

Norman Makes Lunch

July 22nd, A Saturday

Norman looked out of the window. It was a sunny Saturday and the green space across the road was full of families and picnickers. Norman contemplated pulling on some loafers and joining the throng. He imagined wandering among the smilers of the world, petting a friendly dog, and throwing a football. He fantasized about striking up a conversation with one of the ladies sitting alone. Most of them are reading or listening to music on one of those portable devices kids use these days.

Norman didn't like to intrude. He took some bread, butter and ham from the fridge and made a sandwich instead.

Norman Goes to Church Again

July 23rd, A Sunday

Norman, being of sound mind, decided to head to church. It had been a while since Norman had been inside a house of God, so he decided to dress rather simple. He caught the bus to the crossroads, where he stood in front of the church.

"Pretty," he mumbled, stepping into the building.

He sat down in the front pew, adjusting his glasses as he squinted around.

"Can I help you, my son?" An old, wise voice echoed throughout the hall.

"God?" Norman asked, looking up at the ceiling.

"No, but I'm afraid you'll have to leave, we're closed for fumigation." said the old caretaker sternly.

"Oh, alright." said Norman, as he stood up and walked out of the church.

Norman Goes on Vacation

July 24th, A Monday

I deserve this, Norman thought to himself, as he sat looking at the pristine blue waters, and fine yellow sand. The sun was shining down on this beautiful day and Norman could even see a palm tree in the distance. Norman had been working incredibly hard and it was good to finally unwind for a little bit.

Well that's enough for today, Norman thought, as he closed the beach picture on his monitor, and got back to work.

Norman is a Criminal

July 25th, A Tuesday

Norman had struggled with anxiety for some time, and had finally managed to get an appointment with a specialist. The doctor had a ponytail and wore sandals, looking nothing like his regular doctor. He wrote a short prescription for medicinal marijuana and passed it across the desk. Norman folded it up and put it in his pocket.

As he left the office, a police car drove past with its lights on, leaving Norman feeling more anxious than ever. He crumpled the prescription and threw it into a garbage can on the corner. This brush with crime had been most unsettling.

Norman Plants a Garden

July 26th, A Wednesday

On a particularly mundane afternoon, Norman made the decision to create his very own garden. He very much liked the idea of bragging to people he met that he tended his own vegetables. He popped down to the closest greenery shop and got all the things any gardener would ever need, including a pair of bright yellow gardener's gloves, a rubber green hoe, fertilized soil, and a variety of seed packets.

He returned home with his purchases and began to create sections for different plants on his apartment balcony. *This is much harder than I thought it would be,* Norman thought to himself. He completed three plots before giving in to his exhaustion and deciding that three plants would just have to do.

He decided to plant carrots, cabbage, and radishes. They looked easy enough for even Norman to have a hard time messing up. He sprinkled the entire packet of carrot seeds over the soil, before realizing he was supposed to bury the seeds. Shrugging, he moved onto cabbage, making sure to read the directions this time. Satisfied with how his cabbage seeds were planted, he decided to not do radishes. *The carrots and cabbage should be just enough for me,* Norman thought. He watered his plants and promptly forgot about them for the rest of the summer.

Frank Denies Norman

July 27th, A Thursday

For eight hours a day, five days a week, Norman sat with his back facing towards an equally middle-aged man named Frank. Frank was slender, balder, and far quieter than Norman- whose own shyness was something not to be underestimated. For the past nine years, the two men sat solemnly beside each other in the confines of their cubicle. In the morning, they would say "Morning" to each other, and as they packed up their briefcases for the day, they would say "Evening", even though both of them left the office at the same time, rode the elevator at the same time, and even wait at the bus stop at the same time. It didn't help that they lived in the same apartment building, as well as the same floor.

Norman knew very little about Frank. Occasionally he would hear Frank discuss politics with Robert from sales, and from the amount of times Frank ordered in for lunch, Norman could tell he was a fan of Vietnamese food. Norman also knew that Frank had a wife named Josie, and an eight-year-old daughter named Amber. Norman felt that this was his one connection to Frank, if the two ever talked. Norman and his ex-wife divorced when Junior was only seven, and because of that, Norman was jealous of Frank. He was happy for him, but still, a part of Norman wished he were more like Frank.

The change of status quo occurred when Norman received an work-email on a Thursday afternoon.

"Hello everyone,

Just a reminder that today is Frank Jenkins' birthday! Please take a moment in your day to wish him Happy Birthday!"

Norman hesitated, then closed the email, just in case Frank saw it and spoiled any surprise birthday parties, if anyone had happened to plan one for him. Norman then had to consider his options- say Happy Birthday to his face, and risk stumbling over his words, or write a carefully worded, but less thoughtful, email?

After spending an hour of his work hours considering a humorous anecdote for an email and coming up with nothing, Norman decided to just speak in person instead.

"Hey Frank," said Norman, smoothly, "Happy birthday."

Frank nodded in acknowledgement to Norman. Norman felt strange; as if there was a stiffness in the air at followed. Frank seemed down, and Norman wasn't sure why. Norman made note to ask him why, on a day not so important as his birthday.

Norman Watches a Sad Fly

<u>July 28th, A Friday</u>

The little fly buzzed around the ceiling, spinning in circles, aimlessly bumping into the walls. *What is it doing?* wondered Norman.

Soon the fly began to pounce its little bug skull on one particularly blank and un-special wall. If it was a window Norman would understand- but a blank wall? Why?

Perhaps this was a cry for help.

Norman leapt out of his chair, trying his best to scoop the fly in his hands to console it, just for a short while, until it came to its senses.

After ten minutes, Norman successfully caught the fly. Right after Norman named it Melanie, he opened his hand to discover he had crushed her in the crease of his fingers.

Norman gave Melanie a Viking funeral, and the burnt scent of Melanie lingered for the rest of the day.

Norman vs Noodles

July 29th, A Saturday

Norman placed his Maruchan Instant Lunch in the microwave, shut the door, and hit the number three. The light in the microwave turned on, and the Styrofoam cup started its slow rotation.

As the time counted down, Norman looked over at Norman. The cat's eyes were closed, but Norman could hear purring, even over the hum from the microwave. Norman smiled, envious though he was of Norman's contentment and apparent happiness.

Norman started to daydream about what would make him happy, what might kick him out of his rut. He thought about moving closer to his son but was immediately put off by the logistics. What job could he find where his son lived? He considered himself lucky to have the job he had.

He ruminated on how things had ended badly with his ex-wife, and whether he could have in some way been a better person for her. He remembered how their modest honeymoon to Palm Springs had been disastrous when they arrived to find their hotel was being fumigated, and yet, how funny the two of them thought that was, and how they couldn't keep their hands off each other as they slept in the rental car that first night. He smiled thinking of her smile, of her touch. He closed his eyes and was, for a moment, happy.

The microwave's ding pulled Norman back to the present. He opened the door and was met with an unpleasant smell. Norman had forgotten to add water to his noodles, and they now smelled so bad he didn't think he could eat them. He walked them outside to the trash bin and then returned and sat by Norman on the couch. As he started to pet Norman, the cat jumped down, stretched, and curled up on a favorite spot on the carpet.

"That's about right, Norman," Norman said. "That's about right."

Norman's Sick Day

July 30th, A Sunday

Norman woke at his usual hour. He found he had woken up quite congested, with a rather runny nose.

Oh dear, Norman sniffed to himself. He wondered if he should use a sick day. *I don't feel bad enough that I couldn't be productive,* he thought, *but I don't want to run the risk of infecting any co-workers.*

Then he remembered that it was Sunday.

"Thank goodness," Norman sighed aloud. He got up to make himself a mug of Neo-Citran, and was sure to wash his hands before feeding Norman.

Norman Moves his Furniture

July 31st, A Monday

Norman didn't have work today. Once he had finished his chores around the house he felt bored.

"Norman, what should I do now?" he asked.

The cat purred in response. A lightbulb lit up in Norman's head- he could rearrange the furniture!

He spent the next couple of hours moving his furniture into the new perfect position. Afterwards he was tired, so he and Norman went to take a nap. When Norman awoke, he drowsily walked to the kitchen to grab a glass of water. He was thirsty. Before he arrived at the kitchen, he stubbed his toe on an errant piece of furniture. Yelping in pain, he hobbled to the sink for some water.

The next day, he moved his furniture back.

August

Norman and the Promotion

August 1st, A Tuesday

Norman's boss had announced that one of the supervisors was retiring. Norman could not remember speaking to her, although she used to come by and talk to Frank over her morning coffee. She laughed too loud, always wore a pant suit with a shiny pin, and had bright red nails that he thought were too flashy.

As he stared at his desk he listened to the shuffle of those around him over the news. Everyone was happy to know there was a possibility for a promotion. Norman thought he should apply for the position. It came with a small corner office and a raise. He could buy a cat tower for Norman.

Today, he would be different. He would start interacting with people like she had. Norman had to prove his worth. He would start with Frank, his cubicle-mate. He turned around and stared at the back of Frank's head. His mind was blank. Then Frank stood up and walked away.

Norman palms were sweating and he felt stressed. He realized people might come to him more if he had an office and he would have to speak in meetings. He wasn't sure if he would be able to date his co-workers if he was a supervisor. Everyone would laugh if he even applied.

Frank came back and slapped Norman on the back. He asked if Norman was okay, because he'd been sitting and staring at the back of the chair for ten minutes.

Norman shook his head, turned around, and decided it was not a good idea to apply for the position. Norman would probably just play with the box for the cat tower anyways.

Norman Considers Asian Cuisine

August 2nd, A Wednesday

Once again, Norman had burned his microwaveable noodle soup. Distracted by Norman chasing a fly about the kitchen, Norman had forgotten to add water, and now stared disconsolately at the melted, smoking husk of Styrofoam hissing menacingly in his microwave. He decided to order take-out.

Norman was feeling brave, and decided he wanted some sort of Asian food. Not being all too familiar with the local Asian restaurants, or Asian cuisine in general for that matter, he consulted a review website on his computer. He clicked on one promising establishment and read through several brief and lukewarm reviews before scrolling to one that was at least the length of a short essay. Norman read, transfixed.

The review was written like a short story, with a compelling narrative, lots of juicy imagery, and a pervasively snide sense of humor that was somewhat lost on Norman. The review listed a dozen of the restaurant's shortcomings and pleasantries, one describing the soup as being a solid. Revolted, Norman came to the final sentence of the review: "Pu pu platter? More like shit shit platter."

Norman didn't get it. After the thoroughly unappetizing review he had just read, he didn't feel up to eating anything Asian. He popped a frozen dinner into the microwave with a resigned sigh. *Meatloaf...* Norman didn't particularly care for meat loaf.

Norman's Thursday Morning Surprise

August 3rd, A Thursday

It was a Thursday. Norman's morning routine went off without a hitch: brushing his teeth in the shower, and then toweling off in front of a fogged-up mirror. Norman reached for his extra protection deodorant stick and immediately noticed that it was lighter than usual. *No problem,* Norman thought cheerfully, as he had just purchased another stick Tuesday afternoon. Norman used up the antiperspirant under his left arm, until the plastic end-stop rubbed against his skin. He reached for one of the new sticks, and suddenly noticed his mistake: The previous stick had blue labelling, and read 'Cool Sport', while this new stick, though the same brand, was green and read 'Sport Fresh.'

Norman observed his own perplexed expression through the misted mirror. After several seconds of shock, Norman concluded that there was nothing to be done. Norman applied the new scent to his right armpit. He took a moment to smell the new application. It was quite pleasant. Then he took another moment to smell his left side, also pleasant. Norman put on a shirt with a mischievous grin. Today, he had a secret. This was a Thursday full of possibilities.

Norman Saves a Life

August 4th, A Friday

Norman was plodding down a sidewalk on his way home from work. He was a little anxious to get home as the six o'clock local news was on soon and he didn't want to miss a second. Norman approached a crossing and noticed the blinking red hand urging pedestrians to finish crossing. He knew he wasn't going to make it. He stopped.

Suddenly, a young woman passed Norman on the sidewalk, looked to her left and right, and began to cross the street. Norman worried that the woman was going to get herself killed. He then began to think about the news again and how, if he saved this woman's life from certain death, he'd definitely make it on tomorrow's news, maybe even the late-night news. He'd be a hero.

Quickly, Norman reached out towards the woman to attempt to pull her back to safety, but stopped. Norman thought about what would happen if his hand happened to overshoot the woman's arm and grab her chest instead. Nervous, Norman returned his sweaty palms back to the pockets of his pleated khakis, and he watched as the woman safely crossed the street with a second to spare.

Norman arrived home disappointed that he had missed the first ten seconds of the news. He sat and ate a microwaved Salisbury steak dinner in front of the television, daydreaming about one day making it on the local news and how life-changing that would be. He went to bed hour's later thinking about the woman's chest.

Norman is Ready for Bed

August 5th, A Saturday

The episode of CSI dragged on, as Norman eyed the clock, just waiting for it to be over so he could go to bed. Bedtime was Norman's second favorite time of day after all; right behind scratching Norman's ears after work.

Norman purred in Norman's lap, breathing soft and sweet. *Twelve minutes until the credits.* Norman wasn't even sure he'd watch them all the way through. He decided he'd probably shut off the TV when the outro music started. Norman was so tired, he wasn't focusing on the show - the heads were talking, but the words weren't passing through Norman's ears. His mind began to wander, drifting through his day at work. Lisa's sweater, his own coffee stained sweater, Robert's use of nicknames.

Norman came to the realization that, even if he didn't like it, Robert was only trying to be nice. It must feel nice to give someone a nickname.

Suddenly the credits were halfway through. Norman snapped out of his daydream, and lazily turned off the TV. As he slowly stood up, he patted Norman.

"Time for bed, Norm."

Norman felt uneased.

"...Norman."

Norman Orders a Burger

August 6th, A Sunday

It was lunch time on an average Sunday. The cat had just fallen asleep, and Norman had just gotten off his sofa to make a sandwich. He looked inside his refrigerator and, to his dismay, he discovered he was out of cheese! Norman couldn't bear the thought of having a sandwich without cheese, so he sat down, contemplating what to do.

Suddenly, a breeze gusted through the open window in Norman's kitchen and blew a take-out menu off a table. It was from a burger restaurant down the street. Norman took this as a sign that he should order a burger, even though he had never done that before.

He looked through the menu, and decided to order the Number Two: a regular cheeseburger. Norman glanced over at Norman, making sure he was still asleep. He made the call. When the man on the other side of the telephone asked him if he wanted anything on his burger, Norman hesitated, but eventually replied with "no, thanks."

Norman almost ordered bacon on his burger.

Almost.

Norman Says Hello

August 7th, A Monday

Norman was getting ready to leave work. He tucked his folded paper lunch bag into the front pocket of his briefcase and thought about Nancy, the new hire who had sat at the table across from him today at lunch. She had been wearing a necklace with a cat charm and Norman wanted to tell her about Norman. He couldn't manage to work himself into the group conversation but had promised himself he would be friendlier next time he saw her.

When Norman turned out of his cubicle to leave, he saw Nancy walking toward him. She had a smile on her face and offered a happy wave. Norman was glad she must have noticed him in the lunchroom and lifted his hand to wave back to her. Behind him, Norman heard his boss ask, "How was your first day?" and Norman slowly lowered his hand as Nancy walked past him and told Rich all about her day. Norman decided to bring up Nancy's necklace another time.

Norman Buys Chocolate Milk

August 8th, A Tuesday

Norman was grocery shopping early in the evening. When he went to grab his usual half gallon of one percent milk he noticed that the chocolate milk was marked down. He wondered why. He checked the expiration date; the milk expired in six days. That was probably why.

Norman considered buying some chocolate milk. He didn't usually drink chocolate milk, but maybe this week he would buy chocolate milk instead of his usual pint of chocolate dairy dessert, since the milk was on sale. He reached for a half gallon of chocolate milk but noticed that only the full gallons were on sale. Norman knew he would not drink a full gallon of chocolate milk in six days, but he was already looking forward to enjoying a cold glass as he watched television. He bought it anyway.

Norman thought about his chocolate milk on the bus ride home as the condensation on the jug slightly dampened his trousers through the shopping bag. Maybe he would take it to work. Norman couldn't drink a full gallon of chocolate milk in six days, but maybe his co-workers could help him drink it up.

They usually only drank coffee. Maybe chocolate milk would be a nice change. Maybe it would be a nice coffee creamer. It would be weird to bring an opened gallon of chocolate milk to work. He should wait to open it in the office come Friday morning.

Store-bought chocolate milk was always creamier than regular milk mixed with syrup. Norman was looking forward to this chocolate milk.

Seven days later, Norman would throw out an unopened gallon of chocolate milk.

Norman Takes a Trip

August 9th, A Wednesday

Norman lay on his stomach in his kitchen, reaching beneath the cupboards and making kissing noises. He felt sorry for stepping on Norman's tail.

The floor was cold against his cheek, and it felt good. It reminded him of snow. He closed his eyes and imagined being somewhere else. That felt good too.

He woke up in his dark, cold kitchen. His neck was sore from being turned against the floor for so long. He'd missed CSI and since he'd napped, he would lay awake in bed tonight for hours.

Norman meowed from the living room.

Norman Goes Missing

August 10th, A Thursday

It was nearing nine o'clock and Norman was becoming more and more concerned. He hadn't seen his cat Norman since he returned home from work and feared he might have escaped outside and gotten lost, or even hurt.

For hours, he had searched every nook and cranny in his home hoping Norman would turn up somewhere. He checked Norman's bed, the bathroom, the small crawlspace under the stairs, and even Norman's litter box for any signs of his lost friend. To his dismay, Norman was nowhere to be found. Norman was just about ready to start creating missing cat fliers and take his search outside when he heard a familiar purring coming from inside a cupboard under the kitchen sink.

What a relief, it was Norman! Somehow in his search Norman had forgotten to check the kitchen! Quickly, Norman scooped up his dear furry friend and retreated to his living room couch. Together they happily spent the rest of the evening watching television before retiring to bed.

Norman Eats a Peach

August 11th, A Friday

Norman was strolling through the produce section when something caught his eye. He walked over to the peaches, carefully selecting the one he would eat. Norman was never one for peaches, as he'd always fancied himself a nectarine kind of guy.

Today however, he decided to change things up a bit. After buying the peach, which cost exactly eighty cents, he felt like everything was falling into place, as he had had exactly eighty cents of change in his pocket. The universe had been guiding him toward the peach. When he arrived at his apartment, he took a bite of his new treat. As he sunk his teeth into the flesh of the peach, he decided it was too sweet. And there was too much juice. And the peel was gritty. He threw the rest of the peach away and chided himself for not leaving good enough alone.

Norman Sees Something Interesting

August 12th, A Saturday

Norman looked his worst in car mirrors. The convex glass both stunted and fattened his reflection. If he caught himself looking into one, he found it difficult to turn away. At this moment, as Norman stared into his reflection in a parking garage, he stood arrested in his feeling of dismay at the unflattering depiction of himself. He stared so long, in fact, that he saw something that he wouldn't have noticed otherwise.

He saw a bird behind him, just sitting there. Upon turning around and locking his eyes on it, Norman noticed, astonished, that it didn't move an inch. It just stood silent and still. Norman kept looking to see if it even flapped or breathed. It looked unreal. Almost entirely spherical, blue with specks of white, two twig legs holding it up, the bird just rested there completely still, looking like a bizarre Christmas ornament.

After a few moments of apprehension, Norman took a step forward. No reaction, not even a twitch of its head. He took a few more steps. Nothing. *Is it dead?* he wondered. He side-stepped slowly and methodically, the side of the bird coming into view, the front then peeking out. Closer now, Norman could see it breathing. He stood nearly four little feet away. It just didn't make sense. Aside from his cat, the sight of Norman made animals flee. Birds especially tended to avoid him, sometimes pooping on their way out. Norman had his fair share of ruined visors.

"How do you like that," said Norman, taking a knee. "Incredible."

Norman marveled over the bird's expression. That it had one was enough to amuse him. But the expression itself saddened Norman a little. The expression, simple and frozen as it was, evoked sadness. Its head pointed downwards in the fluff of its bulbous chest. Its eyes were less than pea sized, glassy and black. It managed to frown with its beak, *although maybe that's just what all beaks look like*, Norman thought. Norman took out his phone. He couldn't figure the damn thing out, but he could use the camera. So he did, though the image came out fuzzy.

Some people came up the steps. Norman could sense them staring at him. He got up and started speaking into his phone.

"Yes. Yes alright, I've got it. I'm on my way, now."

He left the garage and went on his way to the city park a few blocks away. At the park, a pigeon pooped on his head and he went home early.

Norman Walks on Grass

<u>August 13th, A Sunday</u>

Norman loved his Sunday walks. Norman was on one of those walks around the suburbs, admiring the cars that were better than his. He felt the cool breeze drift across his bald head and heard the people mowing their lawns. It was all very relaxing. Norman decided to relax a bit himself and took his socks and shoes off so he could walk on this stranger's lawn. Norman took his first step.

It was exhilarating! He felt so free! So alive! Norman took his second step and felt a sharp pain in his foot. Norman had stepped on a bee. Norman's foot hurt as he walked home. Norman no longer loved his Sunday walks.

Norman's Day at the Office

August 14th, A Monday

It was Monday. Like all Mondays, Norman was at the office typing away on his Shell computer with the sticky "A" key. It often made Norman type two A's instead of one, requiring Norman to consistently go back and delete the duplicate A.

This had unfortunately been occurring since late last April. It was now August. For a few months, Norman had felt he could live with the sticky A key, and found it quite entertaining, but eventually upon realizing his work productivity had slowed, filed an IT request for a new keyboard in June. He had seen no progress on the new keyboard. Just then, as Norman was typing up another report, Dan, the IT guy walked by. "Hi Norman, how's it going?" said Dan, rhetorically. Norman looked up to say hello, but Dan had already walked away. With a sigh, Norman continued typing up his report, deleting the duplicate A's every few minutes or so.

Norman Books a Cruise

August 15th, A Tuesday

Norman had been nervously excited about today. He recently booked a last-minute singles cruise at his supervisor's request. The last vacation Norman took was years ago, with his ex-wife and her ASL instructor to Palm Springs. Norman grabbed his ticket and billfold and made sure Norman had enough food and water for the next forty-eight hours. Norman locked the front door on his way out, pausing to smile at the satisfying 'click' and then realised that his keys were still inside.

Two hours and two hundred dollars later the locksmith had arrived and promptly let Norman back in the front door. Norman sat on the couch and dialed the cruise number to see about obtaining a refund. The lady from *Great Lakes Cruise Lines* explained that no refund was necessary, since the cruise wasn't for another year. Norman sighed in relief.

Norman Watches Doctor Who

August 16th, A Wednesday

Norman sat in front of his television set. Doctor Who was on. He remembered loving Doctor Who as a kid. "Mom", he remembered saying, "When I grow up I want to be like The Doctor!" His mother had smiled at him, and stroked his hair. His mother was gone now. So was his hair.

Years later he had watched Doctor Who with his son. He hadn't heard from his son in a while now. *I hope he gives me a call soon,* he thought.

Norman Sends an Email

August 17th, A Thursday

Every year around summer time, Norman received an e-mail from his health insurance company to remind him to book his free health assessment. His knees had been playing up lately and Norman was glad he would not have to seek an appointment with his doctor, as he hated disturbing him for such minor ailments.

Just like every year, the e-mail explained that his free check-up would last for about forty minutes and asked him to confirm a suitable date, either over the phone or via e-mail.

Norman checked his upcoming work schedule and decided on the following Friday afternoon. Making phone calls had always been something he secretly dreaded so he clicked on 'reply' to complete his booking.

His hands hovered over his keyboard for a minute. He was not sure how to reply to an automated e-mail.

'Hello, I hope this e-mail finds you well...'

No. That won't do. Norman didn't even know the identity of his recipient. He or she might not be well at all, and still have to come into work. Norman didn't want to come across as insensitive.

'Hello, yes please. I want my appointment on Friday...' That's just rude. Do over.

'Hi!'

Come on, Norman.

He took a deep breath and reminded himself not to make a mountain out of a molehill.

'Hello, thank you for the reminder, is there a way I can book an appointment next Friday please, preferably in the afternoon?
Kind regards,

Norman.'

Norman began fidgeting in his swivel chair. His automated signature seemed a little too formal and business-like. How about 'Best regards"? 'Best wishes'? Or perhaps a simple 'Regards'?

A smile spread across Norman's lips and he decided to make fun of his own indecisiveness:

'Hello, thank you for the reminder, is there a way I can book an appointment next Friday please, preferably in the afternoon?
Xoxo

Norman.'

Norman chuckled. A little ripple of happiness spread through his body, only to turn to horror as the cursor of his mouse passed over the 'send' button while his finger twitched involuntarily.

The e-mail disappeared and Norman went a little pale.

He stared at his computer screen, although '*Xoxo, Norman*' kept flashing before his eyes for what seemed like an eternity.
Eventually, he muttered:

"Yours. Sincerely Yours."
Norman wished he had rung the doctor instead.

Norman Smiles to Himself

August 18th, A Friday

Norman was watching TV while Norman was stretched out on the floor, lying in a warm patch of sunlight streaming through the window. A commercial came on talking about a boat show which was just wrapping up in town.

I've never been to a boat show, thought Norman, *Next year I'll have to go.*

Norman smiled to himself, and thought about how he would have something to talk about with his co-workers if he went to the boat show next year.

It was a pleasant moment for Norman and Norman.

Norman Shudders Deeply

August 19th, A Saturday

It was 8:30 in the morning, and Norman sat at his kitchen table with a newspaper, coffee, and a bowl that earlier had had Wheaties in it. Norman didn't have any plans until 4:00, so he anxiously tried to think of what to do. The laundry was yesterday, he'd paid all his bills, and the apartment was clean. He considered going to see a movie, but then realised that the shelves in the closet hadn't been organized in years.

Energised with purpose, Norman set to work on the shelves. He pulled an unlabelled box out from the back of a shelf. Curious, he opened it. The box was full of items from his youth - yearbooks, journals, photos, trophies, etc. One in particular caught his eye; a scrapbook from when he was young.

In one photo, a seventeen-year-old Norman draped his arm around a guy with a bass guitar slung over his shoulder. There were two other men in the photo as well. One of them had a sticker-covered Stratocaster that he was leaning on like a cane and the other one was crouched on top of some kind of barrel. They all looked disaffected and snotty. A cigarette hung from the side of

Norman's mouth. The setting was a grimy shipyard. This was an early 80's promo for Norman's band '*The Dusty Knucklers*' in a crudely printed zine.

The sight of this hit Norman like a punch to the gut.

I can't believe how close I came to throwing my life away, he wondered. Norman shuddered deeply.

Noreman. Norman? Nore-man.

August 20th, A Sunday

Norman sat in his recliner, listening to the ticking clock. He thought about his name.

Norman. Nor-man? He thought. *Not a man? Noorman.* It was a funny sounding word. It was a funny sounding name. Two syllables. *There's a lot of names with three syllables, like Cameron and Andrea. There's those with one- Zack. Brad. Jessica...is a three syllable one.* Norman re-categorized the thought.

Norman... Norman thought. Like Normal. Norman didn't like that- he didn't want people to think of him as boring.

Norm. Anne.

Norman sighed. He didn't like his name. It sounded funny to him now. *Now.*

Now.

Nah-woo...

Norman Remembers the Office Party

August 21st, A Monday

One of Norman's fridge magnets was faithfully holding a memo. It read, in Norman's scribbly handwriting, 'Office PR party today. Bring soft drink'. He'd placed the soft drink ready by the door three days in advance. It was a bottle of ginger ale.

Norman thought he'd be a little more outgoing today and wear his orange tie. He felt self-conscious leaving the house, so he packed his normal black tie into his suitcase as well. Traffic caused Norman to be a little later than usual. He climbed the stairs to his floor, and paused at the glass doors.

There were a lot of people at the party. They were all talking and smiling. Norman went to the bathroom on the level below and changed his tie.

Norman has a Long Day

August 22nd, A Tuesday

Norman woke up at 5:03 AM to the feeling of Norman attacking his feet under the covers. Norman tried to keep his feet perfectly still but the only thing Norman cared about was getting extra pouncing practice in. After gently pushing Norman off the bed and having a shower, Norman had a cup of coffee and ate some cold cereal before heading to work. Once he got to work he noticed that someone was already in his favorite shady parking spot. *Good for them,* Norman thought.

Norman worked through lunch at the behest of his boss, who had started calling him Norm. His leftover meatloaf and peas had absorbed a generic fridge flavor. *I'd better stop and get more baking soda on the way home,* Norman thought. Once Norman returned home he immediately took his shoes off, sat in his favorite recliner, and started wiggling his toes, marveling at them. Strangely, Norman did not come to visit Norman as he arrived home.

Norman was starving and decided that he would order a pizza to reward himself. The lady at the pizza place sounded beautiful to Norman. He wondered if she would be the one bringing his pizza. Norman secretly hoped it would not be her. At the end of the order the beautiful sounding lady asked Norman if he "would like some complimentary after dinner mints with the order?" Just then Norman came darting out of the shadows at full speed, pouncing on Norman's wiggling toes. Norman let out a surprised shout, despite still being on the phone. As Norman worked to de-tangle Norman from his socks he missed the estimated delivery time.

When Norman's pizza arrived, he noticed a small bag tied on top of the box. The delivery man was not the cute girl that Norman had secretly hoped it would not be. A feeling of relief washed over Norman. As soon as he set the pizza down in the kitchen, Norman carefully untied the bag on top of the box to find that it was full of mints. Norman hated mints, but he thought it best to keep them in case he ever had guests over. Norman opened an unused drawer to his left, and slid the mints in carefully. *I have a mint drawer now,* Norman thought, as he enjoyed his dinner with Norman.

Norman Buys a New Alarm Clock

August 23rd, A Wednesday

On the way home from work, Norman stopped by the store to get some more lavender hand soap for his bathroom because he had noticed it was running low. While walking through the 'Home' section he noticed a sale on a nice alarm clock. Excited that it was an analog clock and had a built-in AM/FM radio, Norman bought it.

Norman rushed home to set up his new clock and set his alarm as he was about to go to bed. He closed his eyes but couldn't fall asleep. He was worried that the alarm on his new clock would not go off and he would be late for work the next day. Norman put the new clock back into its box and taped the receipt to it so he could return it tomorrow after work. He then plugged in his old alarm clock, set his alarm and went to bed.

Norman Meets the Pizza Girl

August 24th, A Thursday

Norman decided to order out for pizza. He dialed the number and asked for a medium cheese pizza and a two-liter bottle of ginger ale. It would be $17.45. Norman sat in front of the window so he would not miss the delivery.

The doorbell rang and Norman opened the door. "Hey man, how's your night going?" A girl proffered the cheese pizza in a box and the two-liter bottle of ginger ale. She had purple hair and a lip piercing. Norman said, "It's good, I'm having pizza." The girl smiled.

Norman gave her a $20 bill, four dimes, and a nickel. She said, "Thanks dude, enjoy your food," and smiled at him again. Norman said, "Thanks, you too."

Norman had three and a half pieces of cheese pizza and two cups of ginger ale. He wanted to watch Dick Tracy but he turned the TV off after thirty minutes. He wondered how many pizzas are delivered every night as he got ready for bed.

Norman Stands up for Himself

August 25th, A Friday

Norman wrinkled his nose as he stood in the break room, watching his lunch spin around in the microwave. The entire break room smelled like fish. *Carol must have been microwaving her leftovers again,* he thought. *It's really inconsiderate to everyone else. Why can't she just make Ramen for lunch like I do? Ramen doesn't smell! I really wish someone would talk to her.*

Suddenly, he was jolted from his thoughts as someone else walked into the room. "Hey man, could you maybe not microwave your goddamn fish in the public area? The whole room stinks." Steven made an exasperated huff as he pushed his way past Norman to the fridge.

"You know Steven, you shouldn't jump to conclusions like that. If you'd just take a second out of your busy schedule, you'd notice that I'm microwaving a bowl of Ramen. The smell has nothing to do with me, so stop being such a jerk about it," Norman retorted to his empty living room as he played the incident through his head, for the fourth time that evening.

Norman Watches his Second Favorite TV Show

August 26th, A Saturday

Norman plodded out of the kitchen holding his plate of spaghetti and eased himself down on the couch. He picked up the remote and immediately wished he'd first wiped the splotch of tomato sauce off his thumb. Frowning because he'd forgotten to grab a napkin, Norman licked the remote clean.

A quick point and press and the television came to life. Norman smiled as he watched Vanna walk across the screen and turn over two 'N's. He liked Vanna. Vanna always smiled. Norman thought there wasn't anyone prettier in Hollywood than Vanna. Pretty and nice. Nice and pretty. Norman felt safe watching Vanna.

This was Norman's favourite time of day. Dinner with Vanna and shouting out guesses at what the puzzle might be. The best time for Norman was when he guessed the puzzle correctly before the contestants did. Norman would slap his thigh and grin at Vanna. He always hoped that Vanna could somehow hear him. If his shout happened to coincide with Vanna smiling on television, Norman's face beamed.

This was Norman at his happiest.

Norman scraped the last of his dinner off his plate and into his mouth. Finishing his dinner just when Wheel of Fortune was ending was perfect timing. At least for that moment. If Norman didn't hurry, he'd hear the music start up for the next show. That ruined everything... so Norman quickly turned the television off.

He'd made that mistake before. He didn't like that music, and he didn't like Alex. Norman didn't think Alex was anywhere near as nice as Vanna. And the puzzles on that show confused him. He didn't know whether to shout out answers or questions. He didn't like Jeopardy. Norman considered himself a Wheel of Fortune man.

Norman Buys Detergent

August 27th, A Sunday

It was a Sunday, and Norman was doing his shopping to prepare for the upcoming week. He was browsing Depo-Mart, and going over the shopping list he had permanently saved on his phone. Up next was "Detergent."

Almost by default, he carted over one aisle from dry-foods to cleaning supplies, and went to the top left shelf where Depo-Mart stored Tide. However, to his surprise, Norman saw a new product next to it: Tide Advanced. Upon further inspection, the product seemed to boast a deeper clean, as well as an advanced formula for a better smell. It was a few dollars more expensive, but seemed to be an upgrade from the product he always used.

Doing some quick thinking, and using his pocket calculator, he realized that he would still be within budget to buy the new detergent this week (there had been a surprise sale on Ticonderoga pencils that day). *But what if it doesn't work?* Norman thought, *and what will I do if I decide I do like it, and don't have the budget to buy it again?* He pondered this for a minute, uncomfortable in weighing his detergent decision. The new product seemed reliable, but Norman always knew what to expect with Tide original. But a deeper clean could provide more power for his money's worth. And besides, a new smell could mean new compliments from his co-workers. Maybe people would notice. Maybe the secretary would notice.

Later on, as Norman was checking out, the cashier grabbed his bottle of detergent and swiped it. "Y'know," she stated, "they just came out with a new advanced formula for this."

"I know," Norman replied, smiling contently, "that's okay. I like what I've got."

Norman Finds a Lucky Coin

August 28th, A Monday

Norman glanced at his watch which told him it was 7:13AM. According to the bus schedule, posted inside the tiny windproof shelter, the bus would not be there for another 27 minutes. "Always pays to be early," Norman grumbled. With his extra time Norman decided to leave the bus stop and look at the fancy topiary across the street. Approaching the opposite side Norman saw a twinkle among the rubbish in the gutter. He bent over to pick it up. A *quarter, brilliant!* Norman thought as he turned it over to examine its date, as was his habit.

1965- his birth year. "Maybe we share a birthday even!" Norman said much too loudly, throwing his arms in the air in a display of triumph to no one but himself. Norman tucked the quarter in his pocket thinking it would be his lucky coin.

After admiring the feline-formed topiary Norman glanced at his watch which read 7:33AM, and decided he should return to his bus stop. At 7:52AM the bus arrived with an earth-shaking rumble and a belch of exhaust smoke. The bus driver, a bearded and slightly deformed looking fellow, opened the doors and Norman stepped on while reaching into his pocket for his bus fare, but all he found was a hole in his pocket. Norman regretted losing his lucky coin as he walked to work.

Norman Sees his Cubicle Mate

August 29th, A Tuesday

Norman was on his way home from the supermarket when he noticed a familiar figure. Norman wasn't sure, but he thought he saw Frank, sitting alone in the park across the street.

Norman was about to go say hello, but then remembered that Frank had once mentioned Tuesday was family night for him. The actual Frank was probably at home, spending time with his wife and daughter.

Shrugging his shoulders, Norman continued on his way home. He didn't want to dilly dally, as Norman was waiting for him to come home.

Norman has a Disagreement with a Co-worker

August 30th, A Wednesday

Norman sighed as he spoke with June from sales.

A few minutes earlier, Norman stepped into the break room to hear June talking with another co-worker. They were talking about their kids, and June specifically wanted to talk about the new vegan diet her family was partaking on.

"Jenny's only three," started June, "but she's loving her steamed broccoli dinners. She doesn't even miss all the sweets she used to have. Believe me."

The other co-worker found an exit opportunity from the conversation when Norman entered the room.

"Hey Norman," he said, "do you have any kids?"

Norman enthusiastically told the two about his son who, despite all the lovely things Norman had to say, hasn't spoken with his father in over eight months.

"Did you feed Junior sugar when he was a baby?" June asked. The co-worker took the chance to flee the room.

"Yes, lots! He could be so noisy, and cry *so* much, but nothing a pop-tart couldn't fix!"

Norman regretted his statement. June spent the next twenty minutes prodding Norman and letting him know all the mistakes he made raising Junior.

"Maybe that's the connection to why he hasn't called you in eight months!" June joked inconsiderately.

Norman laughed respectively but quickly fled back to his cubicle. A tightness was welling in Norman's chest, and although he didn't know what to do about all the problems in his life, he knew one thing for certain- he would be having a large rotisserie chicken for dinner, with a side of ribs.

Norman is Put on Hold

August 31st, A Thursday

Norman picked up the phone and dialed the number that was on the computer screen in front of him. An automated message told him welcome and told him to make a choice in a menu. Norman dutifully listened to the options and picked the right ones.

"Please hold while we transfer you to a representative", the voice on the tape said.

Norman waited. There was no hold music. *Too bad.* After 30 seconds or so, the same automated voice message came back to him. "Your call is important to us. Please hold. You are caller number..." There was a slight pause. "... 4."

Norman frowned and looked at the clock on the wall. Caller number 4, it was right in the middle, wasn't it? Just a little too many people in front of him, but not enough to hang up right and try again later. So he waited.

"Your call is important to us. Please hold. You are caller number..." The pause again. "... 4."

Four callers. How much time would that take? Norman tried to do the math in his head, but decided there were too many variables. Maybe one of the four callers had a rather difficult problem. He had no idea how many people there were to take calls.

"Your call is important to us. Please hold. You are caller number..." "...4."

Norman fidgeted with his hands. What to do in the meantime? He read over the letter again that he'd received. Maybe he had overlooked the answer he was looking for and this call wasn't necessary at all.

"Your call is important to us. Please hold. You are caller number..." "... 3."

Three! Aha! One step up in the queue! Now how long had that taken? He looked at the clock again but hadn't really registered what time it was when he looked for the first time.

"Your call is important to us. Please hold. You are caller number..." "... 3."

He looked around his desk for things to do. For a while he'd meant to learn how to tie some useful knots. The idea had come to him after watching a show on survival on the Discovery Channel, but he hadn't gotten around to finding a piece of string to practice with. *This would've been the perfect time to start practicing,* he thought.

"Your call is important to us. Please hold. You are caller number..." "... 3."

Oh man, how long could caller number 3 take? Should he hang up? He was seriously tempted, but if he hung up the phone now it would even be more of a waste of time since he'd spent these last two (or three? Four?) minutes for nothing.

"Your call is important to us. Please hold. You are caller number..." "... 3."

Norman got a little annoyed. He was a customer, right? At least sort of... He shouldn't have to wait this long, should he? *I'm going to complain to them,* he decided. After they've told him what he needed, he would ask to please be transferred to the complaints department and he would tell somebody there that this sort of behaviour towards....

"Your call is important to us. Please hold. You are caller number..." "... 2."

Oh, two! Maybe it's not too bad, Norman thought. Besides, whoever was out there answering the phones was probably very busy anyway. Maybe a complaint wasn't even necessary.

"Your call is important to us. Please hold. You are caller number..." "... 1."

See? He was up next! He waited again, a little more patiently. He straightened some things on his desk., put his little pencil holder exactly on the edge of it, straightened out of loose paperwork.

"Your call is important to us. Please hold. You are caller number..." "... 1."

It was definitely too late to hang up now, Norman thought, when suddenly a different and distinctly human voice made surprised him a little.

"BT Water Service, thank you for your patience, how may I help you?" A friendly voice, probably a young woman's, piped up.

"Hello, I received my last bill and there was a 4-pound surcharge on it but I don't know what that is", Norman explained.

"Oh yes, that's your annual service charge, they always get added to August's bill", the girl explained in her chipper voice.

"Oh of course! Stupid of me to forget", Norman said. "Thank you!"

"You are welcome sir. Is there anything else I can help you with today?"

"No thanks, that'll be all", Norman answered.

"Then I wish you a very pleasant day!"

She cut off the call before Norman could wish her the same. There were probably too many callers after him for her to wait.

SEPTEMBER

September

Norman Buys an Heirloom

September 1st, A Friday

"World's Greatest Liar", the coffee cup read.

Norman chuckled to himself at the description, as he pondered purchasing it at his favorite knick-knack store. *Greatest liar*, he giggled to himself. *What an exaggerated statement! What a witty cup!* Norman had to own it.

At home, Norman showed Norman the cup.

"It's impossible to know you're the greatest at something so subjective!" Norman pleaded to Norman. Norman meowed in rebut.

Norman knew that a cat wouldn't truly appreciate the brilliance of the cup. He would have to bring it to work this Friday, and show it to all his coworkers. Norman knew it would make him the talk of the office that day.

Later that night, Norman thought more about the cup. *Would Norman Jr. find it funny?* Perhaps he should gift it to his son- no, not now, Norman wanted to enjoy it- perhaps it could be left to his son in Norman's will. When he passed away, Norman Jr. would drink coffee from an incredible coffee cup, from an extraordinarily witty father.

Norman didn't have coffee for breakfast. Instead, he cleaned the cup and packed it into his briefcase.

It's true! Norman would lie.

Oh yes, Hallmark! They're all sold out now. Norman would lie.

I would love to show you more of my humor, at dinner! Norman would say to a woman, given the chance.

Norman reached his cubicle and reached for the cup. Norman pulled the shattered fragments from his briefcase. *Was the road really that bumpy?* Norman wondered. Distraught and upset, Norman tossed away the cup, and sulked his way through the rest of the day.

Norman's Party

September 2nd, A Saturday

That was it- the last balloon was taped to the wall, and Norman sighed in relief. Now all that was left was for the pizza to arrive.

The doorbell rang, and Norman said hello to the pizza delivery boy carrying a stack of seven pizzas.

"Throwing a party?" he asked.

"Oh yes, a busy one," Norman boasted, "With lots of people! Eventually."

"Right on man... Maybe if you were gonna buy seven pizzas, maybe you should have gotten at least one that wasn't Hawaiian. If somebody happens not to like that kind of pizza... "

Norman blushed, then gave a tip and said goodnight to the teenager. He placed the pizzas on the kitchen counter, and then immediately started popping all the balloons that decorated the apartment.

For Norman, it was a fantastic plan- now, he had an excuse to buy a week's worth of pizza all at once, as well as he didn't actually have to entertain guests. *It's better with just the two of us,* Norman said to Norman.

Norman Can't Get Comfortable

September 3rd, A Sunday

Norman lay in his bed, eyes fixed on the ceiling. He couldn't get comfortable. His neck felt like it wasn't quite at the right angle, no matter which way he turned. He didn't want to have a stiff neck in the morning. His room was quite warm, not warm enough to make him take off his checked pyjama shorts, but warm enough for him to mildly consider opening the window slightly. Norman feared being burgled, he daren't open the window.

Norman turned over, and thought about tomorrow's work day. The alarm rang and he jolted awake. His neck hurt.

Norman is Told a Joke

September 4th, A Monday

Norman felt thirsty at work, and decided to get a drink of water. He approached the water tank. His co-worker Robert, resting his arm on the water tank, awaited social interaction on his break.

While Norman filled his cup of water, Robert told Norman a joke: "Hey Norman, remember to not drink too much water. Did you know water is the number one cause of drowning?"

Norman gave a slight giggle and carried on with his work.

Norman did not think the joke was funny. He just wanted his co-worker to feel appreciated.

Norman Makes a Silly Mistake

September 5th, A Tuesday

Norman was in the staff room eating his lunch when Lisa walked in.

"Oh, that smells good!" said Lisa, while walking over to the refrigerator to pull out a diet coke. She then started towards the exit.

"Leftover spaghetti," said Norman with a smile and raised eyebrows. He knew better than anyone how good it smelled, but he didn't like to brag.

"Mmm, well enjoy your spaghetti!" Lisa said, as she left the room.

"You too!" said Norman without thinking. Realizing his silly mistake, he looked up again quickly to perhaps have a laugh about it with Lisa, but she was already gone.

You too... thought Norman, as he was almost asleep that night.

Norman Experiences Existentialism

September 6th, A Wednesday

It was 3:06 AM. Norman awoke to a feeling most unusual. A slight tingle originated from his neck, to his chest, and spread quickly to his left arm. In the two seconds he had been awake, the faintest thought of a heart attack spilled over to the surface of his mind.

Of course not, he mentally whispered to himself. *Don't be silly.*

The slight tingle became a tiny tickle as it made its way down his elbow through to his hand. A second later, he had a realization. It was an ant.

Instinctually, he slapped his left hand with his right hand and the floodgates of his weary, still half-dreaming consciousness poured open.

Birth. Life. Work. Ant. Murder. Death. Clown. Cat. Yarn. Spreadsheet. Coffee. Sun. Yoga. Lisa. Norman.

He turned over and fell asleep again. It was 3:06 AM.

Norman Catches up on Cleaning

September 7th, A Thursday

Norman had been feeling a bit under the weather the last few days, and had fallen behind on housework. He put in a load of laundry, then went to the sink to clean the small pile of dishes that had accumulated. His hands fumbled together for just a moment as he tried to remove his wedding ring so it wouldn't get dirty. As the fingers of his right hand met bare skin he remembered that he hadn't worn one in quite some time.

My throat feels a little scratchy, he thought as he turned off the sink. *Maybe I should rest for one more day before I worry about the dishes.*

A Rainy Day for Norman

September 8th, A Friday

It was 6 PM on a rainy Friday. Norman was sat in his favourite armchair, reading the newspaper from the day before. Next to him in the corner of the living room, a lamp was lit, standing on top a small cupboard. He snickered when he read through the daily comic strip and skipped the next few pages to the weather forecast. He stopped for a moment and gazed through the window. The sky was filled with dark greyish clouds and the rain was pouring. Looking back at the paper, he let out a sigh and turned the page. It was going to rain tomorrow as well.

Norman Sneezes

September 9th, A Saturday

A young and pretty woman sat across from Norman as he rode the train.

Why don't I have the courage to talk to her? Norman asked himself.

He then wished he hadn't asked that question- a lot of reasons came to mind. Norman sneezed.

Part of him wished that the sneeze would grab her attention, but unfortunately, nothing came of it. A minute later, the young woman sneezed.

"Bless you!" A younger, more handsome man said to her.

Why didn't I get a 'bless you'? Norman thought.

Norman felt offended. However, it might have just been a misunderstanding. Perhaps the young man missed Norman's sneeze and forgot to bless him too. Norman decided to test that by giving a louder, more obvious sneeze.

The young man turned to Norman. Norman's heart raced.

"You should cover your mouth when you sneeze." he said to Norman. Norman nodded and agreed, and to tell the truth, he was terribly embarrassed. What would the pretty woman think now?

A moment later, the young man sneezed. Norman enacted his revenge- by saying nothing. He felt petty, but accomplished.

Let's see how this young man likes it, going about unblessed.

"Bless you!" The pretty woman said.

Norman sulked.

Norman Eats Special Brownies

September 10th, A Sunday

Norman was excited.

The brownies he had purchased from the young man yesterday were waiting for him on his kitchen counter. Norman usually only ate a small bowl of yoghurt with granola for dessert, but the young man said they were "special brownies", so he had decided to be adventurous. Norman wasn't exactly sure what was meant by "special".

He must have used an old family recipe, he thought to himself while playing solitaire.

After Norman finished the brownies, he began to feel funny. He couldn't exactly pinpoint what felt funny, but he knew something wasn't right.

Suddenly, Norman's world lit up. He could feel all his worries melting away, as if nothing was wrong in the universe. The sky was brighter. The flowers were more vivid than ever before. The song the birds sang sounded like a symphony.

When Norman woke up, he remembered what had happened and decided to change his life. He decided he would live life on the edge and take every opportunity he could. He decided to live life with no regrets.

Norman was happy.

Norman returned home from work and rushed over to his plate of brownies. The plate had been knocked over, with all of the brownies gone. Beside the plate was his cat Norman, and a trail of brownie crumbs.

Norman ate a bowl of yogurt with granola, watched CSI, and went to bed.

Norman Takes a Shower

September 11th, A Monday

After a long and stressful day at the office, Norman wanted nothing more than to take a nice hot shower and go to bed.

He grabbed a towel from the closet, turned the shower handle to the position that he found made the water the perfect temperature for his liking, and carefully stepped into the stream. He stood there for a moment, eyes closed, letting the hot water calm him. He raised up his arms, opened his eyes, and watched the water run from his shoulders down through his forearm and onto his hand where it leapt off the tips of his fingers and landed with a soft, constant pitter patter on the floor of the shower. He did this for a while.

When he was done with his shower he dried off and looked at the fogged-up mirror. With his index finger, he drew a little smiley face. He chuckled and remembered how he always did that as a kid. Norman was feeling better already.

Norman Visits the Bookshop

September 12th, A Tuesday

Norman stared at the bookshelf for a considerable amount of time. He was inside the small bookshop on the corner that was owned by a little old lady. On the bookshelf in front of him was a bright yellow book. Norman thought it was a little tacky but wasn't one to judge. The book was entitled; "Becoming Confident: Ten Easy Steps to a More Attractive You!" It had a man that looked vaguely like Norman on the cover, except that he was smiling. He also had hair.

Norman grew self-conscious of standing in the same place for so long. He was afraid the old lady might begin to dislike him. He began to walk around the shop, but his mind still lingered on the book. He circled the area around it, moving closer with each pass. Eventually he made up his mind and rounded the corner to where the book was.

It wasn't there. Norman felt a little disappointed. Someone else must have picked it up. But a thought entered his mind. Whoever had picked it up must have needed it more than he did. Norman had a good life. He had a dependable routine. Some people didn't have that, they didn't know what the next day would hold. Norman was one of the lucky ones. Lost in his thoughts, Norman didn't notice that he was in the aisle for cookbooks.

Norman Plays a Game

September 13th, A Wednesday

Norman was bored, causing him to decide he needed some fresh air. While walking out, he invented a new game. He had to walk the same number of steps on each square of the sidewalk. He was having a splendid time, straining every now and again to meet the quota. Eventually, he noticed some strange stares from other people around him.

The other people's stares made him nervous. He quickly walked home.

Norman Thinks About Buying Shampoo

<u>September 14th, A Thursday</u>

Norman had been stressed about the amount of shampoo he had left. He really didn't mind what new type he bought, or about buying conditioner. All Norman wanted was some shampoo to wash his hair. Norman then began thinking about how, if he bought shampoo, he would have to talk to a cashier or even a salesperson. Norman turned on the water and decided he could make the shampoo stretch a little further.

Norman Realizes his Outward Façade

September 15th, A Friday

As the clock struck 4:45 PM, a smile flickered across Norman's lips. Friday had arrived yet again and he was looking forward to a nice, quiet weekend including a visit to Barnes & Noble, an early 90s Schwarzenegger movie marathon, and brushing up on his WWII history via Wikipedia.

Lisa sauntered by his cubicle and the weekly tradition commenced.

"How's it going, Norman?"

"It's going well, you?"

"What can I say? It's a Friday."

Norman chuckled as Lisa returned to her cubicle to whittle away the remaining fifteen minutes. This time, however, Norman realized the entire 'It's Friday' charade was painfully obvious. Not to say he'd been unaware, but Norman could really hear it in his own voice today, as if he were a spectator witnessing it all from a third person perspective. When did his life become reduced to this?

Norman remembered his early to mid twenties. A fuller head of hair, and a confidence that he'd never be a cog in the machine. He used to laugh at the person he'd become. Suddenly, Norman had a thought. He'd need to stop by Safeway after work to pick up some Fancy Feast for Norman.

Norman Remembers his Umbrella

September 16th, A Saturday

Norman looked out the window and saw that it was raining—pouring, really. He considered staying in, but he had promised himself he would go see that new movie they were playing down at the theatres.

He walked to his closet and was pulling out his thickest coat when he saw the umbrella he had bought for his son a few years earlier. It was black, medium-sized, and the handle folded up so it could fit more easily into a bag. He grabbed it and threw the coat over his shoulders.

As he began walking towards the bus stop, Norman realized how enjoyable the rain was when standing underneath an umbrella. It was like there were two worlds—the cold, wet outside world and the warm, dry world of Norman. He might not be able to control the weather, but he could control his own tiny corner of the universe.

Norman Doesn't Wake Up

September 17th, A Sunday

Norman closed the apartment door behind him, locking the door carefully. He took off his coat and stumped over to the kitchen, not noticing the tiny body lying in the corner of the living area.

"Norman?" he said, looking around. "Here kitty."

Norman the cat didn't respond. He laid flat on his side on the floor, not moving. Underneath the window, the last rays of golden sunlight glinted off his still warm fur.

"Norman?" Norman called again, frowning. He was usually greeted by his housemate by now.

He checked on the armchair, on the bed, and even in the cupboards. There was no sign of Norman the cat. Norman the human slammed the cupboard doors a little too hard. He didn't like making noise, but right now he was having trouble breathing for some reason. His eyes watered.

"Norman?" he said one last time, his voice starting to choke.

Norman stood still for several minutes, puffing anxiously, rubbing his face. After a while, he took a deep breath, and then another.

He mechanically shuffled around the kitchen, vaguely remembering that he was hungry. Today was beef day. He was going to have beef stew. He focused solely on these facts--things that wouldn't suddenly leave him--trying to push away the sick feelings of dread and loneliness that grew with every heartbeat.

As soon as he started the can opener, he heard a faint meow. Just as he poked his head out of the kitchen, he saw Norman the cat lifting his head from the warm patch of sunlight under the window, ears perked up.

"Norman! You found a new special spot."

Norman meowed again, trotting into the kitchen.

"Thank you for coming back." Norman said, a smile crinkling his puffy eyes.

That night, both Normans had beef stew.

Norman Buys Alfredo Sauce

September 18th, A Monday

On the way home from work, Norman stopped at the store to buy tomato sauce for his dinner. He reached the sauce aisle, only to find that tomato sauce was out of stock.

Rats, thought Norman, *I suppose Alfredo sauce will have to do tonight.*

Norman cooked his spaghetti noodles with the Alfredo, and was pleasantly surprised. Norman loved the creamy taste of the Alfredo with his noodles. As the night went on, Norman also found that his heartburn wasn't as bad when he had the tomato sauce. How wonderful!

On his way home from work the next day, Norman stopped at the grocery store to buy dinner supplies. He bought one can of tomato sauce to have with his noodles that night.

Seasons Change; Norman Doesn't

September 19th, A Tuesday

After a normal day at work, Norman left the office to walk home. He nodded to the cubicle worker by the elevator, whose name he didn't remember.

On the way home, Norman noticed the leaves were losing colour. Autumn must be on the way. A crisp smell hung in the air, and the shrieks of jungle gym games from an after-school program echoed from Norman's favourite corner, between Elm and Washington.

Even though they were loud, Norman quite liked that the children were having fun. He saw one girl, lost in a daydream, tear the overly eager leaves on the ground into pieces. Autumn was colder than Spring.

I remember when my son was that age, Norman thought, and fiddled with his phone as he continued home.

Norman Stops by the Pub

September 20th, A Wednesday

As he walked to the bus stop with a bag of groceries in hand, Norman passed by the entrance to The Pub.

Perhaps it was the autumn chill in the air, but this evening the lights inside seemed particularly warm and inviting. Norman slowed as he passed The Pub tonight. He paused in front of the old oak double-door entrance. The brass door plate had not been polished in a long time. It was tarnished. Yet the center of the plate was smooth and golden, buffed and polished where countless hands had pushed inside seeking the warmth and companionship within.

Norman stared at the door plate for a few moments. Then he sighed gently, adjusted the collar of his jacket before turning away and resuming his trek towards the bus stop. Norman would be hungry and waiting for his dinner - and if he could catch the earlier bus he might even see the first ten minutes of CSI.

Norman Buys Flowers

September 21st, A Thursday

As Norman walked to work, he passed by the new nursery that had opened last week. An employee was setting up their outdoor floral display and noticed Norman looking over. "Good morning, sir! Would you like to take a look?"

Norman didn't want to be rude, so he agreed. He strolled through the nursery mindlessly, until a plant caught his eye. "That's an Asiatic lily," the employee said. "It's pretty, isn't it? I bet it would brighten up your desk."

Norman surveyed the plant. It was indeed a very pretty plant. Feeling adventurous, Norman purchased the potted plant and took it to work with him the next day. As he settled down at his desk, he carefully placed the lilies by his computer monitor. "It really does brighten up my desk," Norman thought with a smile. He then opened askjeeves.com on the internet and searched up how to best care for his new plant.

Asiatic Lily

They grow best in full sunlight. Keep the soil moist, watering about once a week.

Norman looked around his cubicle and realised he was nowhere near a window. "Well that won't do," Norman muttered to his new friend. "I guess I'll just take you home with me. You can get plenty of light in my kitchen." Satisfied with his solution, he continued reading the webpage:

This lily is toxic to cats.

Norman felt disappointed. In the short time that he's had his lilies, he had already grown fond of them. Norman's health was a priority though, and as a responsible pet owner, Norman would not put him at risk.

Norman picked up his plant and headed over to Lisa's desk. "Hi Lisa. I thought you might like these," he said, as he placed the flowers on her desk. Norman didn't know Lisa that well, but he knew that the lilies would be in good hands; Lisa's work ethic has always shown her to be a reliable person.

Lisa blushed as she thanked him, but Norman didn't notice, as he was already walking back to his cubicle.

Norman Takes Some Pictures

September 22nd, A Friday

Norman was cleaning up his cabinet, something he was had postponed for a long time. He would take a drawer off, choose documents to be kept and others to throw away, dust off the drawer, and then put it back. When cleaning the last drawer, filled with cables, old phone handsets, and manuals for appliances that he no longer had, Norman found a disposable camera.

Norman couldn't remember when he bought it or what pictures it would have. He turned the crank and noticed the film was barely used, and anticipated trouble finding a place that would develop it. However, he thought, if he was going to go through trouble he could take some photos and use up the entire film.
Norman took a picture of Norman entering the room.

Norman took a picture of the view from his window, hoping the clouds would look pretty.

Norman took a picture of two trees so close together they looked like just one, but one of them already had brown leaves.

Norman took a picture of a bird on the ground and, accidently, his thumb.

At night, he saw himself in the mirror and figured he could take a "selfie", but changed his mind. He took a picture of Norman sleeping on the couch, and the film was finished.

On Monday, he took the camera to the office thinking about developing the photos in his lunch break. He hid it in his drawer so others wouldn't ask questions. However, his job was more demanding than usual that morning, and he forgot about it. He forgot to take the camera home as well. The next weekend, he remembered the pictures and looked for the camera everywhere in his apartment, but couldn't find it.

Norman and the Rainy Day

September 23rd, a Saturday

It was a rainy day. Norman had watched the rain outside as he enjoyed morning oatmeal. Norman liked rainy days. Norman liked them because rainy days meant that he could stay at home with a nice cup of tea.

Norman thought of all the nice things he was going to do while enjoying his cup of tea. *First of all,* Norman thought, *I'm going to read the newspaper.* Yes, reading the newspaper was exactly the sort of nice thing that he could do on a rainy day.

Norman went to the front door, opened it and looked for his newspaper.

The newspaper delivery boy did not have the luxury of being able to stay indoors on a rainy day such as this. He had ridden through the rain on his bicycle to deliver the papers and had subsequently become extremely cold and damp in the process. By the time he had reached the street where Norman lived, the newspaper delivery boy had merely thrown the newspapers in the general direction of the houses, rather than placing each paper near the front door as per usual.

The newspaper delivery boy had thrown Norman's newspaper into the apartment complex's front garden.

Norman's newspaper had landed in a very muddy puddle.

Norman went inside again.

He read a book instead.

Norman Finds a White Hair

September 24th, A Sunday

As Norman stroked Norman's soft fur, he was surprised to find a white hair in Norman's usually grey coat. "Well, Norman! It looks like someone isn't a spring chicken anymore," he said with a chuckle. Norman mewed in response.

Norman's reflection in the window caught his eye. He smiled. The sight of his bald head did not bother him as much as usual today.

Norman is Happy

September 25th, A Monday

Norman was sitting inside when he had the idea of going for a walk. He didn't want to waste the whole day indoors, so he went outside, and felt the sun shining on the cold autumn day. There was no sound, except songs sung by birds. That moment, he finally felt at peace. Norman was happy.

After a few minutes, Norman walked home. When he arrived, he found his owner Norman, leaning in his recliner, watching TV. He would probably never experience the happiness Norman felt that day.

Norman Smokes a Cigarette

September 26th, A Tuesday

Norman was out for a walk early one morning, thinking about his life. It was overcast; his second-favourite weather. As he was walking along a street, he saw a pack of cigarettes on the sidewalk. *No harm in looking,* he thought to himself. He picked up the pack, and noticed that there were four cigarettes and a lighter in the pack.

"Well, it has been about ten years since my last one," he said to himself as he put the cigarette to his lips and lit it. After one puff, he started coughing vigorously, and spat with great force. He threw the pack on the ground and walked away, thinking, *at least I'll have a little story for Norman when I get home.*

Norman Buys a Book

September 27th, A Wednesday

Norman entered the bookstore with high hopes of finding a new adventure. Not that he was an avid reader; it would usually take him two to three months to finish the average novel, if at all. The store was charming and small, the books covering every last bit of space, and it all seemed to lack organisation. He fiddled around the store, looking for something that might catch his eye, but not one book looked interesting to him.

That is until he saw Norman. Norman Mailer was the author of *The Naked and the Dead*, and it was because he shared the same name as the author that the book caught his interest. The *'Dead'* part made him feel uncomfortable, and a quick flip through the book for pictures showed there wouldn't be anything to arouse him either. He purchased the book anyway.

Later that night, Norman sat down in his recliner with an ice-cold ginger ale at his side, and turned to the first page of *The Naked and the Dead*. Norman made it through twelve pages before he took a quick nap, and when he woke from the nap he speedily channel-surfed the TV. CSI was on, a rerun, but it happened to be one of his favourite episodes of that particular season. Norman folded over the twelfth page of The Naked and the Dead, and tucked it neatly into his bookshelf full of books he'd only just begun.

Norman Encounters his Old Band

September 28th, A Thursday

Late in the evening, Norman decided to head out to The Pub for a bite to eat. Sure, they had good beers available, but Norman wasn't a big beer drinker. He was a bigger fan of their dish, "Mount Nachos."

As Norman sat at a bar-stool, happily eating his nachos, a band was starting to set up their instruments on the small stage in The Pub. The band members were all older men, somewhere in their forties, and each grunted and groaned excessively as they positioned their drum set, electric guitar, and bass guitar. Then a realization came over Norman.

This was his band from high-school.

It had been many decades, but Norman still remembered the band very clearly. Norman and the three men setting up on stage started a band in the 11th grade, called The Dusty Knucklers, and their specialty was hard rock. First there was Roger, the bass player. Back in the 80's, Roger was a heavy rocker, took style cues from David Bowie, and had a soft spot for Matilda, the bands muse.

Norman also had a soft spot for Matilda and David Bowie, but settled on pursuing neither of those interests, and chose to give up instead. Norman had wondered where Matilda ended up after high-school. He had also wondered where Roger ended up as well- but it was answered for him this very night. Roger's hairline, as well as Tyler and Deacons, had fared well. The show began to start.

"Hello everyone, thanks for coming tonight!" started Roger. He wiped the sweat from his forehead to slick back his long hair. Norman slicked back his hair as well, and wiped the excess sweat from his hand onto his pant-leg. "We're the Wet Knucklers, and we hope you all have a good night. Party hard."

The old band started to play their songs; songs that Norman recognized well. The difference in the songs however, was the lack of Norman's keyboard. Norman wondered if he would still remember how to play a keyboard as well as he did then. It had been so many years...

After an hour of playing, The Wet Knucklers put down their instruments and headed for the bar. Norman's heart began to pound intensely. Would they recognize their old friend?

The three men took a seat beside Norman. Norman's plate was clean. The band ordered a few beers.

"You guys did great tonight!" cheered the bartender, lining up shots for them.

Tyler smiled. "Thanks mate. Always appreciate the compliments."

"So," started the bartender, "I see you guys set up a keyboard every time, but no one ever touches it. Seems like a waste of effort."

"We used to have an keyboard player," said Roger, solemnly, "back when we started the band. But we vowed to never have another one again. Not after Norman."

Norman's heart sank. *Did they not like me?*

"Why not? Did the guy just suck?"

Roger gulped down his beer, shaking his head as he swallowed. "Not at all. He was a great player. But one day he left the band and... well... he died."

"I'm sorry to hear that," said the bartender.

"We heard it was from a heart attack. That happened about a year out of high school... I don't know, mate. It just doesn't feel right to replace him; you know?"

"I understand." said the bartender sympathetically. "Here- let me get you another round of shots."

The bartender poured another row of shots for the band. Everyone was silent- including Norman. Who said he was dead? Did no one look into it? Did everyone from his childhood assume he died?

"For Norman." said Tyler.

"For Norman." said Deacon.

"For Norman." said Roger.

Norman wanted to say something- anything- but he couldn't find it in him. A tightness in his chest stopped him from being able to say a word. He hoped they might recognize him, that they would do him the favor of starting the conversation, but he knew it was hopeless. He looked like a completely different person since high school. He looked like his father. As the band went back up to play a second set, Norman paid his bill and left.

Norman went home, humming the band's old songs.

Norman Tries to Paint a Picture

September 29th, A Friday

Norman was sitting around, watching TV, with Norman on his lap. The commercial on the television displayed a painter doing his thing. The painter used his brush to make swooping, delicate lines that entranced Norman. After watching for a while, Norman decided to try painting. Norman went to his local craft shop and purchased a paint brush, canvas, and some paint. As Norman got home, he decided to paint a picture of Norman. Norman set up the canvas and got out the paints, and moved Norman onto a table in front of them. It was near the end of the day, but Norman was determined to paint a picture. Norman spent all afternoon trying to mimic the master painter's elegant strokes- however, his resolve vanished with the falling sun. Norman and Norman both decided to give up painting and call it a day.

Norman Gets a Call from His Son

September 30th, A Saturday

It was 9:00 PM on a Saturday, and Norman Jr. had just finished eating his microwaved pasta. The guys at the office were at a sports bar, but Norman Jr. didn't care much for sports bars. Upon returning to his bedroom, Norman Jr. sat down on his double bed and reluctantly picked up his cellphone to search for Norman's name in the contact list. It had been a long time since he last called his father, and he felt like he should.

However, Norman Jr. didn't really want to call, because he never knew what to talk about with his father. When he called his mom, she would ramble on about her creative projects and ask him about his favourite TV shows. He found comfort in her voice. With his father, he often found long, awkward pauses in their conversation.

"Hi, Dad. It's me, Junior."

"How's work?" Norman was happy to hear from his son.

"How's work?" It's always the same question from him.

"Work's alright. What have you been up to?"

"Well, not much."

There it was, the long pause.

"There's a-" "What do you-"

"You can go first, Dad."

"There's a little sandwich shop that opened down the street, I would like to go sometime. Also, Norman keeps falling asleep on the keyboard lately, so that's new."

Norman Jr. felt a pang of guilt. Just a simple phone call might have made Norman's day, yet Norman Jr. had been putting it off for so long. He tried to see his father in his mind's eye; a stoic, balding man with weary eyes, edges smoothed down by the weathering of life. He thought about the man who had lifted him and spun him around when he was five. He thought about the man who had dragged him out to play basketball when his eyes were stuck to a computer screen at age thirteen.

Norman Jr. thought about telling his father about his new girlfriend, Jessica. Instead he said, "Oh, I forgot to tell you, Dad. I bought a new pressure cooker other day when I sent out my tax form."

Norman remembered the first time he held Norman Jr. in his arms. He was so tiny, so fragile, and so dependent. He remembered feeling that suddenly, nothing else mattered in the world, and that he had gained a suit of armor and an Achilles heel all at once. *Now, that wide-eyed baby is a fully-grown man, who no longer needs his father.* Norman sighed. *Things will never go back the way they used to be.*

I might never get my baby back, Norman smiled in resignation, *but perhaps I can get to know this man better.*

"If you ever need money or anything, feel free to ask anytime, Junior."

Norman Jr. did not have any money issues, but he was glad to hear that.

OCTOBER

October

Norman Sees Something New at Work

October 1st, A Sunday

The packs of sugar next to the coffee machine at work were normally white, but today, some of the packs were yellow.

Norman asked Lisa what those yellow packets were.

"They're Splenda," she said. "They're like sugar, but with less calories."

"I see," said Norman. He added two yellow packets into his coffee. His coffee was too lukewarm to fully dissolve the Splenda, and the granules grinded against his teeth as he took a sip.

Norman didn't mind. He felt healthy.

That night, he sprinkled a little extra cheese on his spaghetti. He deserved it.

Norman Sees Someone Through the Crack of a Bathroom Stall

October 2nd, A Monday

Norman began his lunch-break by taking a trip to the toilet. After stepping into the bathroom with a single stall and two urinals, Norman surreptitiously undid his pants and took a seat. Norman enjoyed his bathroom breaks; he was certain no one would ask him to file away some new T4 reports, nor ask him how his day was going. The social barrier of the stall door was the pearly gates that Norman had always dreamed of.

A moment later, someone entered the bathroom. Norman held his breath. The footsteps sounded agitated-the other man wasn't interested in the urinals.

He was interested in the toilet.

Norman had hoped the man would see the locked door, leave the room, and check back in a minute, but no-the person paced back and forth, sighed, stood by the mirror, and waited, ever so patiently, for Norman to make a move. Norman couldn't do a thing under pressure like that.

Who would do this to me?! Norman thought to himself in a panicked tone. He tried to peak under the stall to see the shoes of the other man. He knew that Andrew had recently purchased new orange sneakers, and was quite proud of wearing them, despite going against appropriate office attire. Norman bent down and saw the shoes- they weren't orange, as he'd hoped, but black, and scoffed. Are those...

Norman looked up to the crack between the stall door, and there, he made contact. Eye contact. Quickly Norman's eyes flitted away, and the impatient man quickly left the bathroom. It was Frank!

Frank was Norman's cubicle mate. He should have known that the scoffed shoes were his! He saw them every single day!

Norman left the bathroom a moment later and returned to his cubicle. There, he saw Frank, quietly eating his sandwich over his keyboard. Black scoffed shoes leaned against the swivels on his chair. Neither man acknowledged each other.

Norman pulled out his own lunch, and began to eat, pretending that violating act had never taken place... Maybe he should say something. It would spill into rumors eventually. Perhaps he should take hold of it while he can. Norman felt like the Monica Lewinsky of the office place.

Norman decided not to confront Frank- not today. He also felt too uncomfortable to eat his lunch beside him either. Norman carried his lunch into the bathroom and continued to finish eating it in the safety of the bathroom stall.

Norman Dodges Death

October 3rd, A Tuesday

As Norman exited the corner shop, the familiar *bing-bong* of the glass door bid him farewell. The air outside was moist from last night's rain, but the sun was out today which gave the neighborhood a yellowish glow. Norman stopped by the curb and took a deep breath. Today was a good day.

Not great, but good. He felt more energised lately. Last week he had heard from his doctor that his cholesterol had gone down. And on Saturday his son called. Norman felt his head raise a bit higher as he twirled his plastic bag around his wrist with each step towards his apartment.

Just as he turned to cross the street in front of his building, a blue Volkswagen narrowly missed him. Taking a jump back, he clutched his groceries close to his chest. Gathering himself, Norman looked both ways before crossing. With his first step off the curb, he plunged his foot ankle deep into a puddle.

Norman Makes a Wish

October 4th, A Wednesday

After visiting the mall one weekday morning, Norman had some extra time before his bus arrived. He decided he'd use the extra few moments to visit the fountain just outside the mall. He found the sound of the rhythmically splashing water calming.

On his way there, he found a penny on the ground. Excited, he decided he'd throw the penny into the fountain and make a wish. Uncreatively, he wished that something good would happen to him. Optimistic about his wish coming true, he smiled as he stepped onto his bus. The bus driver noticed this and smiled back at him. The interaction flustered Norman and he looked away. He spent the bus ride home looking at his feet and hoping he wouldn't have to speak with the bus driver when he got off.

He'd forgotten about his wish.

Norman Makes a Mistake

October 5th, A Thursday

Norman glanced at the digital clock in the corner of his computer screen. 12:02. *Time for lunch*, Norman thought to himself excitedly. He proceeded to the break room and unpacked his afternoon nourishment: a turkey sandwich, plain yogurt, and bottled water. Norman began enthusiastically unwrapping his sandwich when Steven entered the break room, and asked to join Norman for lunch. This was an unusual request for Norman and he welcomed Steven to join him.

After ten minutes of small talk, Norman noticed his throat becoming dry, so he reached for his bottled water. As he pressed the fitted plastic to his lips, Norman became cognizant of the fact that this was not his bottle of water but, rather, it was Steven's. Norman quickly capped the bottle and placed it carefully in its previous spot, hoping Steven wouldn't notice. Norman then left the break room abruptly, with half a turkey sandwich left and 25 minutes left on his lunch break.

Norman Rides the Bus

October 6th, A Friday

The bus was uncomfortably full. Norman was forced to sit next to an occupied seat. He would stand, but he wasn't sure if that would be rude to the woman sitting next to him. Maybe she would be offended that he would rather stand than sit next to her.

He would get up as soon as someone else boarded the bus. Yes, then Norman could stand slightly to the side of the door and be prepared to exit as soon as he reached his stop.

The bus halted. A young woman climbed aboard. Hurriedly, Norman stood up from his seat and walked toward the door. He looked up and accidentally made eye contact with the bus driver through the rear-view mirror. He quickly averted his eyes, but not before seeing the driver gesticulate at him. He must have assumed this was Norman's stop.

Norman stepped off the bus. He was ten blocks from his home, but the rain wasn't too terrible. It was only as he reached his front door that he realised he'd left his briefcase tucked under the seat.

Norman Looks out the Window

October 7th, A Saturday

Norman stared out the window. The autumn day was cold and grey and damp. It had rained overnight and into the morning and now everything in the outside world appeared limp and defeated in the after-rain of the early afternoon. *Feels like a Sunday*, thought Norman to himself.

It was a Saturday, and Norman was accustomed to waking up at a reasonable hour on Saturdays, but the batteries in the alarm clock had run out overnight. Norman had unfortunately enjoyed an extra four hours of sleep.

The wind picked at the dead and fallen leaves on the ground, pushing them busily about the colourless front-lawn and into the desolate street. As he stared out the window at nothing in particular, Norman saw something fall to the ground from the single leafless tree that stood on the furthest edge of the lawn where the grass met the sidewalk and then became the road. Norman glanced over at Norman the cat, but he was too busy sleeping to be interested in the world outside the window.

Clad in pajamas, with bathrobe and slippers, and with his arms wrapped tightly about himself in an effort against the cold, Norman approached the tree with a shuffling, begrudging curiosity. A dark shape took form on the ground as he shuffled closer. He stopped. On the damp cement beneath the tree lay a small dead bird. Norman looked around. The street was empty and silent except for the wind when it scattered the dead leaves, scratching them against the surface of the road and against each other, and when it howled and came rattling across the spindly limbs of the tree. In that moment, Norman felt very light and weary (and stung with a faint, dull disappointment, but at what he did not know nor stop to ponder) as he looked back down at the broken little body and the tiny perfect beak. And suddenly, feeling with a jump like an uninvited guest at a dinner party, Norman shuffled quickly back to his apartment, where he dressed and promptly thereafter left the apartment to purchase a new set of batteries and a curtain.

Norman Takes a Delivery

October 8th, A Sunday

Norman had returned from lunch to find a brown cardboard box on his desk. It was about the same width as his keyboard and the height of a lever-arch file. It was unmarked.

Norman hadn't ordered, nor did he anticipate receiving anything. Perhaps junk-mail was now being delivered in bulk. He bit his lip and carefully scissored open the seal.

He lifted the flaps to reveal that the box was filled with cassette tapes. These can't have been his. He couldn't remember lending any cassette tapes to anyone. In fact, he couldn't recall even liking this much music. 'The Human League', 'Ultravox', 'Dexys Midnight Runners'. The names all sounded familiar.

It would have been quite the treasure trove if Norman had liked 80s synth music.

Norman wasn't really sure about 80s synth music.

As he delved deeper into the discography he found a folded-over sheet of A4 paper. It was a crayon drawing. The crudeness with which it had been drawn suggested a child's hand. It depicted a man waving outside a house. The man was helpfully labelled Frank. The bottom the drawing was signed 'Amber'.

"Oh." Norman glanced over to his colleague's desk and squinted at his computer monitor. On the desktop was a file labelled 'Amber'.

Norman carefully resealed the box and placed it on Frank's chair. When Frank came back from his lunch a look of recognition played across his face when he saw the box. He picked it up, walked over to where the confidential waste was piling up and dropped it unceremoniously on top. He noticed Norman watching him as he did this.

"It's just 80s guff," Frank said "I never really listened to it."

Norman thought he should say something.

Norman Feels Included

October 9th, A Monday

There was a new coffee machine at work. It had been placed in the break room right where the old machine used to be. Someone had thought up a silly prank and placed a sign next to the new coffee machine stating that it was 'Voice Activated' and included a list of instructions. Norman did not know this was a prank.

Like most mornings Norman waited until the break room was empty before taking his morning break. When he went to make a cup of coffee he noticed the sign.

Well now, what will they invent next? thought Norman.

Norman said politely, "I'll take a small decaf please."

Nothing happened.

"I'll take a small decaf *please*," repeated Norman.

Still nothing.

Unsure of what to do, and not wanting to offend the machine, Norman returned to his desk without his usual coffee.

A short while later Norman heard Shirlene from HR's shrill voice loudly proclaim, "One venti latte with soy milk!"

A few people chuckled, Norman joined in.

It's nice to be included, thought Norman.

It really was an exciting morning at the office.

Norman Plays Checkers with a Friend

October 10th, A Tuesday

It was a cool night at the beginning of winter. Norman was playing checkers with a new friend in his home for quite some time. They were on their thirteenth game. He'd been counting. He was very fond of checkers, although not very good at it.

"King me," Harmony said, as she winked.

"Uh...yeah. Here you go."

He placed the fallen soldier of his foe atop her victorious circle.

"So, you live here by yourself, huh?"

"Ummm, yeah. Just me and Norman."

As if on cue, Norman sauntered by, rubbing his side against Harmony's shins.

"He sure is a cutie," she said, before glancing at her watch, "Well, looks like it's time to go."

She stood up. On her way out, she leaned over and kissed Norman's bald, slightly moist head.

As she left, he realised he had had a very good time. He was rather apprehensive about calling the escort service at first, but didn't regret it. He'd consider calling Harmony again sometime.

Norman Gets his Hair Fixed

October 11th, A Wednesday

Norman was at the barbershop. He always felt very uncomfortable at the barber- the long awkward gazes into the mirror; the hairdresser looking over your shoulder.

Norman looked into his own eyes. It felt weird so his eyes quickly skipped to the hairdresser. This too didn't feel right. He looked at the hairdryer in front of the mirror instead.

After a while he felt it was time to look in the mirror again. He looked at his hair getting cut. He felt this was a safe thing to look at.

The hairdresser stopped: "How is this?" he asked. Norman looked at his hair to the left of his head. Then quickly to his hair to right. He tried to avoid his own eye contact. "Just fine!" Norman answered.

The hairdresser walked away to get a small mirror.

With the hairdresser gone Norman dared to look at the rest of his head. He looked at the big bald part in-between. He wondered if it's getting bigger.

Norman Chases a Fly Out

October 12th, A Thursday

Norman waved the fly away. It buzzed around, all frantic, bumping into the wall and circling the room. Norman went to look for the fly spray in the bathroom. The fly followed him in; he forgot to close the door. "*Bzzzzzzzzt*," it screamed.

"Bzzzzzzzzt."

Norman couldn't find the spray. The fly kept crashing into the closed window next to the one that was open. Norman thought about quitting his job at the office. Then he caught himself in the mirror. Norman walked out of the bathroom and shut the door. "***Bzzzzzzzzt,"*** said the fly through the door. "***Bzzzzzzzzt."***

It'll leave, eventually.

Norman Watches Hockey

October 13th, A Friday

Norman had just finished heating up leftovers for dinner. He had been invited out for karaoke for a co-worker's birthday, but Norman didn't think he was a good enough singer.

As Norman went into the living room with his plate, he sat in his chair and turned on the television. CSI had been cancelled that night because of breaking news about a tornado. Norman didn't want to be sad, so he flipped through the channels. Eventually he came to a hockey game. He'd never watched hockey before.

Florida? Norman thought to himself, *what a strange place for a hockey team.*

Norman didn't understand what was happening in the hockey game, and he had trouble finding the puck. It was moving so fast! Just when he thought he was starting to enjoy hockey, two players began to fight.

Norman turned off the television and went to bed.

Norman Discovers Rubber Cement

October 14th, A Saturday

Norman went to Depot-Mart looking for a new light bulb for his fridge. The bulb in his fridge hadn't burned out; he only wanted to be prepared.

Having secured the proper bulb, he headed for an exit, this time going through an unfamiliar aisle, which was rare for Norman.

Why not? Thought Norman.

Halfway through the empty aisle, Norman saw it.

Rubber cement? Is this some kind of joke? How can something be both rubber and cement? Norman thought.

Norman looked around, expecting to see either Allen Funt or Ashton Kutcher peeking at him from a distance, but he saw neither individual. Norman shook his head in disgust and left the Home Depot, vowing never to return.

Norman went home, sat down, and Norman jumped on his lap.

"Is Allen Funt even alive?" Norman asked Norman.

Norman Wakes up to Snow

October 15th, A Sunday

Norman woke up to sunbeams dancing across his face. The dastardly rays poked through the blinds next to his bed, disturbing his Sunday morning slumber. Norman slept on the radiator in front of the window, softly purring. Norman rolled out of bed and stretched, grabbing his bathrobe to go shower. For some reason, he felt a desire to look out the window.

Norman walked over to the window and moved the blinds apart to peek through. It had snowed last night, just an inch or so. It was pretty, though the snow plows had already cleared the roads. Oh well. He smiled a bit, and scratched Norman's head. Maybe he'll have some hot chocolate this morning.

Norman Takes a Bath

October 16th, A Monday

As Norman readied himself for a late-night shower, the thought of bathing crossed his mind. When was the last time he took a bath? It had to be at least a few decades. It felt like such a childish thing to do; a time to play with rubber duckies and fizzing soap... What was stopping him now? Norman was feeling nostalgic.

Norman filled the bath with hot water and foamy soap. As he stepped into the bath, he failed to factor in his body size, and the first step sent water flowing over the edge and onto his rug. He emptied out a little bit of the tub.

Now it was three quarters full. Norman could step into the water, but as he lowered himself down, even more water poured out. Norman stood up, naked, waiting for more water to drain from the tub. Waiting made him uncomfortable; as he was wet and the chill in the air was unpleasant. The tub was now one quarter full.

Norman sat down, and this time the water didn't flow over. Unfortunately, there was too little water now, and it became cold too quickly. Norman couldn't submerge his legs or his back in the water, and no matter what he did, he couldn't get his belly under either. He splashed water onto his stomach routinely to keep it from getting cold, like an elephant keeping cool in a watering hole.

Norman got out of the bath feeling dirtier than before and quite ready for a shower.

Norman Denies Frank

October 17th, A Tuesday

Norman sat in his cubicle, diligently typing away, when he felt a poke on his shoulder. It was Frank, his cubicle mate. Norman shifted his body towards his leather-faced co-worker.

"Hey Norman," Frank started, "My wife is... out of town for the week. How would you feel about grabbing a few drinks after work at The Pub?"

Norman wasn't normally one to be invited out to social events. Every now and then the office would throw a party, or all head out to grab drinks on the rare occasion. Norman allows his evenings to be quite free, on the rare chance someone might ask him to hang out. However, Frank chose a horrible day to try and be Norman's friend. Norman already has a date with a new episode of CSI.

"Sorry Frank, I'm busy tonight." Norman said apologetically.

Frank nodded solemnly and turned back towards his desk. Norman felt guilty, but he knew that he wouldn't forgive himself if he missed the mid-season mid-finale episode. *I'll have to ask Frank to dinner on another date,* Norman thought to himself.

Norman, of Impeccable Timing

October 18th, A Wednesday

Norman stood at the line for coffee in the office breakroom. Norman was growing nervous that the first pot would be empty by the time he reached his turn. The second pot was slowly brewing- too slowly. Norman would opt to just leave the line entirely if the first pot was empty. Norman sighed heavily as he reached to scratch his-

Just then, a spoon fell from Eleanor's stirring hand. Norman, like a grasshopper, snatched the spoon from the air before it came crashing onto the bacteria ridden carpet.

"Quick moving, Norman!" cheered Eleanor. Norman blushed wildly, speedy to humbly deny his praise as well. Somewhere in the room, a single faint clap appeared. It could have turned into an applause, but Norman was satisfied with the attempt.

Norman sat back down at his cubicle. "Quick moving, Norman", Norman mumbled to himself. Sure, he didn't manage to get a cup of coffee from the first pot, but he knew it was against the point. Norman typed his reports a little speedier today.

Norman Gets Invited

October 19th, A Thursday

"Hey Norman buddy!"

Robert looked down over the cubicle to see the middle-aged man named Norman working at his desk. Robert's friend Chris stood beside him.

"How's it going? Listen, me and some of the guys are going to be having a bit of a shindig at my place this weekend." Robert said, smiling as he did so.

"Just to let you know the whole office is invited, so if you want you can swing by. Get out for once. Meet some ladies maybe yeah?"

Norman glanced up at Robert, and then Chris.

"Should be pretty sweet," chipped in Chris.

Norman appeared to briefly think about it before he made his reply. "Oh, that sounds good. What day is it on?"

"It's this Saturday man!" Robert jovially responded.

At this point Norman's face appeared disappointed. "Oh, I'm really sorry but I've actually got a date that night. I don't think I'll be able to come."

Robert tilted his head slightly and said "Oh, really? Well good for you then Norman! You dark horse you. Next time then aye?"

Robert and Chris turned and walked away from the cubicle towards the break room. Chris raised an eyebrow at Robert.

"You know that's a load of horse manure, right? Why do you keep inviting the fat sack to stuff?"

Robert shrugged. "I dunno. I just feel sorry for the guy. It must be pretty bad spending all your time alone with just some dumb cat to keep you company."

Robert glanced back over his shoulder through the break room window at the cubicle that Norman was in.

Norman felt guilty for lying to Robert, but he was glad that Robert had believed him. Norman didn't really know how to express that he was really looking forward to what was on TV that night without hurting Robert's feelings.

Norman felt a little sorry for Robert. He felt that it must be pretty bad to hate being alone so much that you constantly have to surround yourself with people. Norman briefly wondered if Robert would like to get a cat.

Norman Gets a Coffee

October 20th, A Friday

Megan smiled politely as her next customer approached the counter. "Good morning," she said, as she did every morning.

"Good afternoon, Megan." replied the customer enthusiastically.

"The usual?"

"Yes, thanks."

On the paper cup she was already holding, Megan wrote, 'Norman' and under that 'van lat - whole'. She added the cup to a short queue of similarly marked paper cups, near another barista who was noisily frothing milk.

"Three-ninety-five, please," Megan said as she took the Visa card from the customer's hand. She swiped the card and returned it.

"Thank you," said Megan, smiling politely.

"Oh. Yes. Thank you," said the customer when he realized Megan was ready for the next customer in line.

Norman has a Strange Desire

October 21st, A Saturday

On a particularly cloudy Saturday afternoon, Norman found himself wanting to take a nap.

That's odd, Norman thought to himself.

While the desire to take a nap was not uncommon, it was quite unusual for him to take one earlier than his already scheduled 3:45 PM rest. He looked at his watch.

1:23 PM.

Perhaps I could take a nap, he thought, beginning to rise from his favourite chair.

"Meow," Norman replied.

"You're right Norman," Norman said. "It's quite a cloudy day, isn't it?"

"Meow."

Norman smiled. He returned once again to his favorite chair.

I like this chair, he thought.

Norman played with Norman for several minutes and went to bed at 3:45 AM as scheduled. It was a good day for a nap after all.

Norman Chats on Facebook

October 22nd, A Sunday

Norman was spending a regular Sunday evening in his living room, eating a bowl of leftover pasta he'd brought home from Olive Garden on Saturday night, with his laptop next to the bowl on the table in front of him with his own Facebook page open. Norman had been trying not to use his laptop on his lap recently, since he'd read something that said the radiation from the laptop might cause sterility.

Norman noticed that Tina, one of his college classmates, had just logged onto Facebook. He hadn't seen Tina since they both graduated, but he still considered her a friend. He thought about how nice it would be to hear how she'd been doing lately, so he clicked her name to open a chat window, thinking of opening the conversation with a friendly "Hey!". After clicking, Norman noticed a message that he sent three months earlier: "Heyy!". Tina hadn't responded.

Not wanting to seem like he was bothering Tina, Norman closed the chat window, and finished his pasta. It was warm.

Norman Runs out of Work

October 23rd, A Monday

Norman sluggishly typed away on his keyboard, entering the information into the computer from the stack of papers in his inbox. As he finished his latest sheet, Norman reached over into his stack of paperwork, only to feel nothing.

Norman glanced over, unsure of what to do. *This has never happened before,* he thought to himself. *Now what?* It was only 10:15.

Glancing around his cubicle, he tried to find something productive to do. Rearrange his desk, tidy up his desk drawers, double check all his filing... He had done it all.

Norman stared into the computer screen. He was out of work. It was now 10:18.

Norman Goes to the Bank

October 24th, A Tuesday

Noticing the lack of dollar bills in his wallet, Norman decided to go to the bank. He could always go to the ATM but he didn't want to have to face the pressure of having someone waiting behind him as he waited for his money. He also likes a certain amount of each type of bill in his wallet; one twenty, two fives, and five ones. He felt this was the perfect amount that no automated machine could provide.

He opened the door and noticed the familiar smell of the credit union. He walked up to the teller, a medium heightened young woman, and proceeded to assure his information.

"Will that be checking or savings?" She said with a smile on her face. "Checkings, please." Norman answered.

"Okay one moment plea- oh, it appears you're checking account has insufficient funds." "Did I say checking? I meant savings." Norman said, trying not to appear shaken.

Norman didn't want the money out of his savings account. The teller handed him the eight various dollar bills and Norman rushed the women a goodbye.

He walked to the teller three booths away and puts the money back in his savings account.

Norman left the bank thinking about how he should have considered the ATM.

Norman Answers the Door

October 25th, A Wednesday

It was just after work and Norman was assembling a meal in the kitchen. Just as he peeled back the plastic from his *Anyday Roast*, the doorbell rang.

He quickly stirred his food before approaching the door and peeping through the peephole.

"Hello?" he suggested.

The man on the other side was smartly dressed and carrying a clipboard. "Is that Mr... Um... Is that Nor-man?"

"Speaking." Norman had joined Norman at the door. Norman lifted him up so he could see through the peephole.

"We have a record that indicates you have recently signed up to our Deluxe Life Insurance Policy. I would like to talk to you about our Super Deluxe Life Insurance Policy."

Norman did not recall having signed up to a life insurance policy. And neither had Norman.

"I'm afraid you may have the wrong Norman," Norman shouted politely through the keyhole.

"May I come in for a moment?" asked Clipboard.

"No, I don't think so," Norman replied.

"This is an opportunity for you to leave a loved one assurance and comfort. You would want that, wouldn't you Norman?"

Norman looked down at Norman.

"I think he's probably quite capable of looking after himself. I really must be getting on. I'm sorry. I hope you find another Norman."

Norman felt very guilty as he silently watched Clipboard walk to the door opposite his and start feeling up his neighbour's mail.

Norman returned to his *Anyway Roast*, trayed it up and visited his sofa. He looked at Norman, who was still sitting at the door. "You'd be able to look after yourself, wouldn't you?"

Norman stretched and walked away.

Norman Takes the Elevator

October 26th, A Thursday

Norman didn't tend to go into elevators. He was in a clothes store and after much fruitless searching for a staircase up to the Men's section he submitted to the metallic chamber which promised to whisk him from women's underwear and right into the thick of men's hosiery.

Happily, he didn't need to wait long for the doors to slide open. The elevator was empty; he stepped in. As the Tannoy announced that the doors were closing a hand shot through the gap and coaxed them open again.

It was Frank.

Norman worked with Frank. Their desks were joined. Sometimes important documents would fall through the gap between their desks and Norman wouldn't say anything. Frank would just grimace.

He had no idea whether Frank had recognised him.

They both stared intently at the door in front of them as they each endured the g-force of their ascending capsule. It came to a stop and they waited an unnaturally long time before the doors eased open again.

Frank left the lift first.

Norman realised that he'd been holding his breath for the entire time.

Norman Forgets

October 27th, A Friday

Norman couldn't remember why he had entered the kitchen.

There were many good reasons why his legs had brought him here. Perhaps there had been something that Norman had been meaning to do in the kitchen. That would explain why he was now standing near the refrigerator feeling confused.

Norman looked around his kitchen.

He made himself a cup of tea.

He drank the tea, washed his mug and wiped a small amount of liquid off the kitchen bench with some paper towel, which he placed in the kitchen bin under the sink.

Norman still couldn't remember why he had come into the kitchen.

Oh well, he said to himself. *At least I've had a nice cup of tea.*

Norman left the kitchen feeling triumphant that he hadn't let feeling confused ruin his morning.

Norman Tries "Norm" on for Size

October 28th, A Saturday

Norman got to reading one Saturday and started thinking. Norman thought that, though he could not change his past, he could change his future. So, around lunch time, Norman decided to order a pizza-pie from the local pizzeria, "Local Pizzeria." The phone rang a few times before someone answered. Norman ordered a large, regular crust pizza with regular toppings, for pick-up. The girl on the phone told Norman it would be 25 minutes, 14 dollars, and asked if she could have a name for the order. Norman's heart leaped, raced, and thumped. It was now or never.

"It's Norm."

"Great, see you soon!"

Norm smiled confidently, hung up the phone, and noted the time. Norm did not want to be late.

Norman Goes Back to School

October 29th, A Sunday

One Sunday morning, Norman decided to visit his old university. It was one of those small, quaint schools that was technically a state school but felt more like a community college.

Norman walked to his old dorm building, then to the bookstore, then to the library where he used to study. He picked up a copy of the weekly school paper and sat down on a comfy chair. Before he knew it, he drifted into a peaceful nap.

A few hours later, Norman woke up and saw that it was dark outside. He decided to walk over to the diner where he had met his ex-wife, and took a seat. When the waitress walked up with a menu, Norman said that he didn't need one and ordered a hamburger with a chocolate milkshake.

Norman sat contentedly in his booth, remembering how cute his young had love looked when she laughed at one of his jokes and her nose got all scrunched up. He looked at one of the other booths in the diner and saw a young couple sitting on the same side of the table, laughing together, neglecting their soon-to-be cold food.

The waitress brought Norman his food. He took a bite of his hamburger, sipped a sip of his milkshake, and smiled; it tasted just like he remembered.

Norman Starts a Tradition

October 30th, A Monday

Beginning of winter, Norman thought, as he gazed out his window and watched the leaves bleed from the maple tree in brilliant bright orange. Norman absentmindedly stroked Norman between the ears and decided that today was the day to do something new. To make a tradition.

Norman went to his bedroom and grabbed a heavily sweat-stained work shirt and an old pair of trousers.

"Now...what for the head?" Norman pondered aloud. His gaze fell upon his bed and rested on the pillows.

"Ah, yes that will do."

Norman stripped the pillow of its case. He then trundled to the basement for a piece of rope. While descending the stairs he stepped through a spider web causing him to spit and splutter, violently wiping his clothes to rid himself of the web's inhabitant. Norman was frightened, but he put on a face of determination. He was going to start this tradition and that was that.

Having procured all of the necessary supplies Norman went outside to the front yard of his apartment complex and began piling the fallen leaves around the base of the maple.

"That should be enough," Norman estimated.

After stuffing the pants and shirt to brimming with fallen leaves Norman paused. He couldn't decide how the face should look. After a moment's consideration, he drew a straight line slightly below the lopsided eyes with magic marker. Norman grinned and addressed the pillowcase face;

"Not too handsome are ya there, fella?"

Attaching the pillow case head to the body, Norman propped his creation against the bleeding maple and stepped back to examine his handiwork.

"Now that's a scarecrow," Norman's neighbour observed from behind him.

Norman turned to address the neighbour, but she was already along her way. Norman made a mental note to write an anonymous thank you and slip it under her door sometime soon.

It took Norman a few tries and a few chuckles from the children watching him work before he managed to get the rope over a tree branch, but eventually he succeeded and began tying a noose around the scarecrow's neck. Now all he had to do was hoist it up and let it swing. Hopefully, Norman thought it might even scare away a few of those pesky trick-or-treaters who scared him with their terrifying costumes.

Norman began hoisting. One, two, three hard tugs and his tradition was six feet off the ground. Norman stalled before tying the rope to the base of the maple tree, again examining his creation and feeling proud of making a new tradition for himself. Softly the wind began to blow, rotating the scarecrow's head in his direction.

Norman screamed as their eyes met.

It was no longer a pillow case head he saw hanging from the tree, but his own. His lips the color and shape of some exotic blue caterpillars. Norman let go of the rope and his double crashed to the ground with a thump. Shaken, he slowly approached the body and kicked its shoulder, turning it onto its back. Nothing but pillowcase and marker stared back at him. Norman shuddered.

He removed the rope and carried the limp leaf-stuffed body to the dumpster behind his apartment. He unceremoniously dumped the scarecrow in and shut the lid. Norman lifted the top to throw the rope in and let it fall back into place. *You never know when you'll need a good piece of rope,* Norman thought, gazing upon the bleeding maple tree and thinking of the long winter ahead.

Norman Celebrates Halloween

October 31st, A Tuesday

After work, Norman drove not to his apartment, but to the grocery store. He hoped to beat the rush to the store, as it was Halloween and Norman wanted to get the best candy he could for his trick-or-treaters.

Inside, Norman strolled through the linoleum halls until he found the candy section. Faced with every manner of confection, Norman had a decision to make. Would he go with the full-sized Butterfingers that he normally bought every year, or would he change things up? Wanting to offer even the slightest bit of variety to his future trick-or-treaters, Norman decided to purchase fifty packs of peanut butter cups. He liked peanut butter cups because every time he ate one, he was always a little surprised by the peanut butter flavor.

Norman came back home excited and set the large packs of Reese's Cups into a bowl. It was barely dusk and Norman knew he only had a little time before the trick-or-treaters showed up. Norman jumped onto the counter and pawed at the bowl. Feeling festive, Norman went to the closet and replaced Norman's collar with a bright-orange one.

Norman flipped on his balcony light and watched as, across the street, a handful of tiny ghosts and goblins rang a doorbell. Norman went back inside and sat on his couch. After an hour, he considered calling a co-worker to see if there were any festivities going on tonight, but he thought it was too late. He had talked to Lisa a few days ago, and she hadn't mentioned anything, and even then, what if there was something going on? Would Norman be in the mood for socializing?

Norman was tired and wanted to lie down on his bed. It was much more comfortable than his couch, but he chose to stay in the living room because he didn't want to risk missing a trick-or-treater. Norman thought back to when he was a kid and would ring the doorbell on a friend's house, waiting for them to come out to play. Sitting in the grass, sometimes those moments can feel like an eternity.

It was almost midnight when Norman, eyes puffy from resisting sleep, turned off his balcony light. He took his bowl of peanut butter cups to the pantry. He looked for space to put them and was going to set them on the top shelf when he saw a different bowl full of fully-wrapped peanut butter cups. Norman realized that he had bought peanut butter cups for last Halloween, too.

The Book of Norman

November

Norman and Lisa Feel a Spark

November 1st, A Wednesday

Norman was working so hard he hadn't realized how uncomfortably warm he'd become. *It must be 75, 76 degrees in here,* Norman thought as he rocked back and forth to remove his woolly sweater vest. His shirt became untucked for a moment as his arms extended over his head.

Just then Lisa peeked into his cubicle. She pretended that she hadn't just seen Norman's pale stomach as she smiled and gestured quietly for Norman's attention.

"Oh, hi Lisa," Norman said with an embarrassed grin as he pulled his shirt back down.

"Hi Norman! Say, do you have some liquid paper I could use?"

"Hmm..." Norman thought in silence for a moment. "I think so?" He checked the drawer. Lisa came closer.

"I made a mistake on my report," she explained. Norman chuckled knowingly and continued to look.

"Here it is!" Norman said with excitement. He felt very useful. He wheeled his chair towards Lisa and handed it to her. Just then a shock jumped from his finger to Lisa's wrist. They both jumped a little.

"Ouch!" Lisa said, somewhat playfully. "Well, thank you for the liquid paper. I'll bring it back soon."

"I'm not sure why that happens!" said Norman with a laugh. But Lisa was already gone, and she never returned the liquid paper.

Norman Plays the Lottery

November 2nd, A Thursday

Norman didn't actually play the lottery- instead he would pretend, by recording his lucky numbers by himself, just to see if they happen to win. It was a hopeless hope he had.

For the past seven years, he's always chosen precisely the same numbers- 7, 8, 9, 10, 11, and 13. He thought it was very cheeky to skip 12, for no particular reason. Unfortunately, these numbers have never won once in the past seven years- even if he wasn't winning anything to be begin with.

Today, however, Norman decided to have some change in his life. Instead of writing down the usual 7 to 13 minus 12, he decided to exclude 13- and finally include the lonely number. He wrote this down on a napkin, and again, for the hundredth time, watched the numbers being called on the television.

-today's winning numbers are... 7... 8...

This was already fairing better than normal.

9... 10... 11...

Norman's heart was racing as if he'd just briskly jogged to work. He's never been this close before! Standing, palms sweating, and knees scrambling, Norman held his breath...

... And the final number is... 12!

Norman screamed in joy! All these years of trying 13, all these years of trying to be cheeky- all paid off- but it didn't matter now! Norman jumped up and down ecstatically in his apartment, happy with change, happy with joy in his life, happy to win!

Norman then remembered all he had was a napkin.

Well, Norman thought, *at least there's proof.*

Norman placed the napkin inside his scrapbook full of photos and memories from decades earlier; the happy times. The napkin was right at home.

Norman Buys Donuts for the Office

November 3rd, A Friday

It was holiday season at Norman's work and as usual Norman was covering the holiday shift. On Thursday night, Norman looked at the schedule and counted that only seven people would be in the office on Friday.

On his way to work Friday morning Norman took a detour around the bakery and picked up a pack of nine donuts. It was a better deal to get a full pack of nine than to buy seven individual donuts. Arriving at work in good time, he placed it in a cupboard the kitchen and got back to his desk. Before the rest of the team came in, he sat and composed an e-mail: "Dear colleagues, please help yourself to a donut in the kitchen. Kind regards, Norman." He didn't send it just yet.

Nobody suspected a thing, as he sat in his cubicle working. Then finally at 10'o'clock, he couldn't resist anymore. Norman walked to the kitchen, grabbed the pack of donuts, placed it on the table and opened it. He then hurried back to his cubicle and clicked 'Send' on his message. After a while, he received two replies: "thanks Norman" and, "great way to start the weekend :)". Norman felt good.

Later on that same Friday, Norman sat at home in his couch, when suddenly it hit him that he forgot to take home the remaining donuts. *How many was left? Did anyone get rid of them?*

"Oh dear, I better get in early on Monday to clean up the mess." he said to Norman.

Norman has a Saturday Breakfast

November 4th, A Saturday

It was Saturday, so Norman felt like having a nice breakfast. He made a pot of Earl Grey, fried two eggs and three rashers of bacon. He ate them with a slice of buttered toast.

Norman also had a scrap of bacon.

Afterwards, Norman felt like going for a walk, but it has just started to snow.

Norman Picks up Smoking

November 5th, A Sunday

Norman was normally quite healthy, which was why it surprised him when the words, '*Newport Light*' came out of his mouth. It was the same thing the man in front of him had asked for. He had meant to buy a lottery ticket, but the man had reminded Norman of his son.

The small rectangle slid smoothly enough into his pocket but the sharp edges were pressing on the fabric, leaving an impression.

Well, that won't do, Norman thought, removing the pack and throwing it in the garbage.

As Norman walked home he thought about his adventure.

Norman Watches a Video on his Lunchbreak

November 6th, A Monday

Lunchtime rolled along on this Monday afternoon in the office. Norman, not one to share his meals with anyone other than his cat, avoided the break room and feasted on his ham sandwich in the confines of his cubicle.

Norman perused his Facebook page while he held the stiff sandwich in one hand, and the mouse in the other. A video was auto-playing on the screen, silently, as Norman didn't want to disturb anyone.

But the video was just too enticing. From what Norman could tell, two cats were communicating with each other, lapping their tongues. *What are they saying to each other?* Norman mused. After a minute, curiosity took over him. This was worth the effort to pull out his headphones. Norman stuck the nodes in his ears and turned up the volume.

It was just what he expected, and even then, it was so much better! The tabby cat would meow, then the tortoiseshell cat would also "meow" back! Norman's heart was melting and pooling on his lap. Then it started to feel wet. Norman looked at his lap. It was mustard, from the ham sandwich.

With no time to lose, Norman pulled three napkins and began furiously cleaning. Some of the mustard even made it onto the floor. Luckily Norman had a plastic covering under his chair, so the only negative was having to bend all the way down-

Then Norman saw it.

The other end of his headphones, not plugged in to the computer. *Were they ever plugged in!?* Norman thought.

He muted the video and stood up, peaking his head above the cubicles walls. Everything was silent. It usually isn't this silent.

Norman packed his briefcase and went home early.

Norman Wakes Up

November 7th, A Tuesday

Norman woke to the laughter of children as they passed his window on their way to school. His TV still blared. He stared at his ceiling and listened listlessly to the snippets of conversation drifting by. He tossed restlessly. Norman crept through the door and meowed his hunger. Norman reassured himself he was content.

Norman Goes on a Diet

November 8th, A Wednesday

As Norman dressed for work, he noticed his pants were a little hard to button.

"Guess I need to lose a few pounds," he muttered to himself.

Norman went into the kitchen and poured coffee into his travel mug. He added a teaspoon of sugar. He scooped up a second teaspoon of sugar, thought better of it, and dumped the sugar back into the bowl. Norman screwed the lid shut on his travel mug and headed out the door. As he walked down the sidewalk, he took a sip of coffee. It tasted slightly bitter.

Norman Attends a Seminar

November 9th, A Thursday

Norman had gone to an all-day seminar covering the intricacies of a new software program to be introduced at his workplace. Norman found the seminar interesting, and despite his usual resistance to such drastic changes, was secretly eager to see the new program implemented at the office. The seminar had been hosted at one of the colleges on the other side of town. Norman had had to take three different bus lines to get there. Musing on this new era of workplace efficiency, Norman strolled to the bus stop in front of the psychology building. Norman shuddered. He disliked psychology, mainly because the idea of experts being able to make inferences about his life and personality based on subtle tells made him uncomfortable.

Norman fished his wallet out of his pocket to prepare his bus fare. He was utterly vexed to find no cash within. Norman was certain there had been a small amount left over from what he had spent on lunch, but then remembered that on a cheerful whim he had been rather generous with the tip.

Vexed that he would now have to use his credit card for bus fare (Norman eschewed using his card for frivolous expenses), Norman let his eyes wander, and soon noticed a small pile of cash on the sidewalk several feet to his right. The pile appeared to consist of six or seven ones, quite enough to pay for Norman's fare. Norman saw no one else nearby to whom the money could belong, and thinking it such a paltry amount anyway, he was briefly delighted as he moved to rescue the bills from the ground.

Only then did he notice an observer; a young pretty student was seated at a window of the psychology building with a notepad in her lap. Norman suspected that the money was placed there as part of some esoteric social experiment, and decided he did not want to be part of it. The bus arrived, and Norman sighed as he removed his credit card.

The pretty young student, Emma, had looked up from her work just in time to glimpse a bespectacled middle-aged man drop a small roll of cash as he pulled out his wallet. Shortly after he looked at her expectantly, then turned away. She thought she should run out to tell him he had dropped some money, but then reconsidered. She suspected he might be one of those oddball philosophy professors running some sort of esoteric experiment in ethics, and decided she did not want to be part of it.

The next day, Norman carefully removed the packaging on his new socks and put them on. He looked down at his feet and admired how colourful the socks were. It made him smile to think that while those passing him on the street wouldn't know it, though he might not go on big adventures, or ride a motorbike, when Norman wore those socks he would be reminded that he could be daring too.

Norman Takes the Elevator

November 13th, A Monday

Norman stood alone in the elevator. The dull buzz of the machine hung over his head. No music graced the atmosphere of this elevator, which made Norman a little sad. He'd never really had any strong feelings about elevators before, but he'd always enjoyed the music.

Norman thought about the absence of music. He thought about the sounds that surrounded him, and how they weren't simple melodies. He then thought that maybe the elevator was malfunctioning.

His heart raced.

He thought the machine could stall at any moment, and how he'd be trapped in the small metal box. He thought about the floor under his feet disintegrating and sending him falling to his end. He thought that maybe this would be the last elevator he'd ever be in. He thought that it was unfair that his final elevator ride would be one without music.

Ding. The doors opened. Norman walked out.

Norman and the Girl at the Bank

November 14th, A Tuesday

Norman was out the door 17 minutes early as he was on most Tuesdays. This gave him enough time to go to the bank near the office to take out some money for the week and still arrive to work on time. Norman enjoyed this trip as there was a very beautiful teller who always had a shift on Tuesday mornings. Norman went to the back of the line at the bank and pretended to look at pamphlets until her line was available. He requested the usual; one twenty, two fives, and five ones. As the teller retrieved the money she looked at Norman - "You know, I see you in here every Tuesday, you could take out more at once to save yourself the trip each week - might make your life a bit easier" she offered helpfully. Norman formed a weak smile and took his money. He never went to the bank on Tuesdays again.

Norman Gets DVR

November 15th, A Wednesday

Change is good, Norman thought as the cable guy was bent over his TV, his butt-crack clearly visible. Norman averted his eyes from the sight.

The cable guy stood up and handed Norman the remote. He explained how the remote work worked to Norman, then he left.

The first thing Norman did was find his favorite Thursday night show, CSI. He hit record and a notification popped up to customize the recording. Maybe now Norman could go shopping on Wednesday.

Norman Eats Breakfast

November 16th, A Thursday

Norman looked down at the white plate on the table, and smiled a little. The landscape of ceramic sparsely dotted with toast and potatoes had a smell just strong enough that Norman could appreciate it.

As he ate, Norman tried to remember his dreams from the night before. Thinking of dreaming always made Norman feel a little whimsical, but he thought it was a good way to start his day.

Norman's thoughts were interrupted by a soft brush against his leg. He looked down and smiled at Norman, but during his lapse in thought, he had somehow managed to dip his toast in his coffee.

Norman was pleasantly surprised by the unexpected medley of flavors in his mouth, and he chuckled to himself about his own silliness.

Norman stood up, put his plate in the sink, and left for work.

Norman is Almost Run Over

November 17th, A Friday

Norman was waiting at the level crossing.

He had pressed the button and was waiting for the green man to tell him he could safely cross.

A car zoomed towards the intersection and hastily applied his brakes to stop for the now red light, but the front end of his car went over the white line by a few inches.

"Watch where you're going, you maniac!" Norman muttered quietly to himself.

Norman Saves a Life

November 18th, A Saturday

Norman was having a morning like any other. He woke up and had his tea with non-fat milk (Norman's doctor was worried about his cholesterol levels, and if he was worried, Norman was worried). Norman heard a familiar noise from the front of his building.

Odd... That sounds like Norman, thought Norman.

Norman walked out front and decided to investigate, just like his favourite character from CSI would do.

Norman had left his apartment and was meowing at an unresponsive person laying on the sidewalk.

Norman hastily retrieved his cell phone from the front left pocket of his pajama top, but it wouldn't turn on.

Norman wanted to go inside to call emergency but hesitated; what if Norman ran away while he was inside phoning? How long would they keep him on the line? Would he be fined for having a cat not on a lead in public?

Someone else would call for help. Norman scooped up Norman.

Another tenant came out to see the commotion.

As Norman walked back into his building his neighbour said, "I heard meowing, looked outside and saw the lad not moving. I phoned emergency. Your cat saved that man's life. Why didn't you ever tell me you have a cat?"

Norman acknowledged his neighbor with a nod.

My neighbors are too nosy, thought an exhausted Norman.

Norman took his noon nap early that day.

Norman Does a Crossword Puzzle

November 19th, A Sunday

Norman sat alone at his dining room table with the Sunday crossword spread out before him. The puzzle was nearly completed, but he was stuck on a clue: "What a germ might become." Four letters.

Norman ran through several possible answers, but none of them worked with the letters he had already filled in. He became frustrated by his inability to complete the puzzle, and after a few minutes he gave up.

Later that evening, just as Norman was drifting off to sleep, he realized that the answer he needed was "idea." He resolved to write it down the next day and complete the puzzle, but by morning he'd forgotten, and he threw away the unfinished crossword with the half-eaten remnants of his breakfast.

Norman on the Bus

November 20th, A Monday

On the way home from work, Norman decided to sit on a seat on the bus. Norman sometimes stood on the bus so other passengers could sit, but today he saw that there were no other passengers on. So today, Norman sat in a seat that was situated at the back of the carriage.

A few stops along the bus route, a man stepped onto the bus. The man looked around the carriage. Instantly, Norman stood up to offer his seat to the man. But the man seemed uninterested in Norman and proceeded to sit in another seat on the carriage. Norman tried to apologize but he could only manage to open and close his mouth.

Norman Celebrates Chanukah

November 21st, A Tuesday

Tonight at sundown would be the first night of Chanukah. Norman liked to celebrate as many holidays as he can because it broke the monotony of all the regular days of the year. His favorite was Halloween because he could be anything he wanted; a ghost, a cat, even Gil Grissom!

When he got home from work, he went to his closet and pulled out a decently sized box labeled "Holidays". He dug around past a few Thanksgiving decorations, set aside the pumpkin carving kit, and finally picked out his menorah, some candles, a dreidel, and two small packages wrapped in paper.

He set the menorah on the table, placed a candle in it and lit it. He reached over and set one gift in front of himself and the other in front of Norman. Both labels read *'From: Norman To: Norman'*.

"I wonder what it could be!" said Norman as he unwrapped the gift his cat had gotten him. It was a gift card to a coffee shop Norman often visited. He smiled as Norman pawed at the dreidel.

Norman Meets a Girl

November 22nd, A Wednesday

A year ago, Norman fell in love. As he was in a grocery store, he discovered something magical: Chipotle sauce and Thousand Island dressing worked perfectly together as a dipping sauce for chicken wings. Ever since the discovery, he would learn to savour the mixture, only having it sparsely. Usually he would use BBQ or honey mustard, but those were just the regular flavours. Thousand Island and Chipotle was the diamond in the rough. This occasion was nothing special, just another Wednesday, but it did happen to be the fourth meal of chicken wings this month, and he was ready for some chipotle island.

After picking up a package of chicken wings, the sauces, and bacon treats for Norman, he stood in line behind a cluster of people. In front of him stood a blonde, somewhat large but comfortably curvy woman. Norman noticed she was buying the same kind of animal bacon treats, except hers was marketed for dogs. Also in her cart was Chipotle sauce! Perhaps she was also using it for chicken wings, and Norman could heroically tell her about the concoction he invented.

"Norman?" The woman questioned. Norman looked behind him to see if there were any other Normans behind him.

"Oh my God, Norman! It's me! Dianne, you know, from high school?"

Norman couldn't remember Dianne from high school, but he did remember why he recognized her- E - Harmony. He knew that she was a single lady in his area, and that she was a big fan of Gordon Ramsey. Norman responded with an 'Oh yes, of course,' prompting her to ask, "How have you been?" to which Norman in turn responded with 'Great!'

It turned out Dianne was working as a secretary and had a dog named Dixie. Norman told his life story too, that he worked in an office and had a cat named Norman. She laughed at that, unfortunately. Norman thought Norman was a fine name for a cat.

"Are you seeing anyone?" Dianne asked. Norman shook his head.

"We should hang out sometime. What about Friday? How about that restaurant, L'Impasse? Here's my number. Call me! I'll meet you there. Say hi to Norman for me, Norman!"

Norman stayed in line and purchased his bacon, chicken, and sauces. At home, he cooked up the chicken, doused it in his special flavours, but it didn't appeal to him now. He had too many butterflies stuck in his stomach.

Norman Meets a Girl, Part 2

November 23rd, A Thursday

Norman dug through his closet for something appropriate for his date with Dianne on Friday- specifically, something that could still fit. The closet was stuffed with old pants, shoes and socks, scarves and hats. Nothing terribly fashionable. Norman was used to wearing his black slacks and white short sleeve button shirt to work, and not much else, so this closet filled with miscellaneous items was his only hope to find something. And then he did.

It was an old second-hand suit he had bought, many years ago, when he was just a teenage boy. He clearly remembered the day he wore it- it was with the only person he went on a date with before he met his wife a few years later. Her name was Rebecca. She was in the eleventh grade and he was in the tenth. He'd purchased the suit from a thrift store, costing him well over twenty dollars. It was a beige corduroy with the texture of most sofas, back then in the late seventies. Her father picked him up. Norman had felt nervous.

"You have any aspirations, son?" Rebecca's father asked. Norman wasn't certain what the word aspirations meant, but he knew what perspiration meant.

"Not at the moment, sir." Norman responded.

The date with Rebecca had gone well- Norman treated her to Italian food, and finished the night by walking over to a drive-in movie theater. Norman remembered how much Rebecca smiled at his jokes, and how she rubbed his shoulder every time he offered her popcorn.

"I really like talking to you." Rebecca said. Present Norman tried to remember what he had responded with exactly, but it faded with the last number of decades. *What did I say?* Norman thought. He wondered why he never saw Rebecca again after that night, and then immediately recounted the reason he knew the word perspiration so well. Sexual education class. Puberty. Perspiration. Erratic erections.

Norman tried on the suit that had fit his young, fifteen-year-old self. To no surprise, the suit did not fit. Norman drove down to his local thrift store, and searched through the sports coat and tie sections. Rummaging around, he managed to find a suit uncanny to his first suit, this time much larger around the waist. He tried it on and it was a baggy fit, but he knew that it was supposed to fit like that; that way he would have time to grow into it and let it have room to shrink.

Norman went home and pleaded for Norman's opinion. The cat purred as it shed fur onto the coat, and Norman took that as a blessing.

Norman Meets a Girl, Part 3

November 24th, A Friday

Norman showed up to his date with Dianne roughly 20 minutes early, just in case the restaurant was full and he would need to save them a pair of seats. It turned out the restaurant was terrifically quiet- Norman wouldn't have to feel nervous about strangers listening on, judging him and his poor flirting skills. It was a muscle he hadn't exercised in decades (along with most of his muscles). It would be best if he could do it in private.

A waiter came to Norman with a menu and a glass of water. "Dining for one?" the waiter asked.

"Yes!" Norman said. Norman didn't mean to say yes, but by the time he said it, he figured there was no point in correcting himself. Perhaps when Dianne showed up, the waiter would be impressed by Norman's spontaneity. Norman chewed on the free buns.

As he waited, Norman browsed through the menu.

10 oz steak: $23.00
Potato skins: $20.00
Fillet Mignon: $30.00
Greek salad: $15.00
Arabian coffee: $5.00

Distilled water: $3.00

Norman began to feel nervous. Today was indeed Friday, but he hadn't had a chance to cash his cheque just yet. Eleanor, the accountant who handled payroll, had recently adopted a kitten! Norman was so enthralled in her stories about Little Whiskers attacking the sofa that he had forgotten to leave the office at a reasonable hour. He wasn't sure how much he had in his bank account exactly, but it made him nervous while looking at the prices.

15 minutes after the arranged time, Dianne finally showed up. She wore a dazzlingly purple dress, with her hair pursed up in a tight bun. Norman thought about buns. He realized he felt quite full.

The waiter returned with a pen and notepad. "I see you found company?" he mused. Norman felt incredibly accomplished. Dianne began her order.

"Hi, I'd like to get the steak with potato skins..."

Norman panicked. *She wanted more than coffee?* Dine-and-dashing, if they decided to take that route, would be exhilarating. Norman had read somewhere that you are supposed to make a woman feel an adrenaline rush on the first date. *But*, Norman thought, *that would be incredibly rude to my new friend, the waiter.* He would just have to thick it out. She continued her order:

"... and... uh... how is the distilled water? Do you have a house wine? That would be great. And a salad to start."

The waiter turned to Norman. Norman ordered another glass of undistilled water and a second basket of buns.

"The second basket of buns isn't complementary." said the waiter. He pointed to the menu.

Additional Bread Rolls: 10$

Once the buffet of food was placed upon the table, Norman and Dianne began to share stories.

"Oh my," Dianne huffed, "My Dixie is such a doll. She loves Skittles. The other day, I bought a packet of Skittles, and she ate it! All of it! I was so, *so mad...*"

"Well my Norman is a playful cat. One time I took her to the vet. She was so scared-"

"-My Dixie hates the vet! One time I took her there, 'cause she had worms, and there was this other dog there... It was so cute!"

"One time, Norman found a worm outside-"

"-Dixie loves bugs! She'll crush ones she doesn't like with her paws, but for the most part she just plays with them. She's so friendly."

Norman and Dianne left the restaurant together, after Norman paid the bill and gave a tip to his friend. Dianne carried her leftovers in a plastic container. The container costed Norman an extra three dollars. Norman walked her to her car.

"Maybe I'll you sometime?" Norman said. She smiled and nodded. She drove away.

Norman was hoping for a kiss, or a hug, or a goodbye. *Maybe on the second date,* he thought. He could call a cab, but he figured his bank account had taken enough of a beating for one day. Norman walked home idly, thinking romantically about Dianne. *I hope my breath didn't smell,* he thought.

Norman Eats an Apple

November 25th, A Saturday

It was a warm-ish afternoon and Norman remembered that he had bought a bag of crisp, red apples. He fancied one. Norman walked into the kitchen and got one out of the fridge. He doesn't like biting apples so he would cut them up first. He got out a knife and set up the apple. He cut it in half. And in half again. On the third cut, his knife slipped and sliced his thumb. "Ouch." Norman said passively. He looked down at the blood and fainted. When he awoke, it was night time. *I can't eat the apple now. It's dinner time.*

Norman Checks the Mail

November 26th, A Sunday

One crisp November morning, Norman went downstairs to check his mail. Amid the usual coupons and catalogs, he noticed something out of the ordinary. It was a slightly stiff, square-shaped envelope. His name and address were carefully handwritten across the front. *This certainly isn't a utility bill,* Norman thought as he looked over the mysterious rose-colored envelope. *I wonder who would send me a card? It's not even my birthday.*

Curious and a little excited, Norman tore open the paper. Inside was a glossy greeting card with the words "Happy Thanksgiving!" printed across a picture of pumpkins and autumn leaves. Norman opened the card and read, *"We give thanks for friends, family, and the bounty of the past year. Please visit our website and we'd love to see you here in our dealership. Sincerely, Mike's Dealership."*

Norman exhaled. *What a lovely gesture,* he thought. Norman returned to his apartment and, using a magnet, hung the card on his refrigerator. It was, after all, a nice picture.

Norman Falls Down a Staircase

November 27th, A Monday

It was a Monday evening and Norman had been working late. He hadn't intended to work late but his colleagues had a lot of work to catch up on.

He was alone.

He liked it like this, when he could hear each individual bubble break the surface in the water cooler. He would slip his unshod toes into the short-nap carpeting and lean back in his chair for a moment, his spine and back-rest creaking in unison.

"Oh. Norman! I thought I was alone."

It was Lisa's voice.

And the rest of her.

"Oh," said Norman with the wrong intonation.

"Worried I'd find you relaxing?"

"Yes," said Norman. "I mean no." He slipped his shoes back on. "I guess you been working on..."

"No, not really. I just like it when it's quiet like this."

Norman smiled: "When it's just you and the water-cooler?"

"Water-cooler?"

"Uh..."

"Are you being poetic?" she asked.

"I don't really know. Yes."

Lisa looked to the ceiling: "I like it when all I can hear are the air-conditioning vents."

Norman thought about this, "Don't they turn the air-conditioning off at six?"

Lisa smiled, "That's what I mean."

Norman frowned.

"Follow me," she whispered.

Norman rose to his feet and walked across to where Lisa was standing. She turned on her heel and they walked together to her side of the office. Lisa motioned to Norman to take a seat while she pressed her finger to her lip.

Norman strained. "I can't hear anything."

Lisa screwed her eyes, "It's a different kind of silence. You can hear the emptiness in the vents."

Norman nodded earnestly. They each observed the silence in silence.

It was at that moment that Norman became aware of a sound just beyond the edge of hearing. He looked up to Lisa: "I'm just going to nip to the toilet."

She nodded in encouragement.

Norman left the chair and walked quietly towards the staircase down to the ground floor.

Norman gets Lunch

November 28th, A Tuesday

Norman entered the cafe discretely as possible, not wanting to draw any attention to himself. He read through the menu board three times over from a distance, carefully positioned to establish that he was in fact not in the queue.

Norman approached the cashier who had been watching him in his state of perplexity. He internally recited his order one more time before speaking.

"Hello, could I have a medium coffee and a cheese and tomato Panini please."

"Would you like milk or cream with your coffee?" the cashier chirped.

Norman blurted, "No, thanks" before realising what the woman had asked. He did want milk.

The cashier handed Norman his change which fell through his fingers. He quickly picked up the variety of coins, staring at the floor to avoid seeing how many people had witnessed his blunder.

Norman took his order flag and found a table far away from the registers.

Kylie and Jason

November 29th, A Wednesday

It was snowing outside. Kylie was staring through the frosty windowpane when she felt Jason's eyes on her. He squeezed her hands slightly and smiled warmly.

"Our last dinner before we're husband and wife," he said.

He pushed her engagement ring with his thumb as his smile turned into a sly grin.

"We can finally swap this ring for something less garish, more understated!"

Kylie laughed back, "It is a bit much isn't it? You always overdo things."

The waiter arrived with a vintage Sauvignon Blanc from South Australia and took their orders. Kylie ordered a salmon molee and Jason ordered a pound rump steak called *'The Lion's Kill'*.

"Now that's garish!" said Kylie, throwing her head back and laughing. Jason simply smirked back as he lifted the glass of red to his lips.

Outside, Norman waited for the bus.

Norman Meets a Girl, Part 4

November 30th, A Thursday

It's been nearly a week since Norman had heard from Dianne- and that was the end of the night of their first date. Norman had thought the date went well; she ate lots and enjoyed herself, and Norman didn't mind her interrupting his stories of his cat with her stories of her dog, although Dixie sounded like she would have issues with little Norman, and that made Norman nervous. *Should I call her?*

For lunch, Norman ordered a bagel. The bagel reminded him of buns- what delicious buns they were! He wanted to return to the restaurant to have more. *Perhaps that could be the second date,* Norman thought.

After work, Norman stopped by the grocery store, at the same time he had encountered Dianne the week before. He knew it was ridiculous- if he wanted to find her during a routine he should have showed up at 6PM on a Wednesday, not a Thursday. But he kept his anxious fingers crossed anyway.

Sitting at home, Norman felt he had no choice but to call her. Perhaps something terrible had happened and she was currently in the ER. Norman had made the split-second decision that he would look after her, vegetable or no, for the rest of her life. The phone clanged as she answered.

"Hello?" Dianne said arduously.

"Hi, Dianne, it's Norman... Last week we had a date?"

"Oh yeah! Hi Norman. How are you?"

"Would you like to get dinner again sometime?"

There was a long pause on the other end, that worked into a sigh. "Yeah, I'm sorry Norman you're just... not my type, you know? I usually don't date balding guys.... I thought I would give you a shot, but.... Yeah."

"Alrighty, well, I guess I'll talk to you later."

"Bye Norman!"

Norman felt devastated. For the next few hours, Norman did two things- looking online for a toupee, and trying to fix what hair he had into a respectable fashion. Nothing worked, and no piece of hair was in Norman's budget. Norman sulked.

DECEMBER

December

Norman is Unexplainably Glum

December 1st, A Friday

Norman had been unexplainably glum all day. This wasn't the usual slightly melancholy feeling that sometimes came without explanation. No, this felt disheartening, like something bad had happened and he had forgotten about it.

"What do you think, Norman?" he asked finally, grunting from deep within the cozy armchair.

Norman didn't answer- he was licking himself.

"Maybe I should check the mail."

With great effort, Norman hefted himself out the armchair and wandered out the door, jingling the mail key.

Soon Norman had returned with a handful of mail, which he set on the table.

Among several bills, there was one very pretty card.

The card read 'SAVE THE DATE' and had a picture of a middle-aged woman and an attractive younger man embracing each other. The woman's face matched the one in Norman's wallet.

"Well this explains it Norman." Norman mumbled, after a pause. "The electric bill was due today."

Norman Buys a New Coat

December 2nd, A Saturday

"You'll like this one. I guarantee it," said the old tailor, handing Norman a coat to try on.

Norman hadn't asked for any assistance, but he assumed the old man just wanted to be helpful; and Norman didn't want to upset the man, so he pretended he needed to be helped.

The coat was a perfect fit! Loose around the waist, tight on the chest, and the sleeves were just long enough so that if his fingers were cold, he could easily retract his elbows and stop them from being exposed to the chill. Norman felt he already owned a coat like this one, but knew it to be impossible - how could he forget such a perfect coat?

"I'll take it!" Norman announced. The old man was cheery and delighted for his happy customer.

Norman stripped the coat of tags in the store and wore it all the way home. On this walk, however, he discovered the coat was quite terrible at protecting him from the wind. By the time he got home, his torso was burning from the cold winds, and he switched back to his original coat.

Norman took the new coat and hung it up in his closet. Upon doing so, Norman noticed another coat- the exact same brand and colour - except two sizes smaller.

It'll be better for the Spring, Norman thought.

Norman has a Back-ache

December 3rd, A Sunday

Normans' back had been bothering him ever since he got out of bed. He thought about taking an aspirin, but decided to wait until after he had his oatmeal so he could get some food on his stomach first.

Norman dug out the heating pad from the closet, plugged it in and set it on the couch to warm up while he made his instant oatmeal. After finishing breakfast, Norman went to sit down and put the toasty heating pad on his aching back. However, he saw that Norman had curled up on the warm pad and was purring contentedly.

Breathing a sigh, Norman went to the medicine cabinet, took two aspirin, and sat in his chair until the pain went away.

Norman Says Nothing

December 4th, A Monday

Norman went to work, as he usually did on Mondays, and stumbled through the office entrance with a coffee in hand.

"Morning," Norman said to Lisa.

She mumbled something that Norman assumed was 'morning' too.

Norman noticed his cubicle partner, Frank, was particularly quiet. He didn't say anything all day; no *'hello'*, or *'here's the daily memo, Norman'*, or *'sorry'*, when Frank's chair bumped into Norman's as he left the cubicle at the end of the day. Perhaps tomorrow he would ask Frank what was the matter.

As Norman rested at home, finishing the day by brushing his teeth, a thought came to him: he said nothing today.

Hit only utterance was bidding morning to Lisa... and nothing more. He felt it was strange, and worrisome. Could he lose his voice by not using it?

"Goodnight," Norman said to Norman.

Norman Walks Home in the Snow

December 5th, A Tuesday

Plodding through mushy snow with wet feet on his way home from the supermarket, Norman thought of how warm his apartment would be on his return. He had spent the afternoon optimizing his central heating timer and was confident he had succeeded. He thought of Norman who would be curled up asleep on the sofa. He thought about how the tap water was always pleasantly chilled during this cold season.

As he pondered the things he loved about winter, one of the things he hated smacked him in the face. A snowball. A barrage soon followed. Snowballs landed all around him. Norman curled up- trying to shield himself to no avail. The cruel laughter of children seemed to swirl all around him making him dizzy. One more cold smack on the face knocked him off his feet. The gang of teens cackled and ran off.

Norman lay still on the ground for a long time, staring up at the eddying snow that sparkled in the street lamps. His shopping was strewn all around him. Broken eggs and spilled milk pooled together on the snow.

Without knowing why, Norman began to move his legs in and out. He carved a crude snow angel on the pavement. When it was complete he remained still, arms and legs stretched out across the foot-path.

He laid there for what seemed a long time, wondering about the television shows he was missing in his nice warm home.

Norman has Insomnia

December 6th, A Wednesday

Norman is having trouble sleeping. Norman's clock notes that it is 1:20AM. *Sleep*, thinks Norman.

The room is dark; the lights are off. There is no sound in Norman's room. Norman is fast asleep and curled up at Norman's foot. *Sleep*, thinks Norman.

Norman turns over. *Sleep*, thinks Norman.

Norman checks the clock. It is 2:43AM. *Sleep*, thinks Norman.

Norman decides to start counting sheep, in the hope of falling asleep. *One. Two. Three. Sheep*, thinks Norman.

Norman's throat is dry and he has to pee. Norman fetches a drink from the kitchen, visits the bathroom and crawls back into bed. *Sleep*, thinks Norman.

The clock reads 3:51AM. Norman is dreading work. His alarm is set to go off at 6:00AM promptly. *Sleep*, thinks Norman.

At 6:00AM, Norman turns off his alarm clock.

Norman sees his Ex-wife

December 7th, A Thursday

Norman had been feeling particularly proud of himself today after having been congratulated by his boss for doing an excellent job on this week's report. He decided to treat himself to a night out at a local burger place that had recently opened up.

Upon arrival at the restaurant, Norman sat himself at the bar area, not wishing to take up an entire table for himself. After ordering a Diet Coke with lemon and a well-done Hamburger with no tomato, Norman noticed that his ex-wife was seated at a table with a man in his early thirties.

Embarrassed to be seen eating alone, Norman turned away from them and asked if he could have his meal to go. The bartender seemed surprised but said that it would not be a problem. Norman gave a weak smile and quickly paid with cash and left the bar.

Norman decided that he would not go back to that restaurant again.

Norman is Forgotten

December 8th, A Friday

Norman stepped out of the bathroom. His hands were still damp from washing them, even though he had used two paper towels to dry them off.

Next time I'll use three, Norman thought to himself.

Norman's chair squeaked as he sat down at his desk. Embarrassed, he looked around, and in doing so realised that his entire department was gone. Norman remembered that today was Team Lunch Day, and realized that his team had forgotten him when they went to lunch.

Norman was disappointed, but Norman was also relieved. He liked being around his coworkers sometimes, but he liked being alone sometimes too.

"Today I will enjoy lunch in solitude," he said aloud, to himself.

Norman pulled his sandwich and a bag of baby sliced carrots from his drawer. Norman thought about his ex-wife.

We used to eat together, sometimes.

He stared at his desk while he ate. A framed photograph of Norman stared back. Norman was glad he decided on putting the photo back on his desk. Norman smiled.

Norman wondered how she was doing. He wondered why she didn't talk to him anymore. Norman remembered when they used to watch CSI at their old place, and how she had comforted him when Grissom and Nick found that skeleton under a house, buried in cement. He wondered if she ever wondered about him.

Norman took a deliberate bite, and meditated on the past.

I wonder if she's happy.

Norman finished his sandwich. *I hope so.*

Norman threw away his sandwich bag. Awhile later, Norman's coworkers returned to their desks, and pretended that they didn't notice Norman sitting alone in his cubicle.

Norman Finds a Purpose

December 9th, A Saturday

It was a Saturday. Norman usually read the paper on Saturday morning, but today he was sitting on the couch, staring at the television.

The television wasn't on.

Norman hadn't eaten breakfast. He was still in his pyjamas. In fact, he hadn't moved for a solid two and a half hours.

Up in his head, Norman wondered whether this was what it was like to go crazy. He'd picked up his breakfast spoon this morning, caught a glimpse of his warped reflection in the scratched stainless steel, and stumbled upon an uncomfortable thought.

What was the point?

Norman had elected to sit on his couch instead. He thought quietly and tentatively, his uneasiness about breaking routine pushed to the side for once. He thought about whether he should go to work on Monday. Whether he should drive up to the supermarket. Whether he should get off the couch.

He was halfway through deciding whether to continue thinking at all, when Norman's plaintive cries cut through the silence.

It was 11:32AM. Norman's feeding time.

Norman slid slowly from the couch, and busied himself opening a can of Norman's cat food. After he'd scraped the sloppy chunks into his bowl he was struck with an awareness of how small Norman seemed.

Looking down at the little feline, Norman happened upon another thought; one not nearly as uncomfortable as the one earlier this morning.

Norman couldn't open cat-food cans by himself.
He would go to work on Monday.

A Dollar for Christmas

December 10th, A Sunday

Norman was shopping for presents at his favorite store, Depot-Mart. While exiting the store, he noticed a Sally-Ann man ringing a bell so that people would give money.

Norman had to pass the man on his way to the parking lot. Norman quickened his pace and looked down, pretending not to notice the man. As he passed, the man said, "Merry Christmas and God bless you". Norman pretended not to hear and walked even faster. He made it to his car and quickly left.

When he arrived home, he made dinner and watched the Christmas shows on TV. There was a Salvation Army advertisement explaining how even a dollar can change someone's life.

That night, in bed, Norman thought about the Sally-Ann man at Depo-Mart and felt somewhat guilty. He promised himself he would give a dollar the next time he sees that man. He felt better and fell asleep.

Norman Takes a Piece of Gum

December 11th, A Monday

It was one of those dull gray mornings that made Norman question what horrible thing he'd done to deserve such monotony.

Norman stumbled onto the morning bus and picked a window seat in the back where he hoped not to be bothered.

A bright faced youth hopped on to the bus and sat next to Norman.

Norman was bothered by this.

The youth offered Norman a piece of gum.

Norman didn't want a piece of gum. Gum was too sticky and messy and once he found a piece in Norman's fur that he had to cut out which made Norman mad at him for weeks.

But Norman hoped that if he took the piece of gum from the youth then he wouldn't have to participate in any needless small talk so he took the piece and put it in his mouth.

The gum was sickly sweet and sticky and made Norman's jaw hurt. He wanted to spit it out but he had already shoved the wrapper somewhere deep into his pocket and didn't feel like searching for it.

The youth talked to Norman about a popular television show that Norman had never seen and, after the conversation, never would.

The youth eventually left the bus. By then the gum had lost most of its sickly-sweet taste and somehow managed to get stuck behind one of Norman's molars.

Norman was bothered.

Norman Notices Lisa's Curled Hair

December 12th, A Tuesday

Norman peeked over the top of his cubicle to look at Lisa. Her hair was curled today. As he sat at his desk, he stared at his monitor, pondering this sudden shift of routine and normalcy and he wondered how he felt about it.

He stood to "walk to the water cooler", and as he passed by, he confirmed that her hair was indeed curled.

When he came back to his cubicle with a cup of water, he stopped in front of hers and said, "Hey, Lisa."

She turned around and said, "Oh hey Norman, how're you?"

"I'm well, thank you. I noticed your hair looks different today."

Lisa laughed, which alarmed Norman.

"Well, this is actually my natural hair. I hate how curly it is, but I was too lazy to straighten it this morning. So, it's normal today!"

Norman thought on this for a moment and said, "I like normal."

Norman walked to his cubicle and reveled in his sudden courageousness and his heart felt as though it would burst through his chest. He could not wait to recount his story to Norman when he got home.

Lisa looked at her reflection in her monitor and smiled.

Norman Makes an Unnerving Discovery

December 13th, A Wednesday

As Norman left his laundry room a colorful sparkle coming from the cat pan caught his eye. Before him on a crest of litter sat a bejeweled turd of ruby reds and emerald greens. It was beautiful. Leaning closer, it soon dawned on Norman that Norman had ripped into a bag of Christmas Hershey Kisses, and had eaten several. Fearing for his cat's life, he called the vet. The doctor calmed him down and told him not to worry, as milk chocolate does not contain enough real cocoa to cause harm. Norman breathed a sigh of relief.

Norman Brushes his Teeth

December 14th, A Thursday

It was getting dark and Norman couldn't wait to test out his new toothbrush that he bought for himself. It was an electric one and quite the purchase, really, with a price tag of 60 dollars. However, Norman didn't care. He trusted his dentist's recommendation of buying this specific model. The vibrations tickled Norman's teeth a bit. Happy with his new purchase he looked at himself in the mirror and thought of the funny joke he told one of his female co-workers today.

Today was a good day, he thought to himself. *I look forward to tomorrow.*

Norman Buys Norman a Gift

December 15th, A Friday

Norman was out making his weekly grocery trip when he passed by the local pet store. He thought it would be nice to buy Norman a gift, since it was the holiday season.

Wandering around the store, he saw a cute little cat hat with Christmas trees hanging from it. He chuckled at the thought of little Norman walking around the apartment with the hat on. He looked at the price--$25.

Norman walked out of the store with a bag of cat treats, still chuckling about the thought of Norman wearing the Christmas tree hat. When he got home he found that Norman had vomited in his recliner.

Norman Wins a Car

December 16th, A Saturday

As Norman passed through the mall on one lazy Saturday, he passed by an array of toy vending machines. Claw machines, dollar capsules, sticker slots, the whole lot. Anything cheap and overpriced for a dollar could be found in this junket.

Norman had his eye on one prize in particular: a toy model 1970 Chevrolet, C10, stuck in a bubble capsule. He knew it well - it was his father's truck. Memories of going fishing, loading up the back and skipping school came to mind. He recalled Neil Diamond playing on the radio, and his mother and father together in one place. It brought him an abundance of happy memories. He was determined to have it.

Norman searched through his wallet, and found no coins whatsoever. Through his jacket pocket however, he found an assortment of coins, as well as a lucky quarter he found months ago. He didn't really want to part with it, but perhaps now was the time! To put it to a good use; to reunite himself with an old friend. There wouldn't ever be a better reason to spend the coin than now.

Norman inserted the two dollars' worth of change into the slot machine. With a heavy thud and click, the gears started to work, and Norman kept his fingers crossed until they went pale...

Norman has Leftovers

December 17th, A Sunday

It was the weekend and as per usual, Norman had no plans. As he took some leftover noodles from the fridge and shut the door something caught his eye. A picture his son made for him a long, long time ago.

Norman wondered how many years it's been. He placed the noodles on the counter and took the picture from beneath the fridge magnet for closer inspection. The crayon had faded slightly over the years but was still clear enough to read; 'Mum Dad Me' written messily above the smiling heads of the trio, hand in hand. The sun is shining above the home they once lived in together.

Norman searched the house for a suitably sized photo frame.

Norman Sends Christmas Cards

December 18th, A Monday

Christmas was around the corner. During his weekly frozen food shopping trip, he saw the card section in the store, and a thought crossed his mind. *It would be so nice to send Christmas cards to friends and family*, Norman thought. He decided to be spontaneous and made his way to the card aisle. Three minutes later, he had several cards that he found entertaining in his hands. After putting them on top of the frozen food, he rolled his half-full cart towards the self-checkout machine. He let out a disappointed sigh as he realized the machines were turned off and he had to see an actual cashier. *No problem*, Norman thought. *Not today*. He put on the best smile he could muster up and for once pretended to be happy today, like all the families and couples in the store around him. A couple of minutes passed, and he was now the next person in line. He got lucky this time, lines in his usual store tend to be long, especially on a day like this. The person in front of him started finishing up and Normal braced himself for the imminent human interaction.

"How are you sir?" the cashier asked.

"G-good," stuttered Norman.

"Might want to pay for express shipping with these cards, sir. It's only a couple of days before Christmas."

At that moment, his smile faded rather quickly. As the cashier rang up his food, he looked at his cards, and realized that he can't send them. His attempt at fooling himself into brief moments of happiness backfired. He doesn't have anyone to send them to. But it was too late to back out and leave the store; it would cause a scene. Plus, Norman has had enough excitement for today. He paid for his groceries and walked out of the store.

The Christmas cards waved him goodbye from a nearby bench.

Norman has a Wonderful Dream

December 19th, A Tuesday

Norman couldn't sleep this night, and decided to go for a midnight stroll. As he walked, puddles splashed under his feet, and in the distance, Norman could make out flashing lights, and laughter. A carnival!

Norman wasn't aware the carnival was in town. All around him were laughing children, men selling tickets for hot-dogs and giant bears, with lights spinning and twisting from humongous rides and Ferris Wheels. Norman sat at a bench, still warm from whoever was sitting there last, and watched as a flame-tosser tossed pins on fire in front of him.

Beside him sat a young and warm girl, looking directly at Norman. Norman made accidental eye contact as he glimpsed over, and quickly averted his eyes back to the flame.

"Hi." she said to him.

"Hello." Norman responded.

"What's your name?" she asked.

Norman said Norman.

"Would you like to come on the Ferris wheel with me?" she asked. Norman felt beads of sweat forming on his lip. Norman agreed.

For the rest of the night, the woman lead Norman by the hand, going on each and every ride- even the ones that scared him- and played all of the mini-games. Norman and the woman left the carnival together, with a giant bear in Norman's arms.

"What do you do, Norman?" she asked.

"I'm an astronaut." he responded. He wasn't sure why he lied, but at the time, he thought it to be true. They walked through the city streets mindlessly, holding each-others hand.

She led him to her apartment. Inside was a lively environment, with numerous paintings covering each inch of wall, lamps that twisted and showed more than just a white light, and dogs ran wildly through the apartment.

"Make yourself at home!" she said, as she disappeared off into a hallway. Norman tried to keep himself occupied, fending off a dozen dogs all eager to lick his face. She came back a moment later.

"What are you doing?" she asked.

"... Making myself at home?" he responded dubiously.

"In there, goof." she said. She pointed wantonly to the open bedroom door across the hall. Norman's eyes narrowed and his heart nearly came straight out of his chest. Norman ran into the bedroom.

Norman stripped off his uncomfortable clothes, one by one. Once naked, Norman jumped into the bed and giddily waited for her arrival. He closed his eyes for a moment-

-Norman was back in his own bed, back in his own pyjamas. He rubbed his eyes, terribly confused, and wandered through his home, looking for remnants from the night, but none existed.

Later at work, Norman did a reality check. *Did anything really happen last night?* he wondered. Norman spent the rest of the day thinking about it- the carnival, him being an astronaut, the woman- and he felt odd. He was upset that it was all just a dream… But happy that he got the chance, none-the-less.

Norman Reads a Book Before Going to Sleep

December 20th, A Wednesday

Norman received a nice gift at work from his Secret Santa, who was Eleanor from accounting. It was a pretty big book called 'Dune'. Norman thought he'd heard about it, but wasn't sure.

That night, when Norman went to bed, he decided to start reading it. He started with the editor's note, but leafed past it after a couple of pages.

Norman found the story reasonably compelling. After a while, he counted how many pages into it he was: an even 20. *That's enough for today,* he thought. In a sudden rush of inspired creativity, he folded the top corner of the page, making an impromptu bookmark.

Norman turned off the light and put the book on his nightstand, never to touch it again.

Norman Makes an Omelette

December 21st, A Thursday

Norman woke up early on Thursday and resolved to put the cooking book he had bought to good use. He flipped through the pages and decided upon the *Spring Omelette*, since it looked simple to make. However, upon inspecting his refrigerator, Norman found that he was out of cheese, and only had one egg left.

Norman glanced outside. The sun was shining. He looked at the weather app on his phone, and saw that it was currently 35 degrees Fahrenheit. *It's a nice December day. Maybe I'll walk over to the drugstore to pick up the eggs and cheese.*

Eager for the chance to exercise, Norman grabbed his jacket and snatched his keys from the hook by the door, backtracking for a moment to recover his reusable grocery bag. He trotted to the street, and then made his way towards the drugstore. There were only a few cars on the streets, and Norman met no pedestrians on his way to the store. *It's a shame,* he thought, *that everyone is sleeping through such a beautiful morning.*

He turned a corner and saw a homeless man who had sat himself on a bus stop bench. Norman stopped short, his breath froze in his chest and his mouth pursed. He recovered his composure, and tried to continue, hoping that he hadn't offended the man with his reaction. However, the homeless man noticed Norman approaching, and stood up to meet him.

"S'cuse me boss, but kin you spare a dollar?"

Norman shook his head vigorously and turned his eyes away. He stammered, "I, no, I- I'm sorry. Can't, I've got..." Norman passed the man and hurried ahead, forcing his gaze forward. The man sat back down, unbothered.

Norman continued to the drugstore, his mood noticeably darker. He picked out a fresh-looking carton of eggs and found a bag of pre-shredded cheese. Norman went to the cash register to pay for the items.

The cashier was a middle-aged woman, with greying hair and dark bags under her eyes. She smiled weakly at Norman. He returned the smile.

"Will that be everything?"

"Um," Norman thought for a moment. "Yes."

"Do you have a reward card?"

"No," Norman said, and before she could ask her next question, "and I don't want one." He placed his money on the counter.

The cashier rang up his items and put them in Norman's reusable grocery bag. As she did this, Norman glanced at the "tip jar" that rested on the counter. It was full of ones and miscellaneous change.

The cashier grunted and shook her extended fist at Norman. Confused at first, he reached out and took his own change and receipt.

"Have a good day sir."

Norman nodded in return and left the store.

As he walked home, Norman approached the homeless man again. He entertained the idea of crossing the street to avoid the man, but he doubted that he could make it look natural. The man looked up at Norman and started to speak, "S'cuse me boss, but-" then stopped and settled back into the bench.

Norman paused, reached into his pocket, and extended his fist to the man. "Here. It's all I've got."

The homeless man took the money gently and inspected it. "Bless you, sir. Bless you."

"Yeah."

Norman hoped that the man would spend it on food, instead of drugs.

He walked the rest of the way home. Once there, he put away his jacket and assembled the rest of his ingredients. Norman managed to overcook the vegetables, but the omelette still tasted fantastic. After he cleaned up, Norman placed a post-it note on the page and resolved to try out a new recipe next week.

Norman Sees a Juke-box

December 22nd, A Friday

It was around 8:30PM when Norman was seated at his local Waffle House. He did not feel one way or another about the restaurant, but opted to eat there because it was late and his options were limited. The only other 'open late' option nearby was a McDonalds, but Norman had recently fallen sick from a Buffalo Ranch McChicken there and was thus hesitant to return. So, he decided to eat at Waffle House.

A while after being seated, his order of a chili cheese omelette and hash browns arrived. Midway through his meal, the restaurant's jukebox caught his eye. He walked over to it and examined the available songs. One of the songs in the jukebox was 'September' by Earth, Wind and Fire. The song brought back memories of his first job in the summer of 1981. The job was at a now-defunct supermarket named Eat & Save.

Norman inserted the required fifty cents into the jukebox and selected 'September'. As he ate his meal and listened to the song, he reflected on his memories of stocking cereals and other foodstuffs on Eat & Save's shelves. The chili cheese omelette was surprisingly good.

Norman Ties his Shoes

December 23rd, A Saturday

As soon as he heard the postman's van approaching, Norman excitedly rose from his chair and retrieved his tennis shoes from the hallway.

Checking the mail was one of the most exhilarating moments of Norman's day. It was a sort of low-stakes Russian Roulette; Who knew what Norman would find hidden in the back of his mailbox? A misplaced Victoria's Secret catalog? A letter from his ex-wife? An overdue electric bill? Norman hastily pulled his tennis shoes on and fumbled with the laces.

"Let's see, two bunny ears, one bunny around the tree, then down the hole..."

Norman suddenly recalled a distant memory in which he was kneeling in front of a young boy, patiently guiding the boy's delicate hands across his tiny sneakers... "That's it, first the bunny goes around the tree, then down the hole..."

Norman slowly stood up and frowned. He kicked off his tennis shoes and returned to his comfortable chair.

The mail will still be there tomorrow, Norman thought.

Norman is Named

December 24th, 1997, A Sunday

Norman put down the cage on the kitchen counter. Inside, a little kitten meowed actively, eager to get out.

"Hold your horses, little kitten!" Norman said to himself. Norman then giggled at the joke he just made.

Norman couldn't wait to let the little cat out of the cage. But he knew he couldn't- it would feel like he was opening someone else's gift. It *would* be opening someone else's gift. Norman sneaked little treats through the bars of the cage, until finally Norman Jr came home from school.

"Hey Junior, are you ready for your Christmas present?" Norman announced gleefully. Norman Jr was still busy taking off his shoes, when Norman shouted. The little boy tossed his bag into the air, happily running into the kitchen.

"What is it what is it what is it!" he shouted, jumping up and down. Norman took the cage off the counter, lowered it to the floor, and cracked open the door handle.

Norman Jr was ecstatic! The boy grabbed the kitten up, embraced him in his arms, and gave the feline creature a gentle, loving hug.

"This kitten is no toy," Norman lectured, "it's a living thing. Are you willing to have it be your responsibility from now on?"

"Yes daddy I am! I swear, I'll feed it, I'll water it, I'll take it for walks-"

"I believe you!" Norman cried. Norman Jr placed the kitten carefully down on the floor; watching it waddle and explore the room. Then, Norman Jr jumped to his father, giving him a big hug, the strongest, tightest bear hug he could manage.

"What are you going to name it?" Norman asked his son.

Norman Jr thought carefully. He scratched his head, then a smile came onto his face.

"Norman," the boy said surely.

"You're naming the cat after yourself? That's a little funny, don't ya think?"

"I'm naming it after you, dad. So you'll always be with me."

Later that night, as Norman brushed his teeth, he started to cry. He was proud.

Merry Christmas, Norman

December 25th, A Monday

It was 8:07AM Christmas morning when Norman opened his eyes. The light of the day bounced off the snow blanket in the yard and shone into Norman's bedroom making it a little brighter than usual. Norman was curled up in a ball at Norman's feet. The pleasant vibration of Norman's purring made Norman feel a little extra cozy while wrapped up in his blanket.

Norman checked his phone. *No messages yet,* he concluded. As much as Norman wanted to stay in bed, the tea from the evening last had made itself an overstayed guest in Norman's bladder and quite frankly, felt very uncomfortable. Little Norman was still sleeping on his feet however, which would make Norman feel a little guilty if he disturbed him. Norman did his best to slowly slide his feet out from under Norman's weight, so as not to wake him, and emerged from his cocoon with an advance towards the toilet.

Norman sighed deeply at the simple pleasure of relieving one's full bladder. *It's one of those little things in life that could really turn someone's mood around,* Norman thought to himself. With two shakes, Norman then lifted his pajama bottoms, washed his hands and stepped back into the bedroom.

Two robins flew up to perch outside of Norman's window and caught his eye. Norman scanned the yard below. *It really is a beautiful day*, Norman thought.

Norman sat at his computer with Facebook opened on his browser. He scrolled through the posts of families unwrapping gifts, young couples posing with their dogs in the snow and children trying their hand at peeling carrots in preparation for dinner. 'Merry Christmas' and 'Happy Holidays' dominated the newsfeed. Norman checked his phone. It was 2:38PM on December 25th and there were no messages.

Seeing the smiles on his co-workers' and extended family's faces made Norman feel a little warmer inside. "Let's see what I can make us for dinner," Norman said to Norman, with an uplifted tone. Norman walked into his kitchen and opened the pantry. Two cans of soup - tomato and cream of mushroom, one package of spaghetti noodles and three packages of dried kidney beans were most notable. In the fridge, a half quart of milk, two eggs, one chicken breast and an orange sat amongst condiments. Norman grimaced at the contents of his kitchen against thought of the hearty feasts his Facebook friends were about enjoy. Despite the turkey slices from yesterday, Norman concluded that another trip to the market was in order.

Norman would have his chicken breast with cranberry sauce, mashed potatoes, steamed carrots and a dinner roll. He first entered the market through the bakery section. Walking towards the bread counter, Norman spotted a stand of pies with pine branches, ball ornaments and a 50% discount sign adorning the top. Upon further investigation, he found some tarts - lemon meringue, apple crumble and pumpkin. The temptation poked at him incessantly, and with a deviant smirk, Norman selected a particularly attractive lemon tart and placed it in his basket.

The final item to retrieve was the cranberry sauce. Norman scoured the aisle of sauces and canned goods with no luck. Cranberry sauce was a Christmas necessity, Norman thought, and decided to peruse around the perimeters of the store would be worth it. Norman came upon a "last chance" display where boxes of stuffing, pumpkin pie filling and foil roasting pans waited to be snatched up by holiday procrastinators.

Norman pushed aside some items in search of cranberry sauce, and when it seemed like there were none to be found, he finally spotted what appeared to be the last one. As Norman reached for the can, he bumped into a soft, pale and delicate hand. Norman raised his head to see a conventionally pretty, young, red-haired woman who nervously laughed.

"You forgot cranberries too?" she asked.

"Uh y-yeah.." Norman stuttered also letting out a nervous chuckle. Norman felt embarrassed by this interaction.

"You can take it," said Norman. "I don't need extra."

The red-haired woman smiled cheerfully at Norman. "Oh, thank you!" she said as she grabbed the can, placed it into her basket, and then turned towards the registers. Norman waited a few seconds before also heading toward the registers, and took his place in line at an open one a few meters away from the red-haired woman, so as not to risk making her feel uncomfortable.

Norman's heart sunk a little at the thought of having his Christmas dinner without the cranberry sauce. *At least there's dessert*, he remembered as the cashier scanned the barcode of his tart. Norman paid his total, collected his shopping bag and ambled for the door. At the same time, the red-haired woman walked briskly past him. "Thanks again and Merry Christmas!" she said, smiling. "Merry Christmas to you too!" said Norman and he exited the market with a sheepish grin on his face.

The oven timer alarm sounded, indicating that the chicken was finished cooking. Norman was in the middle of mashing his potato with butter and milk, trying to decide whether he should finish the task at hand, or take the chicken out now. Ultimately, Norman decided that he didn't want to risk drying out the meat, and promptly removed it from the oven and set in on the counter. He turned the oven off and placed his foil-wrapped roll inside to warm it up before returning to mashing the potato. *Everything's coming together nicely!* Norman thought proudly to himself.

Norman tuned the TV on to the public station featuring the holiday Yule Log. Then, Norman set aside some chicken for Norman in a fancy dish. Since this was a special occasion, Norman decided to eat in the living room by the fireside. He brought in his plate and placed it on the coffee table. Norman remembered the cloth napkins left over from an old table set he and his ex-wife owned. He went and looked in the lower cupboard below his pantry, and sure enough, there sat four blue and white checkered cloth napkins. He took one and brought it back to the living room, only to find Norman on the coffee table cautiously sniffing at his meal.

"Norman!" Norman gasped. "This plate is for me!" Norman jumped off the coffee table and looked up at Norman with glossy eyes. "Well I suppose you can have a little more chicken." Norman said. "It's Christmas, after all."

Norman sat down and laid the cloth napkin across his lap. He cut another piece of chicken and handed it to Norman who happily snatched it from his hand and ate it up. Norman checked his phone. It was 7:34PM on December 25th and there were no messages.

Norman closed his eyes and took a deep breath. The fire was crackling on the TV and the lights were dimmed low. He felt extremely relaxed.

After dinner, Norman made himself some tea. Looking out his kitchen window he could see the multicolored Christmas lights on his neighbor's houses and gardens. Bundled up couples carrying wrapped gifts trudged through the snow leading up to the house across the street from Norman's where a party in full swing. Norman took a sip of his tea and quietly relished in his relaxing night at home.

Norman returned to his living room where Norman was laying on the carpet beside his chair. The fire was still roaring on the TV. Norman sat down with his tea and took a sip and in the same moment there was a vibration in his pocket. Norman checked his phone. It was 8:50PM on December 25th and there was one message. Norman opened the message which read,

"Merry Christmas, Dad. Love Norman."

Norman typed "Merry Christmas to you too, son." in response.

Norman placed his phone on the side table and took another sip of his tea. He laid his head back in his chair, shut his eyes and smiled. *Merry Christmas indeed,* he thought to himself.

Norman Receives a Gift

December 26th, A Tuesday

Norman heard a knock on the door. His joints creaked as he peeled himself off the sofa and slowly made his way to the door. He fumbled with the keys and finally managed to unlock the door.

Standing upon his doorstep was a young, skinny man wearing a FedEx cap, clutching a large box in one hand, and piece of paper and pen in the other. Norman took the pen and paper and signed for the box on the dotted line. The skinny man handed him the box and left without a word.

Norman's usually dull face lit up with excitement. His heart pounding, he placed the box onto the coffee table and tore open the box, eager to find what was inside. Soon, he held up a festively-decorated card. It read "To Norman. Merry Christmas!"

He recognised the handwriting as his ex-wife's. His heart suddenly doubled its rhythm, and he found himself shaking. He felt his smile could not be any bigger.

He quickly threw the card down onto the table, and grabbed what was inside the box...

Cans and cans of cat food.

Norman looked around in confusion. *What did this all mean?*

His eyes came to rest on his furry companion, looking up at him curiously. Norman's face fell and he sighed. The gift from his ex-wife wasn't for him.
It was for Norman.

Norman Wakes Up Early

December 27th, A Wednesday

5 AM. Norman's eyes opened slowly and drew in the faintest hint of a soft morning light from the nearby window. For Norman, it was easy to tell he had awoken too early- the light was too dim, he heard no cars passing on the street outside his apartment, and in his peripheral vision he caught a glimpse of the leading number on his digital alarm clock. It was a five. "It should be a seven," Norman thought to himself. *Just a digital dash and a half short.*

He reluctantly turned over and flipped on the lamp sitting atop his bedside table.

It was then he remembered his copy of *Dune* he got from Secret Santa. Perhaps reading a bit of it could help him back to sleep?

He reached for the thick book sitting under the light of the lamp but... as his arm neared the book he realized he in fact felt no real desire to read it at all.

Norman's next course of action was to drag himself out of bed and to the kitchen - regretting not just closing his eyes and drifting back to sleep.

Norman Gets Ready for New Years

December 28th, A Thursday

Norman decided he was going to have a party at his house for New Years. It would not be anything extravagant; he just wanted to invite a few people from work over to have a drink or two and watch "Dick Clark's Rockin' New Year's Eve."

He woke up early before work on December 29th and made a list of supplies he would need for the party. He could go to the store after work.

He began writing:

1. Coke
2. Chips
3. Champagne

He chuckled to himself, realizing all of the items on his list started with a "c." He wondered whom he should invite and began to make a list for that as well. After a few minutes, he decided he would rather not have a party.

Norman's Chance

December 29th, 1994, A Friday

The year was 1994, and Norman had just come home from work. The day went well- the best any first week could go when starting a new job. It was his first office job, after finishing an internship at a separate branch, Norman was promoted to an entry level position. After Junior had been born, Norman was nervous about how the bills would be paid with his wife on leave. The job was a tick on a list Norman was eager to check. However, what Norman hadn't had on his list of things to fix, was his marriage.

Things weren't going well. Bills were one thing the baby brought, but it also brought Norman and his then girlfriend of three months into a very difficult situation.

"Maybe it's for the best," Norman said when they first learned the news. She nodded optimistically, sitting in the hospital waiting room. "Adoption is always an option too, you know."

"Norman..." she started, but didn't finish. Norman took a deep breath, squeezing the palm of her hand.

Two years after that, the year was 1994, and Norman had just come home from work. Junior played in his baby bouncer as Norman's wife prepared dinner, chicken breasts and rice. Norman wasn't a fan of chicken, but he wasn't one to complain to his wife. *She has enough on her plate as is,* Norman thought.

Dinner was served at the table as the three of them craned their heads towards the living room, absent-mindedly watching America's Funniest Home Videos as it played on the television, still muted from before. A small dog ran into a plate glass window. Norman chuckled softly, and Junior, a toddler, laughed so hard that he spewed up the chicken back onto the plate.

Norman only managed a jerk forward motion to clean up before his wife took the lead. She took the plate out of Junior's reach and tossed it into the kitchen sink, clanging violently with the dishes from the day before. She then went over to Junior, pulled his shirt off, and stomped over to the laundry room.

"Need any help?" Norman muttered. No response.

She disappeared into the laundry room, shutting the door behind her. *What's she doing in there?* Norman wondered. Norman continued to eat his dinner. Ten minutes later the episode of AFV had finished (the plate glass dog had won the ten grand), and Norman's wife still hadn't come out of the laundry room. Norman wondered if she was angry at him, if it was something he said. He didn't see why that would be- he barely said anything at all this evening. Was it his socks? He did do a lot of walking about today, and perhaps the stench was getting to her.

Norman walked quickly past the shut door and headed for the bedroom, finding a fresh pair of socks to put on. He then sat down in his recliner. He picked up Junior and placed him on his knee, rhythmically bouncing the little boy as he flipped through the channels, looking for something different to watch.

Norman has a Date

December 30th, A Saturday

Norman dusted off the table cloth he stored in the bottom of the duvet closet, draping it over the kitchen table. He didn't use the cloth often, so the smell which presumably was once *Spring Fresh* now smelled more like *Musty Carpet.* Norman didn't mind musty carpet smell; it reminded him of church, and recitals, and the basement of his parent's home, where as a teenage boy, often hid dirty magazines under the stairwell. A sinking feeling entered his stomach as he realized those magazines were forgotten in that stairwell, left behind to surprise the new home owners.

Norman cleared his conscience by turning his full attention to basting the chicken that had just come out of the oven. After that, Norman prepared the store-bought buns by placing them in the microwave for fifteen seconds, and the lit two oblong candles sitting on the dinner table.

Norman saved his bow tie for special occasions, but as the year closed and he struggled to find significance from any one event, he decided today would be a day worth remembering.

Which is why Norman set a plate out for his cat as well.

The cat, after some luring by clapping the seat and following a trail of tuna bits, jumped up on the chair across from Norman. The cat quickly found the chicken, and after a moment of hesitation, began to enjoy the meal along with Norman.

Norman smiled, humming his favorite song as he chewed a chunk of fat. He knew how he looked right now- having a bow-tie dinner with a cat- but Norman didn't care what people would think of the situation. He loved his cat, and his cat made him happy. The bow-tie made him feel handsome. What more could he ask for?

Norman set the timer on the camera to twenty seconds, to give himself plenty of time to sit back down at the table and smile. Norman realized twenty seconds was far too much time after it took him three seconds to sit back down. A bead of sweat ran down his head, and from the corner of his eye he watched his cat, hoping he would look up to the camera in time as well. The cat was engrossed by the chicken.

At the last second, the cat looked up, and Norman's stiffly held smile finally paid off. The photo looked washed out from the flash, but it captured the moment, and that's all that Norman wanted. Norman took a magnet and placed the new photo on the fridge, proudly. The two finished off the last season of CSI before heading to bed.

The End

December 31st, A Sunday

Norman stood awkwardly by himself, near his cubicle, heavily focused on the punch in his hands. *Tastes the same as last New Year's punch*, Norman thought to himself. He remembered running out of punch during the last countdown, so he was certain to slow his drinking speed; determined to have something to do during the kissing and the cheering segment that would end the year. Not too far away, Norman could hear his coworkers Frank, Robert and Steven converse.

"This has been a great year for me," started Steven, "I bought a new truck, I lost ten pounds since last New Year's, and I've managed to put away a few grand into my savings, for when Micah gets into college!"

"I'm happy for you," said Robert, "What about you Frank?"

Frank looked sullen. "This hasn't been the greatest year. My wife left me, Deborah. It wasn't working out. Then Amber with her... not good."

"I'm sorry to hear that, man." Robert put his hand on Frank's shoulder. Without having anything to say, the three men cheered their beers for the New Year and kept drinking.

Norman felt bad for Frank. All this time, he was going through issues that Norman could relate to. All year he shared his cubicle with him, and he had no idea. Then again, Frank never wanted to talk before, but that might've had to do with how blue he was feeling. Norman decided that once everyone was back to work, he would try to relate to Frank. He knew he could.

After hearing how their year went, Norman thought back to his own. *It was an okay year,* Norman thought. His car broke down and never recovered, so that was a negative. He had a date with another woman, the first in years! Even though it never went farther than a first date, Norman was still proud he progressed that far in his love life. Maybe next year he'll have another date, with that newfound experience and confidence. His cat was a joy, as was every other year, and although nothing changed, he was still happy for the company of his cat. Someday Norman won't be around, and he'll be grateful for everyday he has with him now. The thought of Norman now only made him wish he was home.

Norman was also glad to hear from his son again, twice this month alone. He wished his son would call more often, but at the same time he doesn't want to be greedy. *Jr calls when he can, so don't bother him too much,* Norman thought. Norman took a sip of his punch drink.

The countdown would be in five minutes. The drinking was picking up, and as usual, the older crowd were the first ones' drunk. Norman looked at his punch. It was still a quarter full. *I'll make it*, Norman thought excitedly to himself. Just then, Lisa approached him.

"Hi Norman." Lisa said. In her hands was a tightly gripped glass of punch.

"Hi Lisa. How's the party?" Norman shifted his body's full attention to Lisa.

"It's good, it's good. I missed last years, so this is all new to me. People are having fun."

Norman nodded.

"Are you having fun?" Lisa asked. Norman wasn't sure how to answer that.

"I'm having a good time." he responded. To Lisa, he sounded uncertain, but he didn't know how to address it any other way. Then he remembered: "How about yourself?"

"I'm enjoying it... Listen, Norman..." Norman listened. He was nervous. Was she going to ask him to move? This was Norman's cubicle, but perhaps he was blocking the way to the bathroom-

"... I know you're not seeing anyone, well maybe I don't, I don't want to make that assumption, I was just assuming, but I don't want you to feel offended if I said that-"

Norman started to develop beads of sweat on his brow. She didn't need to use the bathroom. She was asking him something else.

"- but, I'm also, not currently, seeing... Anyone. So, I was just going to ask, since there's five minutes to the countdown, that if you would like to, when it comes-"

"-Okay." Norman said. His body twitched. Her eyes went wide, as in shock, but also in relief.

"Okay?" She asked.

"Okay." He confirmed.

Norman felt like he knew what he agreed to, deep in his heart, but in reality, he didn't quite understand the implications just yet. He opted for the stand in silence route. So did she.

The party continued on, completely unaware of the events unfolding between the middle-aged man and woman standing near the bathrooms. *Don't Stop Believing* blared on the speakers. Norman loosened his grip on his punch glass to wipe the sweat off his hands.

"Twenty seconds everyone!!" Robert shouted from the other side of the room. People began to scurry to their places, setting themselves up to where they'd want to be for the countdown. Norman and Lisa stayed put- they were exactly where they wanted to be.

Norman looked at his punch. He still had a quarter of a glass left. He didn't need to have the drink anymore. He gulped it all down in two goes, the second ending in a coughing fit. He felt embarrassed, but when he looked over, Lisa was laughing nervously with him.

"Ten seconds!"

Norman and Lisa positioned themselves a little closer, not facing each other just yet, but close enough for their shoulders to touch. Lisa finished off her punch too, a little more elegantly than Norman, then wiped her mouth.

"5... 4... 3..." The room counted down together. Lisa and Norman didn't count along, only looked at one another. Norman's heart was skipping beats. *This is going to be a better year*, he thought to himself. *I'm going to make sure of it.*

"2... 1..."

Acknowledgements

First and foremost, I'd like to thank the community of /r/lifeofnorman. Never before have I had the pleasure of being a part of such a polite, kind, and modest group of people. Every delay I've ever announced, groans I gave, and sub-par stories I've written have always been met with a grandmotherly boost of confidence and support. Love you guys. I'd like to thank Riley Miller, who was my first confidant for the book, who helped listen to even more of my groans and whines. Not only that, but he came along for the first rounds of edits, where dozens of others failed to commit with me, and after a year of listening to me slowly tackle this book face first, he agreed to do the front cover illustration, and delivered wholeheartedly. I'd like to thank Jack Harvey, who had the pleasure of being the first person to read the book on paper, and gave it the editorial spanking of a life time. Over many beers and hurt feelings (especially after I asked him, "What did you like about the book?", responded, "Boy... *Like* is such a strong word..."), Jack helped get the book over it's biggest hurdle- grammatical errors and misused past-tenses. I'd like to thank all my friends, with specific shout outs to Angela Protzman and Jarom Strong. Despite never having read the book, your utmost confidence that things will be fine is idiotic- but appreciated, always. And finally, thanks, Norman. Life hasn't been the same, only better, since I met you.

List of Illustrators

Front Cover- Ryley Miller

Back Cover- Kody Urban

January- Krista Gibbard

February- Patrick Doody

March- Aron Larsson

April- Natasha Buck

May- Angela Protzman

June- Katrina Epp

July- Katrina Epp

August- Max Lisimachio

September- Jack Harvey

October- Gustav Hammerth

November- Caitlin McPherson

December- Chelsea Chen

The Long List of Authors

Something I mentioned in the preface of this book, and paid no attention to until here now, is the mentioning of how this book was written. It wasn't written by me, but by hundreds of people; all writers from the subreddit. I felt it would have been a little too cluttered to include the names of every writer at the top of each story; it wouldn't have helped with the façade that Norman is not a highly orchestrated character, as well as some of the usernames being less than... how do I put it... wholesome. But now, here at the end of the book, I wish I could stress just how lovely all these people are. Over the years, I've asked for permission and collected nearly 800 stories, many just cutting and replacing older ones, for ones that are a better fit for this book. From all the years of asking and collaborating, I've only had one person tell me no. All these people agree to the book and the cause, and while editing these stories together into one big story was a headache, reading these stories, and working with this group of writers, was not. I appreciate the hell out of their cooperation, and if you liked their story in particular, send them a message and let them know! They deserve it-especially since I can't afford to buy them a copy of the book. Sorry everyone. Thanks for all your work.

March 23rd- Norman Walks Home in the Rain
By Penangpenis

March 24th- Norman Messages Ted on Facebook
By andaseeker

March 25th- Norman Wins the Lottery
By RamsesThePigeon

March 26th- Norman Makes Hot Chocolate
By 1-forest-1

March 27th- Norman Wakes Up Early
By CasualFrydays

March 28th- Norman Uses a Public Restroom
By cactusmcduck

March 29th- Norman is Proud!
By soupmeister

March 30th- Norman Walks in on a Meeting
By shlewkin

March 31st- Norman has a Joke for his Coworkers
By Jankman01

April 1st- Norman's Birthday Dinner
By reburrito

April 2nd- Norman Feels Proud
By Cameron Crane

April 15th- Norman Makes a Salad
By cardern

April 16th- Norman Goes to Church
By canteen007

April 17th- Norman's Special Evening
By Incompatibert

April 18th- Norman Buys New Shoelaces
By toesarestilltappin

April 19th- Norman Goes to the Talent Show
By pelviselvis19

April 20th- Norman Pours a Good Glass of Water
By themanoftin

April 21st- Norman's Missing Meatball
By HansBrixOhNo

April 22nd- Norman's Childhood Toy Set
By dylorean

April 23rd- Norman's Rainy Day
By Harasoluka

April 24th- Norman has a Sick Day
By Jolly_Line_Rhymer

April 25th- Norman Almost Gets Hit On
By Lewis N. Price

July 15th- Norman Goes to the Pictures
By PUBE_FACE

July 16th- Norman Reminisces
By raphay

July 17th- Norman Reads the Paper
By Twisted-Biscuit

July 18th- Norman Writes a Bestselling Novel
By protagonizer

July 19th- Norman Steps Out
By Future-Turtle

July 20th- Norman Goes to the Movies
By ireloyal

July 21st- Norman Misses Out
By Cameron Crane

July 22nd- Norman Makes Lunch
By skrinklelada

July 23rd- Norman Goes to Church Again
By DenversReddit

July 24th- Norman Goes on Vacation
By Bathtubhero

July 25th- Norman is a Criminal
By bumblebee851

July 26th- Norman Plants a Garden
By Lochness123

August 7th- Norman Says Hello
By IDontItsCinnamon

August 8th- Norman Buys Chocolate Milk-
By hasafewbuckstospare

August 9th- Norman Takes a Trip
By AtomGray

August 10th- Norman Goes Missing
By Jeffan

August 11th- Norman Eats a Peach
By ninjarabbit14

August 12th- Norman Sees Something Interesting
By breakfastmagic

August 13th- Norman Walks on Grass
By RoonilWazilbob

August 14th- Norman's Day at the Office
By itskindafucked

August 15th- Norman Books a Cruise
By hotshotjosh

August 16th- Norman Watches Doctor Who
By JohanDeWitt

August 17th- Norman Sends an Email
By PunishHerForMeErrol

August 18th- Norman Smiles to Himself
By Jims_Law

November 7th- Norman Wakes Up
By Julz_Mor

November 8th- Norman Goes on a Diet
By zebrapotamus

November 9th- Norman Attends a Seminar
By dudalas

November 10th- Norman Orders Poached Eggs
By VoodooAsparagus

November 11th- Norman Runs a Bath
By consciousclone

November 12th- Norman Buys Socks
By Kinhead

November 13th- Norman Takes the Elevator
By Jarom Strong

November 14th- Norman and the Girl at the Bank
By corseting

November 15th- Norman Gets DVR
By insanebatcat

November 16th- Norman Eats Breakfast
By Tetrithoven

November 17th- Norman is Almost Run Over
By AtWorkwithNoImgur

November 18th- Norman Saves a Life
By Bromosexual87

December 23rd- Norman Ties his Shoes
By UsuallyHonest

December 24th- Norman is Named
By Cameron Crane

December 25th- Merry Christmas, Norman
By Ruth-Less

December 26th- Norman Receives a Gift
By JumbaTheMartian

December 27th- Norman Wakes Up Early
By MovieTimePopcorn

December 28th- Norman Gets Ready for New Years
By MississippiBurning

December 29th- Norman's Chance
By Cameron Crane

December 30th- Norman has a Date
By Cameron Crane

December 31st- The End
By Cameron Crane

Norman's story isn't over yet. To read new stories everyday, and to write your own, head to:

reddit.com/r/lifeofnorman

CSI

10827863R00337

Printed in Great Britain
by Amazon